PRAISE FOR

BLACKOUTS

"Evidence of Boyko's obvious talent can be found on virtually every page. His diversity of voice, subtle wit, loving attention to milieu, deft characterizations . . . each of these elements shine throughout. . . . *Blackouts* marks an auspicious arrival."
– *Edmonton Journal*

"Stealthy, seductive. . . . *Blackouts* will provide thought-fodder, not to mention good old-fashioned pleasure, for months."
– Montreal *Gazette*

"[An] accomplished debut. . . . Boyko's range and playful versatility [are] impressive. . . . An inventive writer who's willing to try almost anything." – *Toronto Star*

"Boyko excels at [bringing his characters] to a tipping point between longing and obsession, love and hate, fact and fiction. . . . Elegant and compelling." – *Winnipeg Free Press*

"Boyko's gifts for characterization and dialogue compress whole relationships – whole lives, even – into tight narrative packages. . . . What results is refreshing. . . . Boyko's not interested in exploring the contours of the same old garrison. And why should he be, when there's so much else to see and he's such a gifted guide?"
– *The Walrus*

"When you're caught up in stories as clever, imaginative, and absorbing as Craig Boyko's, you could either take a [break] after each one or simply forget where you are until you've turned the last page. . . . Unexpected, captivating. . . ." – *Georgia Straight*

"Craig Boyko's 'OZY' is funny, bittersweet, and very moving. . . . Boyko somehow manages to capture, celebrate, and mourn the passing of childhood and also to reflect upon the enigma of mortality. . . . The wisdom of this [story] is stirring and irrefutable."
– David Bezmozgis, introduction to *The Journey Prize Stories 19*

BLACK

CRAIG BOYKO

OUTS

STORIES

EMBLEM
McClelland & Stewart

Cloth edition published 2008
Emblem edition published 2009

Emblem is an imprint of McClelland & Stewart Ltd.
Emblem and colophon are registered trademarks of McClelland & Stewart Ltd.

LIBRARY AND ARCHIVES CANADA CATALOGUING IN PUBLICATION

Boyko, Craig
Blackouts : stories / Craig Boyko.

ISBN 978-0-7710-1671-4
I. TITLE.
PS8603.O9962B53 2009   C813'.6   C2008-904198-4

We acknowledge the financial support of the Government of Canada
through the Book Publishing Industry Development Program and that
of the Government of Ontario through the Ontario Media Development
Corporation's Ontario Book Initiative. We further acknowledge the
support of the Canada Council for the Arts and the Ontario Arts Council
for our publishing program.

Typeset in Garamond by M&S, Toronto
Printed and bound in Canada

ANCIENT FOREST
FRIENDLY

McClelland & Stewart Ltd.
75 Sherbourne Street
Toronto, Ontario
M5A 2P9
www.mcclelland.com

1   2   3   4   5   13   12   11   10   09

FOR MARY JANE AND RANDY
AND ROLAND AND ERIKA

♡ CPBOYKO

CONTENTS

Acknowledgements

Earlier versions of some of these stories appeared in *Grain Magazine*, *The Malahat Review*, and *PRISM international*. I am grateful to their editors and to those at *Descant*, *The New Quarterly*, *The New Orphic Review*, *filling Station*, *Pottersfield Portfolio*, *Queen's Quarterly*, and *The Journey Prize Stories* for their support. And I owe a special debt of gratitude to my editor, Anita Chong.

A great deal of this book was written with the financial assistance of a grant from the Canada Council for the Arts.

*

The quotations on page 170 are from Francis Bacon's *Sylva Sylvarum, or A Natural History in Ten Centuries* and Charles Darwin's *The Descent of Man*. The poem quoted from on page 206 is James Joyce's "I Hear an Army Charging Upon the Land." A slight paraphrase of a line from G.W.F. Hegel's *Logic* appears on page 216. The excerpt on page 218 comes from Henri Bergson's *Creative Evolution*, translated by Arthur Mitchell. The quotation on page 275 is from Lord Byron's *Don Juan*. The sentence from Ralph Waldo Emerson on page 276 is from his essay "Self-Reliance." Finally, on page 277, there is a glancing reference to Arthur Schopenhauer, who, in his essay "On Thinking For Oneself," wrote, "If Nature had meant man to think, she would not have given him ears."

BLACKOUTS

ASSISTANCE

It began the Easter long weekend. I'd been looking forward to being alone, to having the house to myself. In fact, if only half consciously, I saw it as a precious opportunity, a chance to perform a test of sorts. An experiment in solitude, if you like.

So once Alice and Becky had left I tried to luxuriate in my freedom. I slept in late and left the bed unmade, I took a long bath and threw my wet towels on the floor, I left the television on even when I wasn't in the room. But it wasn't working. Something was wrong.

The house felt too large, too quiet, too empty. To distract myself, I kept my mind occupied with obvious and trivial thoughts: "I'm frying some bacon, I like bacon, I like it well done, I wish Alice made bacon more often, but she always undercooks it." Or, while painstakingly perusing the newspaper: "This isn't a very good column, I've never liked this guy, he uses too many paragraph breaks, I wonder what's on television, but it's better to catch up on my reading, it's important to know what's going on in the world, even if only to give yourself something to talk to other people about."

This worked for exactly one afternoon. But as soon as the sun went down, the heavy feeling in my chest, the tickle at the back of my throat, and the sour ache in my jaw, all of which I'd been successfully ignoring all day, became unignorable.

So I went from room to room, even Becky's, and switched on all the lights. I turned on the coffee maker, the stereo, the empty dishwasher.

But it was no good. I sat down, clutched my head as though to restrain it, and heaved a phlegmy sigh. "Christ," I thought. "I don't fucking believe it. I'm *lonely*."

This thought was unbearable. Not because the loneliness was unbearable – nothing that I knew would end in seventy-two hours could be truly unbearable – but because solitude had been my secret last hope. The fact was that I was miserable and had been miserable for a long time. I hated my life. But until that weekend I had unconsciously convinced myself that my wife and my daughter were all that were standing between me and an eventual return to happiness. The truth, I now realized, was that solitude was a gateway to nothing but a different kind of misery. There was no way out.

Becky returned first, Sunday afternoon. I had no trouble, after all, restraining myself from running out into the street to greet her. A boy who looked too young to be driving pulled up to the curb in front of the house. Carrying a small overnight bag and no trumpet case (she was supposed to have been out of town, playing with the school band), Becky promptly climbed out, almost before the car had come to a complete stop; and the boy, without a word or a glance, promptly drove off, almost before she had slammed the door shut. I thought the manoeuvre looked practised, choreographed. But I refrained from interrogating her when she came into the kitchen and, in lieu of a salutation, asked what there was to eat. Becky was old enough to be having sex and doing God knew what kind of dangerous new drugs they had these days, and I was sure that the quickest way to get her to start indulging in these activities, if she hadn't yet, was to let on that I suspected she already had. So, in lieu of a welcome, I informed her that there was leftover bacon in the fridge. She sneered at the fridge and, apparently not so hungry after all, clomped upstairs to her room. A shrill wail soon descended the staircase: "Has *somebody* been in my *room?*"

And so the tightness in my chest dissipated. The ache in my jaw disappeared. Loneliness was instantly replaced by its opposite – something like suffocation.

And later that night, when Alice turned out the light and asked – her voice muffled by pillow, fatigue, and indifference – if I'd had a nice weekend, I had no difficulty lying.

"It was fine," I said. "Quiet."

A couple weeks later I found myself in my office after hours, lingering absentmindedly over the yellow pages. I was working late again, or pretending to, and had just ordered a pizza. Now as I slowly flipped backwards through the phone book, postponing the call home, I wondered if Alice would begin to suspect that I was having an affair. I almost wished that I were. Or rather, I wished that I wished that I were.

I found what I hadn't known I'd been looking for between Assembly & Fabricating Service and Association Management.

There were four ads. They were virtually identical. One featured the word "accredited." Another, in a tiny, sloping font, said "100% legal." All four claimed to be "professional" and "discreet."

They could offer little more than costly consultation, I thought. Probably they would provide me with nothing but a list of legal drugs, recipes, LD50s. Or did they perhaps target the old, the frail, and the timid, by offering to facilitate the act? But how could they do that?

They couldn't. Assistance was an illusion. Because ultimately the decision had to be made by me alone. There was no way to delegate that responsibility. The only question was a pedantic one: Which step would I call my last? At what point did the process become irrevocable? Whether I pulled a trigger, signed a form, or picked up the phone, it would still be my effort – my will seeking its own termination.

Was there a paradox there? Was it inconsistent to want to stop wanting? To decide to stop deciding? Was it hypocritical to use my will to destroy it? Was it not like launching a war on violence, or casting your vote for the abolition of democracy, or using language to decry the inadequacy of language? No. There was no paradox. To use some tool to dismantle itself made perfect sense, if it was the best – or only – tool for the job. There was nothing illogical about detonating dynamite to get rid of it, and there was nothing hypocritical about killing yourself. You were not deciding that there should *never* have been such a thing as decision-making; only that there should be no more of it, not for you.

Anyway, it was not, I believed, the action itself that posed any difficulty. I had in my life swallowed many a pill; I had started my car in the garage countless times. It was only the context that would be different. Naturally I – or my body, rather – recoiled from the possibility of pain, but there were certainly ways to avoid that. And cessation, mere nothingness, held for me no terror: for a man who never remembered his dreams, it would differ not at all from sleep. No, I decided, it was not the end, but what would follow the end that filled me with fear.

For one thing, Alice and Becky would never forgive me – not for the hurt my death would bring them, but rather the embarrassment. What would Becky tell her classmates, or the nameless boy in the car, or the boys who would follow? Then there was Alice's family, who had never really accepted me; their confident, self-assured contempt would surely poison what little remained, or would remain, of Alice's feelings for me. That thought was, somehow, intolerable – even though my own feelings were now much closer to hatred than love. But I could remember a time . . .

My own family would perhaps be more sympathetic. Elton, at least, always flaunting his boundless empathy, would take up the role of apologist; he would probably quote Hume or someone at the funeral. (Would there be a funeral? Of course: I had no religion eager to condemn me.) Evelyn would simply be mystified, but would pretend to be overwhelmed; I could picture her over-eating and snapping at the children. My mother, though – terminally, incorrigibly on my side – would be shattered; probably she would blame Alice.

Not least of all I had to consider my friends, my co-workers, even my fucking neighbours, and what they would say. I knew so many people; so many people knew me. And yet not one of them would understand. Not one of them would try to. They would see only the flawless exterior of what I'd left behind – the lovely wife and the talented daughter; the two-car garage and the secluded summer cabin; the list of famous clients and the six-figure salary – and they would conclude that I'd been crazy, that I'd acted without reason, like a puerile, selfish coward. Perhaps if I'd had more reason to believe that my suicide would be respected, I would have had less reason to commit it.

But suicide was not childish: children had been known to murder other children, but never themselves. It was not selfish: nothing that obliterated the self, and in such a spectacularly invidious fashion, could be called that. Nor was it cowardly: death was never the obvious, and certainly never the easy solution. Surely it was going on living – by default, out of habit, despite the grief that life engendered – that was the safe and craven act. My problem was not that I was too much of a coward to go on living; I was too much of a coward to die.

An hour later I found myself driving aimlessly and, as it were, autonomically through glowing, rain-glossed streets. I'd forgotten the pizza. I'd forgotten to call home. Somehow, though, I remembered the phone number from the first of those four ads.

Late one night the following week, I stopped at a 7-Eleven on my way home from work. I bought milk and bread and a *Harper's* that I wouldn't read. Back out in the parking lot, at the edge of which a single tree shimmered lethargically beneath a single lamppost, I lifted the receiver of the payphone and, with wilful thoughtlessness, dialled the number I'd memorized. The line purred once and then, somewhat to my surprise, a woman's voice answered. I became aware of the blood beating in my head. I waited a moment to make sure the voice did not belong to an answering machine.

"Assistance Associates," repeated the voice. "This is Tracy speaking. How can I help you?"

"Tracy?"

"That's right."

"I'm sorry. I didn't think you'd be open. I thought maybe there would be a recorded message, or . . ."

"No," she said. "We've always got someone here answering the phones."

"Ah," I said. My mind remained stubbornly blank, overloaded with a hundred potential but unrealized thoughts. "I was just wondering," I said, "that is, I had some questions, but I'm not sure this . . . I'm at a payphone and . . ."

"Would you like to schedule a consultation with one of our Assistance consultants?"

"I don't know," I said. My ears were ringing. I cleared my throat. "I don't know. Actually, I don't think you can help me."

"There's no fee," said Tracy softly, "and there's no commitment."

"I just want to know one thing. Tell me, can you arrange it, the uh, the . . ."

"Yes?"

"This will probably sound crazy, but can you arrange it so that no one knows?" I felt, in my cheeks, the sting of gathering tears. I closed my eyes and took a deep breath. "I don't want anyone to find out."

The next day I took an early lunch and drove across town for my free, no-commitment consultation. In a modest but comfortable office on the fourteenth floor of a nondescript high-rise, I met with a tall, blandly handsome, well-dressed middle-aged man named Clint Markam. He shook my hand with polite efficiency, sat back down behind an artfully cluttered desk, and invited me to take the chair opposite. His manner was crisp and businesslike, not morosely solicitous or cheerfully therapeutic, as I had feared.

"You've probably got a lot of questions," said Clint Markam. "Everyone does at first. To a certain extent it's inevitable. The nature of the service we offer here, as I'm sure you can appreciate, prohibits publicity." Clint Markam enunciated a little too clearly, as though taking care not to bite any words as they left his mouth.

I shrugged. "Tracy explained a lot over the phone."

"Of course." Clint Markam seemed a little disappointed by this news. He began rummaging through the papers on his desk. "Before we get any further, there is one little formality . . . Here we are." He handed me a sheet of paper and a stubby pencil.

"Is this like an IQ test?" I asked. "Or some kind of psychological thing?"

"Yes," said Clint Markam simply. "It's very much informal and unofficial, of course. You will have to complete a much more exhaustive profile at a later date, should you decide to continue, which helps us ensure that, among other things, you are acting autonomously and that psychologically, as you say, you fall within the acceptable parameters."

I grinned with part of my mouth. "What parameters would those be?"

"Those that the government outlines for us."

"In other words, I'll have to take a test that proves I'm sane?"

"That probably sums it up, yes, if a bit coarsely. But this questionnaire will give us a general idea of whether or not we will, in fact, be able to assist you. I find it saves time in the long run, you see, to get it out of the way early on. So if you don't mind, it should only take a few minutes."

"Of course." I pulled my chair forward, to the edge of Clint Markam's desk, and read over the form.

For each section, mark with an "X" the *one* statement that best describes you.
(Remember that there are no right or wrong answers.)

1.
___ I have felt remorse for things left undone
___ I have felt depressed without knowing why
___ I have drunk to excess and later regretted it
___ I have felt despair at the thought of the future

2.
___ I have not made friends easily
___ I have imagined problems where problems didn't exist
___ I have felt overwhelmed by events that were beyond my control
___ I have wished for the impossible

3.
___ I have felt nostalgic for an unspecific past
___ I have preferred my own company to that of other people
___ I have disliked myself
___ I have been overly critical of myself and/or others

4.

___ I have failed to communicate my ideas clearly

___ I have been unable to see how things could be improved

___ I have wasted my time

___ I have avoided crowds and/or crowded events

5.

___ I have indulged in regret

___ I have been uncomfortable in unfamiliar situations

___ I have had more worries than most people

___ I have allowed bad situations to continue

6.

___ I have been selfish more often than selfless

___ I have taken few risks

___ I have been unable to make up my mind on important issues

___ I have focused on my failings instead of my strengths

7.

___ I have carried on with habits that I knew were harmful

___ I have had strong mood swings

___ I have used sleep as an avoidance tactic

___ I have found it difficult to unwind

8.

___ I have felt ill at ease

___ I have manipulated people to get my way

___ I have been bothered by noise, ugliness, and/or disorder

___ I have been a poor listener and a poorer speaker

9.

___ I have been overwhelmed by doubts

___ I have failed to react

___ I have felt desperate

___ I have made a mess of things

10.

___ I have felt trapped

___ I have told people they were right when I knew they were wrong

___ I have not stood up for myself

___ I have made matters worse

I looked up from the exam. "Do I really have to choose just *one?*"

Clint Markam sat there placidly, patiently. A sympathetic smile flickered upon his lips. "I'm afraid so."

After a minute of deliberation, I began putting X's beside the statements that seemed slightly more true than the others. Frequently I scribbled out my first X – the pencil had no eraser – and put another beside a different statement. It must have taken me fifteen minutes or more to answer all ten questions. With an apologetic shrug, I held out the sheet to Clint Markam. He grasped it with a clean, ringless hand, glanced at it for less than a second, and put it aside.

"What's the matter?" I asked.

"Nothing. It's fine."

"I thought there were no wrong answers," I said with a small huff of embarrassment.

"You're righter than you realize," he said. "Don't worry, you 'passed.'"

"Oh." I pushed my chair back to where it had been.

Clint Markam spread his hands slowly, as though measuring some object from memory. "Now," he said. "I imagine you have a question or two."

"Yes," I said and, without intending to, leaned forward in my chair. "How can you make it so that if I go through with this, no one will ever know?"

Clint Markam nodded. "We have many plans that accommodate that desire," he said, so unemphatically that, for the first time, I began to hope that it was possible. "It is," he said, "a very common request." Again he rummaged through the papers on his desk. He found what he was looking for almost immediately. "Here we are," he said. "The Replacement Plan."

I took the brochure as far as my car, but – remembering the time I'd "hidden" Alice's tenth-anniversary gift in the glovebox – decided not to leave the parking lot with it.

The pamphlet praised me for taking the first brave step towards making an extremely difficult decision, then thanked me for having the wisdom to put my trust in Assistance Associates, who had been proudly providing a wide range of creative, highly personalized, competitively priced, and technologically cutting-edge Assistance plans to their clients for more than fifteen years. As one of the pioneers in the field, AA had been . . .

Impatiently, I flipped the page.

The AA Replacement Plan

At Assistance Associates, we realize that there are nearly as many reasons for seeking Assistance as there are stars in the night sky. In fact, only a small percentage of our clients suffer from debilitating or incurable diseases. And today's hospitals, staffed with ever more compassionate nurses and enlightened doctors, have been increasingly able to provide the terminally ill with the nominal Assistance they require.

Typically, it is the "healthy" whose Assistance needs continue to be overlooked and ignored, even in today's supposedly Assistance-friendly political climate. The sad fact remains that only a very narrow, very arbitrary spectrum of justifications for Assistance has been generally accepted as legitimate. *The AA Replacement Plan* has been specifically designed for the Assistance-seeking individual who suffers from none of these "approved," because visible, afflictions . . .

I skipped a few more paragraphs.

It may come as a surprise to learn that all humans have over 99% of their genetic makeup in common (scientific corroboration of the old adage that although there are only small differences between people, those differences matter a great deal!). It is this principle that allows us at AA to produce an exact genetic replica – a Replacement – of a client in a very short amount of time.

Without going into too much technical detail, the procedure involves transferring first your unique genetic information, and later, your particular brain state, including all your memories, skills, and attitudes, to a generic *tabula rasa* (or "blank slate") – that is, a body of your sex and approximate age, but with only the first 99% of its genetic code "filled in." (*Tabula rasas*, as you may know, are most often used today as organ and blood donors. Don't worry. They can't feel a thing! Besides lacking an active brain, and thus any form of consciousness whatsoever, *tabula rasas* are not even technically human beings.)

Incredible as it may sound, it's not "science fiction"! Recent advances in psychogenetic engineering, magneto-electroencephalogrametry (or, if that's too much of a mouthful, MEEG), and synthetic neurotransmitter feedback loop transfers have made the dream of creating your very own *doppelganger* (or "double") not only a possibility, but a confirmed reality. Already, we at Assistance Associates have successfully produced and seamlessly introduced Replacements into the lives of over *300* of our clients – thus freeing them to receive the Assistance they need without guilt, shame, or regret.

Indeed, *The AA Replacement Plan* has rapidly become one of our most popular Assistance packages. In fact, we think of it as our specialty. Other Assistance firms offer elaborate Accident and Disease Plans that can be as risky as they are potentially painful – for both you *and* your loved ones. And no mere mishap or illness, no matter how dignified, can spare you the inescapable ignominy of your no longer being a part of the human race.

Clearly, *The AA Replacement Plan* is the plan of choice for those who want everything to go on exactly as it is – but with one key difference.

I got out of the car, crossed the parking lot, and dropped the brochure into a garbage can. Back in the car, I was appalled to see that, according to the radio clock, I was already twenty minutes late for my two o'clock teleconference.

*

Less than a month later, everything was in place for what Clint Markam had called the "insertion." I had undergone the requisite scans and passed the necessary tests. I had signed countless legal forms and intoned into a tape recorder a prepared statement affirming that I was compos mentis and acting of my own volition. I had traded in some stocks and cooked our bankbooks – it gave me a kick to do this for myself, for once – to free up the money to pay Assistance Associates without arousing Alice's suspicion. And I had done nothing else.

Clint Markam had warned me not to behave any differently in the days leading up to the insertion. It was imperative that I resist any urge to say my goodbyes. I was advised not to call old friends, apologize for things done or undone, visit graveyards, weep, call in sick to work, go on trips, give away my belongings, discuss with friends or family their plans for the future, or do anything else that might appear out of the ordinary.

And I had behaved myself. At worst, I may have been a little more patient with Becky, a little more amiable with Alice, a little more industrious at work. I couldn't help myself. The truth was, the only person I felt any real temptation to bid farewell to was myself. My valediction – my elegy – took the form of good behaviour: I tried a little harder to be the person I'd want to remember myself as.

On the day of the insertion I took care to wake up at the usual time, brush my teeth with the usual listlessness, drink the usual three cups of coffee, and yell through Becky's door the usual warning that she was going to be late. I may have stood in the doorway for a moment too long, watching

Alice attack the clogged sink with a butter knife . . . But I clamped down on those thoughts, and muttered the usual perfunctory goodbye. (She didn't even look up.) My heart was clattering in my chest as I drove off to work. But I was proud of myself. I'd given nothing away. I took the usual route at the usual speed.

At the office I was unable to do anything more than pretend to go over the work I'd finished the day before. At around eleven o'clock I told my secretary I felt a migraine coming on and was going home. Her face crumpled with concern, at which I nearly burst out sobbing. Instead I mumbled a sullen "See you tomorrow" and got into the elevator.

My appointment at AA was not until one, so for an hour or so I drove aimlessly through the suburbs, taking only right turns at prime number intersections: after the first right I took the second right, then the third right, the fifth right . . . When I was forced to take the fourth right instead of the eleventh because the street I was on came to an end, I quit playing the game. I pulled into a nearly deserted shopping centre parking lot. I went into the bookstore and browsed blindly for forty minutes, not even bothering to open the books I held in my hands. I caught one of the cashiers eyeing me suspiciously, so I bought a calendar of old sports cars – whose days, I realized with maudlin relief, I would never have to wake to – and left. Then I drove to the Assistance Associates building.

Clint Markam was waiting for me in the reception area. He clasped my hand briefly between both of his. His look of confident expectation faltered for a moment.

"Everything all right?" he asked.

"Perfect," I said. I'd been crying in the car. "Everything went well."

"Excellent. Then follow me."

He led me into a small, unfurnished room. Inset in one wall was a wide mirror. Clint Markam closed the door and switched off the lights, and the mirror became a window. I stepped towards it.

In the room on the other side of the glass was a man who looked like me. He sat in a chair, feet together, hands folded loosely in his lap, his head tilted back slightly, his eyes closed. He looked as though he were trying to remember someone's name. "Is he asleep?" I whispered.

"No," said Clint Markam. "Not exactly. He's in a hypnotic trance."

"What for?"

"We don't want him to remember being here. We want him to think he's been at work all morning, and that he came home with a migraine. Now what I need you to do is take off your clothes."

I stared at him.

He gestured towards the mirror. "For him. Then we'll drop him off at your place."

"Right," I said. "Of course."

"There are some clothes in that closet. Put on whatever's most comfortable. It should all fit you. I'll be back in a minute." He exited the room.

I studied my doppelganger. He was not facing the mirror but an adjacent wall, so that I had a view of his profile. There was no question that he resembled me to an uncanny degree, but I was not convinced that he was my exact duplicate. Something about the shape of the head . . . The chin, perhaps . . . Surely Alice would notice the difference . . . I told myself that I was mistaken, that I had simply never seen myself in full profile before, or, for that matter, with my eyes closed.

I got undressed.

Clint Markam had provided me with three bugs to install in my house. I'd put one in the kitchen, under the sink, one in the living room, under the couch, and one in our bedroom, under the bed. They looked and felt like little pebbles, so even if Alice or Becky (or, I supposed, my doppelganger) found them they would just toss them out. They only had to remain in place for a few hours – until I was satisfied that the insertion had gone smoothly.

I sat alone in Clint Markam's office (he'd cleared all the detritus off his desk and locked its drawers). I sat there and fiddled anxiously with the knobs on the radio receiver. From the bugs in the kitchen and living room I heard nothing but somnolent static. From the one in the bedroom I could hear my doppelganger lightly snoring.

I did not snore.

Did I?

At about three o'clock I heard a door being unlocked, opened, closed, and locked again. Then I heard voices. One belonged to Becky. The other I didn't recognize, though I guessed it was the boy who'd dropped her off after her spurious band trip.

"We should be good for an hour and a half," Becky said.

"Cool. Do you got anything to eat?"

"No," said Becky peevishly. "I mean, what, you're *hungry*?"

"I guess not. No. Not really."

"I mean, we can eat later. Can't we?"

"Sure. Of course. Yeah. That's cool. I don't care."

There followed a minute of silence. Then, in a sarcastic tone, as though extending a challenge she hardly expected him to meet, Becky said, "So do you want to go upstairs?"

"Yeah, of course," said the boy with factitious bravado. "If you want."

"Well, I mean, we might as well."

"Yeah. Okay."

The sound of footsteps receding up the stairs. I switched to the bedroom channel. The snoring had stopped. I heard a door click faintly, then the creaking of bedsprings – too clear to be coming from Becky's room. My doppelganger was getting up.

I heard a distant knocking, then Becky's voice, muffled but noticeably shrill with alarm.

"Do you mind opening up?" said a third voice. It took me a moment to recognize it as my own – or a variation on my own.

After half a minute a door was opened. Then Becky, guilty and flustered, said, "What are *you* doing home?"

Ignoring this, my double said, "Hello."

"Hey," said the boy, his bravado gone.

"Dad, what do you want?"

"I don't believe we've been introduced."

"His name's Kevin, now do you mind?"

"I was just leaving," said the boy. "I'll see you later. Nice to meet you."

"You don't have to go," said Becky. "Oh forget it. *Bye.*"

A drum roll of footsteps down the stairs.

"There. Are you satisfied?"

"Why should I be satisfied?"

"You come home early from work just to spy on me now?"

"I just hope you're using protection."

"Oh God. I can't believe you just said that."

"If you think you're exempt from catastrophe, you've got a big lesson coming."

"You are so . . . *aggravating*. You don't know anything about me."

"Whose fault is that?"

"Did you ever hear of privacy? Could you now please get your foot out of my doorway?"

"All right. Fine. Never mind. I don't care what you do."

"Good. Then maybe you can stop spying on me."

"For your information I came home because I had a headache."

"Well you seem to be pretty all right now."

"*I am not all right!*"

"No, you're not! You're crazy!"

A door slammed.

I turned off the receiver and went to find Clint Markam.

"Well?"

I shook my head reverently. "It's absolutely amazing," I said. "How does he know to say what I would say?"

"Remember, he's not an actor. He's not an imposter. As far as he's concerned, he *is* you."

"I see." At that thought my admiration for him was adulterated somewhat by pity. "Well, I've got no complaints. He's perfect."

"I'm glad," he said, and sounded it. "Now, unless there's anything else . . ."

He'd explained to me earlier that I could back out at any time, but that once the insertion was complete it would be considerably more problematic. The bottom line was that any interference with the new me – who was now, as far as the law was concerned, in fact the old me – would be impossible. I could not go back to my old life, and it would be difficult, even foolhardy, to leave town and attempt to start a new one. What Clint Markam was asking me, then, was whether I was having second thoughts.

"No," I said. "I think I'm ready."

"Good man," he said, furrowing his lower lip in an approving, supportive expression.

He showed me into what looked like the lunch room of a family-run company. It was small without being cramped, characterless without being sterile. There was a mini fridge, a table and chairs, a comfortable-looking couch, a dartboard, a television, a telephone, a magazine rack, and a good view through the one window of the downtown core. "I can see my office from here," I said, pointing.

"If you need anything, just pick up the phone," said Clint Markam. "There's an assortment of beverages in the fridge, also some fruit if you're hungry. There's also a small pill bottle," he said.

I looked at him.

"Three should be plenty," he said. "I'd recommend you take four or five."

"Do they . . . Will I . . ."

"You'll begin to feel groggy. Possibly some pins and needles in your extremities. A warmness in your chest. Vision will blur a little. Nothing unpleasant. Within fifteen minutes you should drop off to sleep."

"And that's it?"

Clint Markam turned back to the door, as though physically evading my question. "Again, if you need anything . . ." He pointed at the phone.

"Well," I said. "Thanks for everything."

He smiled with grim encouragement, like a coach sending his star player in to save the game in the last minute. Then, without any further word, he stepped out the door.

I removed an orange juice and the pill bottle from the fridge. There were only five pills, five milky green capsules. I swallowed them all. Then I sat down on the couch to wait.

I closed my eyes and took a long, deep breath. I imagined first my feet, then my legs, then my torso, then my arms, and finally my head turning to heavy stone. I exhaled.

Then an unpleasant thought occurred to me: What if *he* decided to kill himself?

Well, I supposed he would probably do what I'd done. Eventually he'd discover the same page in the phone book, and eventually he'd call one of the numbers. Just like I had. Just like the next one would, if there was one.

Just like the one before me had, if there had been one.

Anyway, I hoped, dimly, for his sake, that he didn't try to do it alone. But I didn't really care anymore, one way or another.

I started to feel pins and needles in my fingertips. I wondered if my life would flash before my eyes. I rather hoped not.

THE PROBLEM OF PLEASURE

The first night they unpacked the stereo and the coffee maker. Their plan was to stay up all night and watch the sun come up, as she put it, over the slums where the little people lived.

They played tic-tac-toe on the balcony window with their saliva until she was convinced that two winning strategies inevitably resulted in a tie. They cleaned the glass with yellowing newspapers he found beneath the sink.

She took a shower and emerged with one towel draped around her body and another coiled in her hair. She had to look in the mirror to show him how it was done. He took a shower and put his dirty clothes back on.

They smoked the remainder of a rumpled joint that someone had shared with her at an audition for a chewing gum commercial. She stood on the sofa and delivered her one line with ecstatic glee, with slack-jawed forgetfulness, with shock and revulsion, with Shakespearean gusto: *What's that taste?* She hadn't gotten the part.

He turned off the lights, crouched next to her on the sofa, and traced his index fingers down the ridge of her spine.

How many? he asked.

Two, she said. No, one. I don't know. I have a stomache, she mumbled, making it one word. Too much coffee.

My head hurts, he said, as though by way of consolation.

Your head hearts?

My head hearts, he agreed.

He brought out his camera. She pressed the backs of her hands against her forehead histrionically, like an ingénue. When she reached for him, he stepped away, raised the camera to his eye, and said: Click.

She fell asleep soon after the sky began to turn blue. He didn't wake her. Instead he made more coffee, turned off the stereo, and unpacked his computer from a box she'd labelled FRAGILE.

They had a rule: They were not allowed to say "I love you too."

He'd said it once, and she'd said, Ah – no. Not allowed.

What do you mean, "not allowed"?

Empty and/or automatic reciprocation not allowed.

Okay. I love·you.

Maybe. Maybe so. But how do I know you're not just saying it because it's what I want to hear? Wait a few minutes and try again.

A few minutes later he said, Oh, by the way. It just so happens that I love you.

Sorry. Too soon. I saw it coming. You need to surprise me. Or you won't know that I mean it?

*

Her sister liked him. Her brother liked him. Her father liked him. Her mother loved him. Jen liked him. Marco liked him. Hélène said he was cute. Roger thought he was intelligent. Elle said he seemed a little shy – but charming, definitely charming. Nan claimed he had "nerd chic." Janice liked him. Wynne liked him. Heather liked him.

Caryn liked him, or said she liked him. She teased him, jabbed him with her knuckles, mussed his hair, called him the Hemogoblin – all playfully, of course, all in good fun. Or was it?

Caryn had liked Anthony better. Anthony had been wild. But it didn't matter.

Riding home in the crowded, silent, creaking subway train, he made lists.

The colour of her hair when it's drying.

The loose, wrinkly skin that appears at her elbows when she straightens her arms.

The way she intentionally bruises her apples before eating them, tap tap tapping them on the counter or tabletop.

The way she doesn't turn around, like most people, to glare incredulously at the crack in the sidewalk she's just stumbled over, but walks on, seemingly unaware of having stumbled at all.

Her fuzzy earlobes.

Her face.

She taught him how to cook, cut his own hair, buy pants, and play guitar.

He taught her how to get free cable, make mix CDs, register her own domain name, and operate Unix, which she referred to as Eunuchs.

Because she always wanted to come along, and because he could not refuse, sometimes he stayed late at work so that he could take his after-dark walks alone, before going home.

On the phone to her sister he heard her say: No, I *am* still looking. It's just that you have no idea how much time auditioning takes . . . Of course I don't, you know how independent I am. But it's not like *he* minds that I . . . You know, if everything you do is just the opposite of what Mom did, if everything's just a knee-jerk reaction to the old-fashioned . . . It has *nothing* to do with feminism, Laura . . .

And then she softly closed the bedroom door.

Would you still love me if I was fat?
Yes, he said after a pause.
Would you still love me if I was ugly?
Of course.
Would you still love me if I was a hundred years old?
No question.
Would you still love me if I was five?
Would you still love me if I was a man?
If I couldn't speak any English?
If I didn't have any arms or legs?
If I was just a disembodied head?
If I was made out of cheese?

Absolutely.

All of the above?

You mean, would I still love you if you were an ugly fat boy's head, made out of cheese?

Who couldn't speak English.

He pretended to consider it. Then: *Yes*, he said bravely. Yes, I think I would. All of the above.

Would you still love me if I didn't love you?

Sometimes Caryn came over to watch the *Sunday Night Sex Show*.

He hated the bloodless, clinical, cheerfully candid way that the host reduced sex to a game of skill or an intellectual problem, the sort of puzzle that, with the latest playbook and a little earnest application, you could not fail to solve.

The girls thought it was hilarious – though he noticed they didn't laugh quite so loudly when he was not in the room.

It's not that bad, she said quickly, to conceal her annoyance. I don't mind as much as I maybe used to. He just has a different outlook than I do. Different experiences. I'm only his second girlfriend, you know. It probably just takes time. But I'm not complaining. It's not a big deal. It's not the most important thing in the world. What? What are you smirking at?

I just wish the you of two years ago could hear the you of today, said Caryn. Or vice versa.

Okay, well, with Anthony maybe it *was* the most important thing in the world, because that was the extent of our world. He had nothing else going for him, I mean at all. He was an asshole. I hated his guts, really.

Which was precisely why the sex was so-good.

I love you, he said.

She looked up from her cross-stitch and smiled gratefully.

I'm very pleased to hear it, sir.

One night he walked home, forgetting it was Friday. Teenagers shouted "fag!" at him from passing cars, laughing groups bound for downtown bars edged him off the sidewalk, men with their dates stared him down, then magnanimously challenged him to a fight.

He wondered if there was something particular about him. Did he look like a dog asking to be kicked?

It never happened when he was with her. Something about her elicited people's respect, almost reverence.

He hurried home.

She was riding home on the subway late one night when three young men sat down next to her, though the car was almost empty. They were drunk. They talked about her loudly and appraisingly, like shrewd consumers. She stared fixedly at the reflection of a Clairol ad in the window. She had pepper spray in her bag but didn't dare make a move to reach for it. She focused on the sound of her clanging heartbeat and pretended she was deaf. Eventually they lost interest in her, and offered only a few parting gestures and perfunctory self-gropings when their stop came.

Was there something about her that invited this treatment, she wondered, or was it simply that she was alone, and therefore vulnerable? Vulnerable and therefore contemptible?

She hurried home, her keys clutched in her fist, her eyes stinging.

He was already asleep.

At night when he walked, so many of the windows were bright, unobstructed and inviting, lit up like the grid of flickering television screens in an electronics store.

Well, how do I look? she asked.

He stepped back and crossed his arms.

You look great.

Good, she said, and kissed the corner of his mouth. Then let's get going.

Why is there a password on your computer? she asked. Don't you trust me?

Of course not, he said.

What have you got on there, porn?

Yes. Kiddie porn. Gigabytes of kiddie porn.

Hmm, she said. Can't say I approve of *that*.

I love you, she said.

He transferred the receiver to his other ear and looked over his shoulder.

Yes, that is most definitely good news, he said.

At first he assumed it was a joke. But the mischievous solemnity with which she made popcorn and turned down the lights told him otherwise.

She giggled and kept looking at him sidelong to gauge his reaction. He pretended not to notice.

I don't understand humans at all, he said at the end of the first scene.

Well, it is kind of silly, she admitted.

It's disgusting.

Watch one more?

I have to piss.

Should I pause it?

No. I'll be right back.

Later, she joined him in the bedroom.

Can I turn on the light?

If you must.

Wordlessly she crawled in between the sheets.

You don't have to do that, he said a minute later.

I don't mind, she said.

He said nothing.

Correction: I *like* to, she said.

It just seems a bit silly, he said, half the syllables coming out as whisper. He cleared his throat and added: Now that we're living together, I mean.

It was her turn to say nothing.

So it's okay, he said. Don't worry about it.

What do you mean, now that we're living together?

Just that you don't have to . . . try to impress me anymore.

You don't like it?

I don't *dis*like it.

You don't like it.

I just don't feel like you should have to, that's all. If you don't want to.

And if I do want to?

I'd just prefer you didn't.

If I'm doing it wrong you just have to tell me what to do differently.

That's not it.

Then what is it?

He flopped onto his side. You don't find it a little demeaning?

What? For who?

It looks silly, he said slowly. It makes you look silly.

She allowed a few seconds for this to sink in, but it would not. The light is off, she said at last.

It's just not necessary.

And what about me? What if I want *you* to?

Instead of answering he said: Should we just go to sleep?

So she let him roll on top of her the way he'd done all the other nights.

Afterwards she whispered: I guess you wouldn't want to try anything we saw in the video?

He wrapped his arms around her tightly, as though she were a waif he'd pulled from a river, and said sternly: Listen. I *love* you. Get it?

I love you too, she said automatically. That's not –

Ah – no, he said. Not allowed.

And he kissed her forehead brusquely.

And you? she said. How's the new stud treating you?

Oh God, said Caryn. He's wearing me out.

That's good, isn't it?

I *guess*. The problem is he won't go down. His idea of pleasuring me orally is to tell a knock-knock joke.

There were two girls he watched for. One lived alone in a creamy, spartan apartment on the third floor of a condo on Eighteenth Avenue. She moved around a lot, from room to room, tidying or rearranging, pausing occasionally to think, with arms akimbo or the fingers of one hand lightly cupping her chin.

The other lived in a cramped, colourful garret in a rickety house on Seventh Street, which she shared with at least three roommates, two of them male. She spent most of her time reading, sitting in a deep chair beside the window with a book propped against her knees. Every few minutes she would turn and stare out the black window, as though mentally measuring the discrepancy between what she had read on the page and what she knew, from experience, to be really out there.

They were both lonely and beautiful. They both seemed to be waiting for something.

Why do we do this? she asked Caryn. Oh, sorry doll, your lips are too thin. Oh, sorry babe, your lips are too puffy. You should *probably* lose about four pounds. You're just a *little* too malnourished. Your eyes are too wide – I actually had someone say that to me the other day. Not too far apart, but too wide, whatever that means. What would you look like with green contacts? Or red hair? Or a C-cup? Or a different head? Why do we do it? Why do we put ourselves through it?

Because, said Caryn, sucking offhandedly at a cigarette, we want all the world to love us, presumably.

Not me. Not anymore. After two years of this I'd settle

for loving myself. If I ever get back to that point, I'll quit.

And do what with yourself? Raise babies? Little hemo-goblins?

Sometimes I think it's not that we want to be famous or recognized or whatever by *other people*. Sometimes I think it's more about making it easier to recognize and understand and, I don't know, maybe even like *yourself*. Like, maybe if you saw your own face splashed across bus shelters, or if you saw yourself on television or in magazines once in a while, maybe then you could finally –

Finally see yourself for what you really are. Sure.

I *know* I'm attractive, she said defiantly. Directors don't know anything. Agencies don't know anything. I'm always getting compliments.

They don't count if they're from your boyfriend. Oh, I *know* –

No, from all kinds of people. From photographers, hair-dressers. Even strangers. In the street, on the bus . . .

You're a goddess, said Caryn, crushing her cigarette beneath the heel of her boot. I was just teasing.

I know.

Let's go back in. Maybe they're almost ready for one of us.

He said his back hurt, so she asked him about work.

I'm sorry, he said. It's just been pretty hectic lately . . .

It doesn't matter. But tell me *about* it. Tell me what you're doing right now. Details. Inundate me with techni-cal jargon.

The only project that interested him at the moment was the new video compression codec. He'd always been intrigued by the possibility of shrinking data, making something large small. In high school he'd spent a cola-fuelled weekend in front of his C compiler, reluctantly coming to terms with the logical impossibility of recursive compression – compressing an already compressed file. But the disappointment was only temporary, and the challenge eternal: how to express the greatest amount of information in the most concise way. What it came down to was patterns, the recognition of recurrent patterns in a set of data. If some string, some phrase, appeared three times – "I love you I love you I love you," for instance – you could store it once and recall it twice – "I love you" (repeat 2x). The tricky part was that repetitions rarely came sequentially, so you could search the entire world for another instance of "I love you," wasting valuable time, and it might never reappear. The breadth of your pattern search always had to be weighed against the time required to perform it. Speed came at the cost of quality compression, quality at the cost of speed.

She watched his lips as he spoke. She wanted to lean over and brush them with her thumbs.

You're yawning, he said. I don't blame you.

I wasn't. I'm listening. I can yawn and pay attention at the same time. But I wasn't yawning.

Well, the codec we're working on is for live webcam feeds. With those the picture doesn't usually change very much. Often as not it's just some guy's empty dorm room. So there might be shortcuts. We might be able to cheat and – Never mind.

Sorry. That was a yawn. I confess. Not because it's boring. Go on.

No, you go on. Tell me about the photo shoot. Was it a photo shoot?

Ah – no. Not allowed. Still you.

There's nothing else to tell.

What about that gadget you brought home? Is that one of these camera deals?

Yeah. Prototype from the client. I thought maybe I'd point it out the window, down-at the street or something. Just to get some different data to work with. I've got hard drives filled with the back of Nathan's head and the inside of the server room.

So you'll, what, be able to watch it from work?

Well, yeah, if I leave my computer on.

Will anyone else?

Not without my password, no.

Then why don't you just, I don't know, put this one in the corner over there or something?

What? Why? So I can spy on you? Is that –

I don't know. I kind of like the idea of you watching. Even if you're not watching. It'll be like having you here, maybe, a little bit.

At first she seemed guarded and self-conscious. She did not look directly at the camera – she was too much of a professional for that – but every time she went into the bedroom her awareness of the device permeated all her movements, tainted them ever so slightly with an air of deliberateness and calculation.

But soon enough the self-consciousness faded. Soon she seemed to forget that she was (at least potentially) being watched. Soon she was spending most of her time in the bedroom.

And soon he found her every gesture, her every pose, her every facial expression, endlessly gripping, inexhaustibly fascinating.

Do you have a picture of me on your desk? she asked.

No. But I have three in my wallet, he said, as though it were only a joke.

Well, she said, now you do.

For her birthday, Caryn bought her a toy.

For when you're out of town, Caryn told him.

But neither of them found it funny. So Caryn gave him one for his birthday, too.

For when she's out of town.

He threw his away. She kept hers, hidden beneath shoes and books in her closet.

I love you, he said.

She rolled over and blinked at him with pink eyes.

What time is it? she asked.

Colin told them about an implausible liaison with a policewoman who had almost written him a speeding ticket. Geoff related an Ecstasy-fuelled night spent with a cute green-haired girl he'd met at a rave in San Francisco. Nathan recounted in great detail the predilections and perversions of a high school chemistry teacher who'd approached him – "practically tackled" him – in a bar,

He was surprised that in each of their stories the girl had been a complete stranger. Their best experiences had all been one-night stands.

Then it was his turn.

I don't know, he said. I guess it would have to be with my girlfriend, but –

They all groaned.

Well, okay, but there was this one time that was pretty . . . exceptional. We were both sick. We both had the flu. Fever, runny nose, sore throat, nausea, the whole thing. Mountains of used kleenex all over the floor. Anyway . . . I don't know. It was just memorable. She was so *hot*. And the whole time I was having these hot flashes and cold flashes, alternating one after the other. Goose pimples appearing and disappearing in waves across her skin. Both of us just dripping with sweat. The sheets were soaking. And the whole time we were coughing and laughing and our noses were running all over each other . . .

Jesus Christ, said Nathan.

But no, it was nice. I don't know how to explain it. Like huddling around the fire when the wind's howling outside. Only the wind and the fire were both there, inside us, at the same time.

They stared at him incredulously.

Something like that, he muttered, and lifted his beer.

The way she punches only multiples of eleven when using the microwave.

The way she fidgets in her sleep. And when she's not tossing or turning, when she's completely still, the way she seems to be biding her time, planning her next move.

Her habit of quoting herself. Not elaborately or pompously, but reflexively, almost apologetically. As though she doesn't want anyone, even herself, to be able to accuse her of unoriginality. As though her biggest fear is that someone should roll their eyes at her.

Her tendency to weep.

Her tendency to exaggerate.

Her use of the word "whatever."

The bloody floss she leaves floating in the toilet.

Jackie liked him. Susan liked him. Rachael liked him, Fiona liked him. Elisabetta liked him. Penny liked him. Casey liked him. Quinn liked him. Paula liked him.

He didn't like her friends. He thought most of them were obnoxious egomaniacs. He didn't understand why she surrounded herself with such people, or indeed why she wanted to be an actress. She was too intelligent to dedicate herself to the glorification of wine coolers or luxury sedans or athlete's foot powder, and too modest to act like a star – to cultivate, in her own person, a monument to her everlasting greatness.

He never said any of this, of course. But he didn't have to.

Now he often stayed late at work to watch her. One night his heart plastered itself against his chest when she suddenly looked up from her magazine, turned to the camera, and plaintively mouthed the words, Where are you?

One night he watched her until she fell asleep. He had been waiting for her to grow anxious and alarmed. Waiting for her to call him, to ask if he was all right, would he be home soon? Waiting for her to begin waiting.

Use your hands a little more, she whispered.

How?

Here. And here. Good. Only not so . . . mechanically.

It's hard not to act mechanically when you're giving me instructions.

I'll shut up then. Do whatever you like.

I thought I was doing that.

And your mouth too.

Can we turn out the light?

They had made a kind of game of it, he realized. They blurted the three words not like an endearment but as an incantation or a hex, one that would only take effect if the victim had let their guard down.

But the game had spoiled the sentiment. Instead of "I love you," all he heard now was "Sorry, not fast enough," or "Tag, you're it."

On her bedside table he found a piece of paper on which she'd been experimenting with her signature. Just once, as though by accident, she'd scrawled his last name instead of her own.

On his desk she found a piece of paper on which he'd written

The problem of EVIL. Never the problem of GOOD?

The problem of PAIN. Never the problem of PLEASURE???

Sometimes I think I can tell when you're watching.

T E L E P A T H Y ? he spelled out with his finger on her belly.

No. I don't know. Just that sometimes I'm aware of it and sometimes I'm not. Sometimes I suddenly *become* aware of it. Like eyes staring at the back of my head.

O N E E-Y E, he spelled.

Is it always on? Is it on right now?

N O, he spelled, then said: Well, not exactly. It only sends when someone – when *I* log in to the server. So it's on, but the picture's not going anywhere. It's not recording or anything.

This wasn't precisely true. In fact, his computer at work saved everything, but he often deleted the previous day's footage without watching it.

Could you? she said after a minute.

W H A T, he spelled.

Could you turn it on? So that it was recording?

W H Y.

She looked at him. I don't know, she said knowingly.

F I L T H Y S L U T, he spelled quickly.

What?

L O V E Y O U.

Oh. Thanks, she said, and fell silent.

I'm surprised your boyfriend doesn't do this.

Well, he does do *that*, she said, laughing metallically. In fact, he's usua – He's the only one who does.

The photographer pursed his lips in a little moue of playful disappointment but withdrew his hands from the collar of her dress, which he had been arranging.

Not for lack of offers, I hope.

I wouldn't know, really. Lack of interest, rather. On my part.

I find that almost equally difficult to believe, he said through a leer. Before she could object, he went on: Of course I was referring to the delicious headshots in which we are about to immortalize your immortal visage.

She blinked at him. Her mouth was dry. She felt dizzy. What? she said.

He put one hand on his hip. You said he was a photographer, didn't you?

Oh. No. Did I? Well, he's not really. I mean he is, he does, but only as a sort of hobby. Not professionally.

I see, he murmured, retreating as far as the nearest spot-lamp, which he began fiddling with to no obvious purpose. And what does this tyro hobbyist of yours shoot?

What? Oh. I don't know, really. Landscapes and objects, I guess.

And do you fall under either of those headings?

Do I – what?

Surely not even the most bumbling neophyte could resist the temptation to, how should I put it, map out some of that exquisite geography?

He fixed his eyes on her. She couldn't find her voice. Suddenly he laughed, a low, booming laugh that belied the delicacy of his speaking voice.

Why so pale and wan, fond lover? You know of course that I'm only playing with you. You must be familiar with the method by now. A little innocuous flirtation, a little insincere badinage. It puts some colour in your cheeks. There are certain effects you can't simulate, you know. It's why men dominate this industry, I'm afraid. Heterosexual men, I might add. We have our tricks.

She caught a sigh and stretched it into a normal, nonchalant exhalation.

So, she said hoarsely, you weren't trying to seduce me?

It beggars belief, does it not? I think . . . Well, perhaps not. I was about to say that you'd know with absolute certainty if I were attempting to seduce you. But I'm not sure it's true. I'm not even sure, in your case, whether I'd know myself. Would you mind putting this strand of hair here behind your ear, I think? Like so. Almost. May I?

She cleared her throat, trying to make it sound like an expression of dubiousness. In my case? she said.

He stepped back, crossed his arms, and looked her up and down.

You're very much my type, you see, he said abstractedly. Very much indeed. Naughty in all the right places.

Now that, that's the method again, right? Putting a little colour in the old cheeks, is that it?

Of course, he said blandly, almost impatiently. He retreated behind his camera and sighed: I don't suppose you'll ever reconsider vis-à-vis the nudes?

How do I know they wouldn't end up on the Internet?

My dear, he said, you should *be* so lucky.

The girl in the garret had disappeared. Someone else was living there now.

He felt responsible. He had been away too long.

At least he had pictures.

He caught her looking in the mirror one day, evaluating herself methodically from every angle, for nearly an hour.

What's that? said Nathan, suddenly behind him. Porno?

Nothing, he said, closing the video window.

Live nude girls? Barely legal coeds?

Just data, he said. Just collecting some new data.

Nathan slapped him on both shoulders. This is a great job we have, isn't it? Say, you coming with us to the Grove tonight?

I don't know. I don't think so.

Nathan peered at him, as though at some rare insect.

He straightened his posture and said: It's just that the wife is dragging me to a goddamn play or something.

That's right. I keep forgetting. You've got pussy at home. Why eat out?

They threw a party to celebrate the airing of her first commercial. Thirty of her friends crammed themselves into their two-bedroom apartment. They all hooted and cheered when at last her face appeared on the tiny television screen, smiling archly yet admiringly at the computer-generated anthropomorphized cereal bar who was showing her, and a number of other young on-the-go professionals, how to slam-dunk a basketball.

When it was over, she took a solemn bow. Someone called for a speech. Others began tapping the rims of their wineglasses with their fingernails.

Six hundred dollars, she said slowly, with drunken fastidiousness, six hundred dollars . . . for two seconds . . . of screen-time.

That's on par with Naomi Watts, you know. Second by second.

Well, Meg Ryan, maybe.

Rebecca Pidgeon, anyway.

Kirstie Alley, at least.

Just imagine what you'll make for your first feature film.

Or solo commercial, for that matter.

Later she cornered him on his way out the door and asked him what he really thought.

You were good, he said. Real convincing.

And what is *that* supposed to mean?

I don't know. You looked like you were, you know, really feeling it.

It's just a commercial. It's not supposed to be a great work of art. She poked him in the chest with an index finger, sloshing white wine onto his shirt. You know what you are? she said affably. You're *jealous*.

Yes. And you're drunk.

In the other room Caryn had climbed onto a chair and was launching into what was apparently an elaborate toast, one which for some reason began with a not much abbreviated account of her own childhood.

Not *envious*, mind you. But *jealous*. There's a dicstinct – a distict – dis-*tinct*-ion. You're possessive. You want to own me. You don't want anyone else to . . . own me. Where are you going?

I'm going to get some fresh air. He kissed her quickly at the corner of her mouth and ducked out into the hallway.

And why aren't you drinking? she shouted.

Yes, said someone behind her, doors are notorious teeto-tallers.

Anthony! She flung her arms around his neck. When did you get here?

Just a couple minutes ago. I guess I missed the big event. Will there be an encore?

Supposedly it's going into regular rotation. But it doesn't matter. It's dumb. It's nothing. And I know how you feel about TV and all that.

Maybe I've mellowed in my old age. You look great, by the way.

So do you. As always.

Ah – no, said Anthony. Reflexive reciprocation not allowed. Do me a favour and tell me I look great in twenty minutes or so.

You look great in twenty minutes or so. Can I find you something to drink?

After the tongue-lashing that door received, I don't dare say no.

The next day he fast-forwarded through most of the evening. The guests had generally stayed out of the bedroom. They stood silhouetted in the doorway, their heads bobbing and hands fluttering at triple speed, then drifted away. Occasionally, individually or in pairs, they would venture a rapid reconnaissance of the room, glancing critically at the books on her shelves and the software on his, peering cautiously into the tangled junglescape of her closet or the cluttered drawer where he kept his "valuables": diplomas and certifications, expired prescriptions, the journal he had kept for six weeks while in Montreal four years ago, every letter and note that she had written him and most of the ones he'd written her.

But one couple who entered the bedroom lingered longer than the others. These two displayed little curiosity about the room or its furnishings.

She stretched out supine on the bed while the other one paced languorously. They talked for a few minutes, animatedly but without eye contact. Then the other one, the ex-boyfriend, nudged the door shut with his toe.

He watched the next five minutes of the video very carefully. Then he watched it again. Then he watched it three more times.

Before he left for home he logged on to his news server and uploaded the clip to the alt.binaries.multimedia.erotica group, inserting it amidst the garish promises and nauseating claims of "Amateur teen sucks off two guys at once," "World's biggest transsexual orgy," and "Cumswapping brunettes get-DP'd."

"My girlfriend," he typed, "caught cheating. (5 minutes, 15.5 MB.) Comments welcome."

You can either be famous, said Anthony, or the cause, in a small way, of everyone else's fame. You and I have made our choice.

Sure, said Anthony, everyone is the star on his or her own stage. That's obvious. And every one of us is also a bit player in everyone else's show. But this is really a most efficient arrangement, after all.

To paraphrase Freud, said Anthony, the one thing that everyone wants is, basically, to feel important.

Other than sex, you mean, she said through a yawn.

Well, yeah. Other than sex. Obviously.

She remembered now why they had broken up. He was an obnoxious egomaniac and he bored her silly.

Speaking of which, she said, how's Kimberlee with two E's, or whatever her name was?

Kimberli with an I. I have no idea how she is. Can't say I care, either.

I can't believe you left me for a Kimberli with an I. It's disgraceful.

I didn't *leave* you. As I recall, you told me you never wanted to see me again.

Yes, because of assorted shenanigans involving Kimberli with an I. I hope she was at least more fun in bed than I was.

You know that no one was more fun than you, he said softly.

Oh, don't, she sighed. You shouldn't say such things.

Why shouldn't I?

You'll make me believe it yet.

Maybe you shouldn't be lying there like that and not expect my mind to wander down certain avenues.

She lifted her head and looked at him through narrowed eyelids.

I can lie here any way I like, she said slowly, with drunken fastidiousness. Thank you very much.

Is that so? said Anthony. And he nudged the door smoothly shut with his toe.

Attn: Vulcan.

Re: My girlfriend, caught cheating.

Picture quality rather poor, no? Way too dark & low contrast. Good clip otherwise. Your girlfriend's totally hot!

More light next time please! Sound too!

He walked for four hours. He took more than a hundred pictures.

Hey! someone shouted. What do you think you're doing?

She left the curtains open, he muttered. They all leave the curtains open.

*

I love you, she said, with a slight rising inflection.

Super, he said.

You seem a little spacey tonight.

Do I?

Maybe a little.

Just thinking, I guess.

What about?

He lifted his head from the pillow. That camera, he said.

She propped her head up with one bent arm and looked at him. What about that camera?

He lowered his head again. I don't know. Maybe we should use it sometime.

Use it in what way, she said slowly.

Maybe we should shoot ourselves.

She was silent for a moment. He gave her a sour glance.

You know what I mean.

In flagrante delicto? she asked, beaming at him.

He tossed a sheet over her naked body.

What's that for?

I don't know. You look . . .

Like I've just been ravished?

Cold, he said.

Should we watch it? she asked.

What, right away?

Sure. I want to see us.

I guess. But put something on. It's not exactly summer.

She hovered on the edge of the bed, wrapped in bedsheets. He sat on his swivel chair, in boxers and T-shirt.

On the computer screen, she was crouched on hands and knees upon the bed, wearing only her underwear. She twisted her head to one side and looked back in the direction of the camera. She said something and laughed. Then she lowered her head and pushed her backside into the air.

You look good there, he murmured.

I think you enjoyed this part the most, she said. Playing director.

On the screen, she struck a few more poses. Then he stepped into the frame, gripped her throat delicately with both hands, and pulled her face towards his.

They watched themselves – he with growing disgust, she with growing regret.

1:	1500000	WWJ
2:	1200000	NEF
3:	1000000	RTP
4:	750000	BQD
5:	500000	TYO
6:	250000	GMV
7:	150000	DSA
8:	100000	HIV
9:	75000	THG
10:	50000	MKE

The scores were fake. They were too even, too rounded. Tenth place, bottom rung, was exactly 50,000 points. Ninth was exactly 75,000. Eighth exactly 100,000. Fifth was not a point more nor less than half a million. First place would cost you exactly 1,500,000.

"It's goddamn impossible," said my brother after his first game. He'd scored 17,455.

If the highest scores seemed too big, the lowest were too small. The top ten were spaced out in neat exponential increments, like currency – or prizes.

Even at twelve, I was old enough to know that progress was made not in great, smooth leaps but in clumsy, painful steps. I'd played piano for six months, taken swimming lessons for three, and been a scout for about two weekends – and if I'd ever found myself stranded on an island ten metres from the mainland with nothing but a Swiss Army knife and a Casiotone keyboard, I'd have died of hunger or poison ivy in about twelve hours flat and wouldn't even have been able to perform my own funeral dirge.

Genius was not a gift. Talent was not innate. Practise, and only practise, made perfect – which was just to say that the long road to perfection was paved with bumpy, potholed imperfection. If some kid calling himself "WWJ" had really scored one and a half million points, there should have been countless others who'd only made 1,450,000, 1,464,000, 1,485,975. For every Edmund Hillary who reached the peak there should have been dozens of frozen carcasses littering the mountainside below. The lack of evidence of any such carnage in the hygienic high-score list was proof of its artificiality.

And that offended something in me. I was insulted. And from my brother I'd learned a useful self-defence manoeuvre: Take every insult as a challenge.

I told him to give me a goddamn quarter.

"Suck a turd, midget."

I could tell by the mildness with which he said it that he was out of money. So were the others. We lingered around the machine like smitten suitors, jiggling its joysticks and tapping its buttons, already reminiscing over past exploits and sketching out the fiery mayhem we would unleash in the near future, until Mr. Kacvac, invoking his dead wife's long-suffering soul, told us to get out of the store. Our loitering was scaring away paying customers.

Everyone but me had great handles. Some – Donnie Werscezsky (DON), James Thomas (JIM), and my brother (LEO), to name but a few – had been blessed from birth with names exactly three letters long. Others – Gob McCaffrey and Pud Milligan, for instance – had had such names bestowed upon them by inadvertently generous peers. Even those whose names seemed at first glance to be as unabbreviatable as my own had little difficulty re-christening themselves. Hank Lowenthal, who occasionally claimed British heritage and could quote entire scenes from *Monty Python and the Holy Grail* as proof, embraced his pedigree with ANK. Sanjeet Kastanzi, who everyone called Sanj, had a number of options: SAN was safe if rather dull, ANJ was bold if a little risky, and KAS had a nice rough-and-tumble ring to it. (SNJ was tacitly off-limits; we all wanted our names to be sayable.) In the end he went – a little overweeningly, I thought – with JET.

And Theodore Mandel, a friend of my brother's, tried on labels like they were shoes. Indeed, I sometimes suspected that the challenge of textual condensation was the only reason he played – just as I sometimes suspected that the only reason he hung around with my brother, Leo, was so he could refer to the pair of them in rhyming third-person.

Theo tried on TEO first, then DOR. But you could see the self-dissatisfaction of the artist in his eyes. When he discovered that numerals were permissible he came up with 3OH ("Three-oh"), 3A4 ("Three-a-four"), and finally, his *chef d'oeuvre*, 0EO. The zero, he explained to everyone in the store, stood for the Greek letter theta, which, in the International Phonetic Alphabet, was the symbol for the "th" sound. We responded to this little lesson with a different sound. Marcel Kacvac (MUT), who we all looked up to in fear and awe because he was in high school and had a tattoo, a car, and acne, started calling Theo "Oreo" and then, because "Oreo" was not offensive enough to ever catch on, "Cookie." But Theo defused the danger by pretending to be delighted. For a week he insisted that everyone call him Cookie and for a week everyone refused. "Piss off, *Theo*" even became a schoolyard catchphrase. One night I used it to greet him at the door to our walk-up and was swatted for it later by my mom, who, seated upstairs in the kitchen, had neither heard him call me "Oozy" first, nor seen him ruffle my hair afterwards.

I was supposed to have been OLD. O.L.D. really were my initials. Fortuitously, they spelled a recognizable word. And old was something I wanted to be anyway. OLD was perfect.

I crept onto the high-score screen with my very first quarter. Naturally I took this to be an omen, a sign that I'd been earmarked for greatness. But my triumph was short-lived.

LEO – whose hard-won 76,450 points had been propelled into the abyss by my seemingly effortless 78,495 – immediately pantsed me. This was to be expected, and wouldn't even have been humiliating if Mrs. Schrever, my brother's History teacher, hadn't been in the store at the time. Because she was, Mr. Kacvac felt obliged to loudly reprimand my brother – and me – for our deplorable behaviour. Normally

he didn't give a damn how we comported ourselves so long
as merchandise got paid for. He believed Mutt's generation
to be so far beyond redemption that it didn't even trouble
him anymore. On the contrary, he seemed to relish each
fresh confirmation of our wickedness. When there were no
adult customers in the store he encouraged us to deride vol-
unteerism, team sports, and homework. Once, home from
school with a feigned illness, I wandered into his store in the
middle of a weekday afternoon and Kacvac rewarded my
waywardness with a free handful of gummi fruits. But that
day, with Mrs. Schrever in the store, he had to condemn my
brother's wanton cruelty and my obscene immodesty until
the grown-up finally paid and left.

The charge of wilful obscenity was, I thought, a little
unfair. It's not that I wouldn't, but *couldn't* pull up my pants
right away. There was a high score that needed claiming; I
had to enter my initials first.

Whether in my excitement or because everyone was
laughing at the threadbare state of my skivvies, I overshot
the D and put an E in its place. The mistake proved irrevocable. So I pretended I hadn't made a mistake at all. When
Theo demanded to know what the heck "Olé" was supposed
to mean, I just shrugged enigmatically but with tight-lipped
significance, as though we were really talking about some girl
I'd banged, and whom I was too much of a gentleman, or
depraved pervert, to slander by disclosing the garish details.

In the end it didn't matter. My low high score was wiped
out, to my secret relief, a mere twenty minutes later by
DON. OLE was dust.

But so was OLD. That name was now forever tainted. It
was just as well, I realized. OLD was a stupid, terrible name.

Mrs. Schrever was old. Mr. Kacvac was old. And did I really want it getting out that my middle name was "Leslie"?

OSS seemed the obvious choice but I didn't like it. It looked amputated. Standing on their own like that, the first three letters of my name gave no clue to their origin, their context, their pronunciation. Future generations would suppose that OSS rhymed with "floss" or "gloss" – words not known to strike fear into the human heart.

I could fix this problem by substituting Z's for the S's but I didn't like OZZ any better. It looked ugly and asymmetrical; the second Z was technically superfluous. Besides, I hated "Oz," with all its childish connotations: witches, wizards, flying monkeys, munchkins, a girl named Dorothy and a dog named Toto, for crying out loud. Yes, I had made a habit of kicking the shins of anyone who called me Oz and who was not my brother.

So what did that leave?

OSI? OZI? OZE?

Ossie's needs had been modest. He'd spent his meagre allowance on little more than junk food, model airplanes, and elastic bands and paper clips – which he and Philip O'Toole (POT) stopped firing at human targets after Jill Alistair's mom complained to their moms.

OZY, on the other hand, was always on the lookout for money.

I dismantled our sofas. I stuck my fingers inside pay-phones and pop machines. I trawled the gutters in our neighbourhood with my eyes. At night I stole quarters from my mother's purse and, in the morning, obfuscated my crime by demanding an advance on my allowance. (After all, no thief in his right mind would return to his victim the very next day as a supplicant.) I upturned my peanut butter jar and converted its former contents, my life savings, into a roll of pennies, two rolls of nickels, and a roll of dimes – nine dollars and fifty cents in all. At the bank I watched, red-faced, as the teller removed, with a long red fingernail, two quarters from a roll before cheerfully handing it over to me. It felt like a slap on the hand. But my mood improved as soon as I stepped back out on the street with thirty-eight quarters in my pocket, weighing the left side of my cords down almost past my hip.

Unfortunately, there was no one in Kacvac's but Kacvac. I felt the need to flourish my fortune at someone, so I squandered one play – three whole lives – on a dozen gummi fruits. Fussily, but with good-humoured resignation, like someone who has grown weary of the bank's empty promises to make their coins easier to get at, I peeled a coin from the top of my roll and slid it across the counter like a checkers pro.

"Mazel tov," said Mr. Kacvac gloomily, and in his perpetually damp eyes I saw not the dysfunction of lachrymal glands – a medical condition that my mother had warned me not to mention – but a keen, unadulterated – and unadult – envy.

In no hurry to shatter my adversaries' records in their absence, I sauntered up to the machine, performed a few limbering calisthenics, looked around the store, smiled companionably back at Mr. Kacvac, peeled off another quarter, and inserted it into the slot. *Ballistic Obliteration* chimed happily, like a baby robot gurgling at the sight of its mother.

I exchanged a grim nod with my reflection in the store window, like two rugged highwaymen crossing paths out on some lonely mesa after midnight. Then I reached up over my head, gripped the joystick with one hand, and slapped the START button with the other.

It was not respect that we sought. Those who were better than you could not respect you, and those who were worse could not even like you. Those who did not play – my mother, our teachers, the President of the United States of America – did not really exist.

It was not respect that we were after but immortality. I dreamed of taking all ten high scores. I dreamed of an army of OZYs slaughtering anyone who would deny them their rightful place in eternity.

It never occurred to us that our high scores might not be immortal. They were as indelible as a Guinness World Record or the Permanent File that Principal Ballsack kept locked in the cabinet in his office – and which he promised to show no one but such colleges, potential employers, and juries as might someday need to be disabused of any notion of our goodness or worth. Our high scores were the high scores of all time and space. We assumed they would last forever.

For disabusing us of this notion, Roger Parker (ROG) was systematically ostracized: we put dead gophers in his locker, we squashed his lunches with our textbooks, we tied his gym shoes together and wrapped them around the football goalpost like a bola, and then – worst of all – we left him alone.

ROG had been one of the real contenders, one of the Obliterati. He'd been with us from the beginning. He'd been the first to "get HIV," with 104,895 points. He'd also been the first to kill the underwater-level boss, a giant robotic octopus that sprayed clouds of ink that would freeze you to your spot for five seconds while it – rather implausibly, I thought – lobbed fireballs at you.

Leo smacked me in the side of the head and said that obviously *grease* fires could burn underwater. Phil, who was supposed to be my best friend, backed him up, saying that everybody knew that the army had flame-throwers on their attack subs. I asked if he meant the navy, and Leo smacked me again.

"*Ow* – what was *that* for?"

"For being a smartass."

"I wasn't," I said truthfully. (*Wasn't* it the navy who had subs?) I felt the first prickle of tears gathering somewhere beneath the skin of my cheeks. It was not hardship or cruelty but injustice that made me emotional.

"Oh shit. I was just teasing. Don't pull a Kacvac on us."

One afternoon Roger was in striking distance of usurping Jim Thomas (JIM) for sixth place. We were all cheering him on. Jim Thomas was almost eighteen and, like MUT, far too old, in our opinion, to be competing. Shouldn't he have girls to bang? we asked ourselves.

This was approximately one month after the machine had first appeared in Kacvac's, dumped indifferently, as though by some giant stork, at the front of the store between the rotating display of birthday cards and the three shopping carts that no one ever used because they were too wide for all but the frozen foods aisle. None of us ever really paused to wonder where the game had come from. Though battered and scuffed with age and rough use, it seemed to us to have simply materialized out of thin air, like some sort of divine challenge – like Arthur's sword in the stone. Some of us must have realized that Mr. Kacvac owned Kacvac's, but he never seemed like anything but a worn-out and mistreated employee in his own store. It was inconceivable that we had him to thank for *Ballistic Obliteration*.

A month after it appeared, the bottom five scores were history. MKE was long forgotten. THG's thing had fallen off. DSA had, of course, caught AIDS from HIV. We were unable to do much with GMV or TYO – which was suspicious. Indeed, with the exception of HIV, none of the default high scorers' names spelled anything even remotely dirty. They even seemed to have been chosen to rule out offensive acronyms. Not a single DIK or TIT or AZZ among them – another sure sign that they were fakes.

Then again, none of us ever resorted to such vulgarity either. We took the game, and our fame, too seriously. To pass up the chance to take personal credit for your score would be more than a tragic waste; it would be a gesture of disrespect, more obscene than any three-letter word could be. Donnie Werscezsky (DON) – who later became my principal rival, next to Gob McCaffrey (GOB) – did once enter POO after losing three lives in quick succession to the dragon on the lava level (who at least did not breathe water at you). But no one so much as smiled at POO. It had been a gesture of peevishness, we all knew, not rebelliousness. DON had two better scores on the list already, so maybe it didn't matter. But there were kids – my brother, for one – who'd have killed for what Donnie tossed so dismissively aside – namely, 589,140 points.

*

At the time of ROG's last game, the bottom five scores were 545,770, 532,225, 528,445, 500,000, and 476,610. They belonged to JIM, GOB, OZY, the imaginary TYO, and ROG himself. Watching him play were GOB, OZY, POT, and Wally Hersch, who never had a moniker because he never made it onto the high-scores list. The kid was hopeless. His hand and his eye were apparently operated by different brains altogether. And he never got any better despite all the quarters he plugged into the machine. We serious players respected neither his ineptitude nor his conspicuous wealth, so we never let him play unless we were all broke or he promised to lend us money – which he did gladly for anyone who would play doubles with him. But this we refused to do.

Two-person play was, at least among the Obliterati, tacitly prohibited. It was easier to get further when playing doubles, and while the points that piled up had to be split two ways, the extent of player one's contribution to player two's success and vice versa could never be teased apart. Doubles scores were an inaccurate and therefore invalid measure of one's skill. A *high* score that came out of a doubles game was deemed not just worthless but in fact immoral, because every illegitimate score displaced a legitimate one. It didn't matter if your partner *was* Wally – that is, if he contributed nothing, if he died off before you even got as far as the wild boar boss at the end of the forest level. It was a question of precision. Of honour.

I once walked into Kacvac's to find Donnie Werscezsky playing alone. I watched him mutely for ten minutes. Suddenly he let out a shriek and swiftly committed hari kari.

"Why the hell'd you do *that*?" I wanted to know. "You were creeping up on bottom rung with two damn lives left."

"No shit – why d'you think I killed myself?"

Evidently Mutt Kacvac had been labouring over the machine when Donnie came into the store. MUT never played if anyone was around. He didn't like being watched. He was not a real contender, and he concealed his lack of skill behind a mask of derisive indifference. When Donnie came in, he suddenly remembered he had to be somewhere and asked DON if he wanted to take over. Donnie hesitated, so Mutt casually crashed his ship into a toxic chemical vortex, then turned and strode out of the store without another word. Donnie couldn't bear to let most of a quarter go to waste. But nor could he claim a high score that was not completely, 100 per cent his own. When he backed away from the machine after his *felo de se*, he kept shaking his hands as though they were dripping wet and muttering to himself, "That was close, that was a real close call."

By the time Jim Thomas came into the store, Roger had 521,915 points. He'd secured ninth place and was sneaking up on me in eighth. He'd made it to the electricity level – a nightmare landscape of sparkling capacitators and fizzling dynamos swept with gleaming acid showers and arc lightning that only a few of us had ever seen with our own two eyes – and he'd done it without losing a single life. He had 521,915 points, his Faradization upgrade, ten nukes, a triple forcefield, and three ships left. He was on fire.

Gob, Phil, Wally, and I fell silent. Even the buzzing coolers in the produce section seemed to hold their breath. JIM, our current scoring leader, pretended not to notice what was happening. He made a lazy circuit of the store like an old lady searching for discounts. He stood in front of Mr. Kacvac and deliberated out loud over which brand of cigarettes he should try today. In the end he bought nothing but a newspaper, which he folded neatly and tucked under his arm before finally strolling, lackadaisically and as though quite by chance, in our direction.

"What's this?" he asked primly.

"It's a video game," Gob said quietly. "Never seen one?"

Casually, and with the inattentive air of someone lighting a pipe, Jim asked, "And how's old Rog doing?"

"Fine," Phil said.

"Amazing, actually," Wally said. "He's got ninth place."

Roger muttered something under his breath.

Jim stooped forward slightly, turned his head to one side, and blinked rapidly out the window. "Hmm? What's that he said?"

"Eighth place," Gob said. "He just got eighth."

"There goes Ossie," said Phil.

I exhaled. Something tight in my chest loosened up.

"Suck a turd," I said.

"Holy, what kind of power-up is *that*?" asked Wally breathlessly.

"He's right on your ass, Jim," said Phil gloatingly, "and he's got three lives."

At precisely that moment, Roger's ship exploded. He swore loudly. Mr. Kacvac, perched on his stool behind the counter, looked up from his crossword puzzle and cleared his throat threateningly. (Mrs. Howard, a friend of my mother's, was palpating lettuce heads in the produce section.) Out of respect for the dead, and not because we were cowed by

Kacvac, we fell silent for a minute. Jim, who'd been about to say something, let his mouth hang open like someone anticipating a delicacy. He brought his lips together at last:

"Two," he said. You could tell the word tasted good. "Two lives left."

Phil sent Gob a quick commiserative glance. "He's on you. He's right on you. Oh man, he's – that's it. You're toast."

"Nice one," said Gob.

"He's got seventh place now," Wally explained. "He just passed Gob."

"Seventh place," said Phil, "and he's got two lives left."

Roger's ship erupted into flames. He swore. This time Kacvac cleared his throat inquisitively, as though politely inquiring which of us would most like to be kicked out first.

"You guys are goddamn jinxing me," Roger said under his breath. "Stop saying how many lives I have goddamn left."

"Why?" said Jim brightly. "What's the matter? Are we *jinxing* you?"

He was chuckling but there was an uneasiness in his voice. His eyes, like the rest of ours, were locked on the screen, where Roger's score continued bit by excruciating bit to rise.

"How many lives do you have left anyway? One? Just one?"

As though on cue, Roger's ship hurtled into a giant electrified razor-wire barrier and blew into pieces.

He did not swear. He slammed his palms down on the buttons and spun around to glower at Jim.

Jim grinned. Gob, Phil, Wally, and I gasped in horror. Roger's game wasn't over yet. He needed less than four thousand points to beat Jim and *he had turned his back on the game.*

He was back at the controls before we could scream at him, but the one- or two-second interruption proved fatal. Before he knew what was happening, his right wing had been grazed by a deadly blue will-o-the-wisp, sending a geyser of black smoke up into the poisonous atmosphere. Roger pulled away too late and too hard: overcompensating in space for what he'd failed to do in time, he rocketed from one side of the screen to the other and came too close to a giant electromagnet, a device that looked as harmless as a giant bedspring but was as deadly as a coiled cobra. The magnet pulled him in slowly, almost gently. Then it injected him with a billion volts. The screen went white.

GAME OVER.

545,385 points. Seventh place.

Roger spun around. Jim was bent double, clutching his newspaper to his chest. It looked to me like he was only pretending to laugh.

"You goddamn jinxed me."

Jim straightened, took a deep breath, and fanned himself with his paper. At length he brought his eyes to focus uncertainly, as though without recognition, on Roger.

"*Twice*," said Roger through his teeth.

"Hey Roger," said Wally. "Your name . . ."

The game gave you thirty seconds to enter your initials. Roger had twenty left.

He made no move. Jim stopped smiling. This was serious. Roger was going to throw his score away. He *was* throwing it away. We were watching him do it. He was hurtling towards the edge of a cliff and defying anyone to intervene. He just stood there, glaring at Jim.

Jim glared back. He was angry now too. But he was nervous as well. His eyes kept darting to the screen. Fifteen seconds.

I couldn't breathe. Wally looked ready to pee himself. Phil had to put an arm out to prevent him from rushing forward to enter the R, O, and G on Roger's behalf.

Ten seconds.

Jim flinched first. The spell was broken. A goofy, panic-stricken grin spread across his face. He lunged past Roger, dropping his newspaper, grabbed the joystick and began jiggling it madly. He managed to tap out the last letter – an M – with less than a second to spare. Then he stepped back to admire, and invite the rest of us to admire, his work.

Phil, Gob, and I were too upset to speak. Wally appeared to be working himself up to a Kacvac. Roger just peered wordlessly at the screen.

Jim sensed he'd committed a faux pas. He became defensive. "Hey, it's just a joke. He was going to waste it. Jeez, it's just a *game*."

Mr. Kacvac had time to say "Hey, you kids –" before Roger reached around behind the machine and pulled the plug out of the wall. Wally shrieked. Gob closed his eyes. Jim Thomas's face went white. Then he stepped forward and punched Roger neatly and expertly in the stomach, like a paramedic administering the Heimlich manoeuvre. Roger reeled back, then tipped forward, using his momentum to head-butt Jim in the chest. They collapsed together into the display of birthday cards. Mr. Kacvac sprang over the counter and, perhaps by invoking his dead wife's name, or perhaps by brandishing a baseball bat, persuaded all of us to come back another time.

*

I couldn't stay away long. The next day, under the pretense of having been delegated by my mother to purchase some goat's milk, I was able on my way out – empty-handed as planned – to confirm my fears.

MKE, THG, HIV, and DSA had made miraculous recoveries.

ROG, JIM, GOB, and OZY were no more.

Gone. Just like that. Without a trace. In the blink of an eye. Forever.

So what was the point?

That night I lay in bed, struggling to fill my mind with the idea of forever. I took a single summer day spent rambling through our neighbourhood with Phil, taking apart bugs, collecting pop cans, melting popsicles on our tongues, browsing through his dad's old CB radio catalogues, practising our ventriloquism, throwing rocks at stray cats, chalking our names on sidewalks exposed to the naked sky – I took one day like that and tried to hold it in my head all at once. Then I shrunk it down to a dot, a mere speck, and populated the vacated space with a hundred dots, a thousand specks. A sandstorm of days – as many as I'd ever see in all my life. I compressed the dust cloud too, squeezed it down into a tiny cube and pushed it to the very edge of my imagination. I began lining cubes up next to it, slowly at first, only one or two at a time, to give me a chance to grasp the enormity of the addition. Then I began adding half a dozen blocks at once, then half a dozen half-dozens, then a long undifferen- tiated row of blocks spanning the entire width of the space behind my eyes, then half a dozen rows, then half a dozen half-dozens.

I sensed that I was cheating; for each time I moved to a higher level, the detail of the lower levels went out of focus, so that I was no longer really multiplying the multiplied multiples of multiplied multiples but just pushing around individual blocks again, solid pieces that could only regain their plurality at the cost of their unity, parts of a whole that I could not simultaneously see as wholes of yet smaller parts. But I continued until I realized that everything I'd imagined so far, every multiplication I'd performed, could itself be condensed to a single infinitesimal cube and put through the very same process, from start to finish. And *that* entire process could be taken as a unit and run through itself, and so on, and so on, forever and ever. There it was: no matter how long you imagined forever to be, your idea of it was to the real forever as a split second was to your idea of it. This truism remained true even if you took it into account when formulating your idea of forever. Even if you took *that* into account. And that. And so on, forever and ever.

Forever, then. Forever was how long dead people stayed dead. It was how long my dad and my mom's dad and my aunt Sharon and Leo's hamster, Delorna, and Theo Mandel's mother and Jill Alistair's brother Geoff and Mr. Kacvac's wife, Eleanora, would stay dead. Forever was how long gone things stayed gone. It was how long my switchblade would stay at the bottom of Konomoke Lake, how long my magnifying glass would stay smashed (thanks, Leo), how long the key I'd lost to our old apartment building would stay lost, how long our cool old car would stay sold to a fat salesman from Wisconsin. It was how long the Alistairs' house would stay burned down, it was how long World War II would stay finished, and it was how long JIM and ROG and OZY would stay gone from the *Ballistic Obliteration* high-scores list. It wouldn't matter when the power went out or when the plug was pulled. It didn't matter if it happened tomorrow or a hundred years from tomorrow. Forever would wait.

Every message is a message to the future. The feverish, grandiloquent *billet doux* stashed with trembling hand in the coat pocket of the girl you're in love with; the casual note to your wife jotted in haste and posted to the fridge before you leave in the morning; the drunken, desultory jeremiad left on your ex's answering machine – they will be read or listened to, if they are read or listened to at all, by people of the future. Even the thought scribbled carelessly in the margin of whatever novel you're reading is a variety of time travel. Every mark we make, every trace we leave is a broadcast sent out into forever. We think of our footsteps as receding behind us, but really they are beacons sent out before us.

So listen:

I was good at something once. Great, even. It was a long time ago. I was twelve. Now I'm forty-three and not good at much of anything.

I'm not complaining. You're only forty-three and not good at anything for a short time. But you will have once been twelve and good at something forever.

I can't prove it, of course. I have no evidence, no documentation. Three weeks after I obliterated Gob McCaffrey's top score by a margin that should have established my supremacy for – well, for a very long time, our neighbourhood experienced a brief power failure at about four-thirty in the morning. My mother's alarm did not go off; the three of us slept late – a real treat for Leo and me but a catastrophe for Mom, who crashed into our room bellowing and clutching her head as if bombs were being dropped on the neighbourhood.

We had to pass Kacvac's on our unhurried way to school. Power failure. Blackout. 12:00, 12:00, 12:00.

I had to go inside. Leo swore at me and continued on to school, not because he minded being late but because the decision to be late, or to do anything else, always had to be made by him.

They were gone, of course. All of them, gone forever.

Or were they? Might there not persist, etched upon the air we breathe, though we haven't the sensitivity to detect it or the wit to decode it, the mark of some mark, the trace of some trace?

The universe is thought to be without memory, existing only for an eternally renewed split second. Like a sprung trap, the immediate past is supposed to inexorably propel the present into the immediate future. But I think what the past really does is stand nearby, at the present's elbow, and whisper in its ear, give it counsel, suggest how a future might be made. We listen but we don't always hear everything. Not the first time. Not right away. But there might be echoes.

I put a quarter on the counter. Mr. Kacvac held out the pail of gummi fruits. I counted five, showed him. He glanced at his wristwatch. It must have been well past nine.

"Oh, go on," he said. "Take a handful." And he slid my quarter back across the counter.

I stood before the machine, the coin resting in my loosely cupped palm.

Forever would wait. So, let it wait.

I dropped the quarter into my left front pocket. "Later," I promised, and hurried to school.

JIM and ROG, LEO and 0EO, GOB and OZY – they're gone now. Only briefly did they stir from the dust. For a short time, a time that seemed long while it lasted, they made marks that were read and left traces that were followed by others who made marks and left traces of their own. Among the marks they left were the following.

BALLISTIC OBLITERATION

** HALL OF FAME **

TOP TEN HIGH SCORES

10:	98505	MUT
9:	212005	JET
8:	299385	0EO
7:	398510	LEO
6:	545385	ROG
5:	545770	JIM
4:	784605	POT
3:	1246325	DON
2:	1597425	GOB
1:	2069100	OZY

Yvonne hadn't warned the man about Richard. Most people, if not warned in advance, could be counted on to make fools of themselves. They would raise their voice; they would stammer; they would talk about her husband in the third person as if he wasn't there; they would shake his elbow instead of his hand; they would ask gallantly if he wanted to feel their face. At the very least they would act uncomfortable, or, what amounted to the same thing, make a show of just how comfortable they were. And that, of course, made Richard uncomfortable – though he was good, too good, she thought sometimes, at pretending not to mind.

So she warned only those applicants she herself approved of. She did not approve of the man. She didn't know why a man would want to apply at all. No other men had applied. There had to be something funny about him. She wouldn't even have bothered introducing him if Richard's office door hadn't been open.

She could never have guessed that they had once known each other, years ago. Nor could she have foreseen the easy grace with which the man would size up the situation when Richard's eyes failed to find his:

"It's gotten worse, then?"

Richard grinned lopsidedly. "Didn't Yvonne tell you?"

Richard was used to surprises. Every encounter was an unexpected interruption, every "hello" a flash of lightning out of the void. He had trained himself not to act surprised by these surprises. He had become passive: he did not ask his sudden visitors where they had come from or what they wanted, any more than he asked callers where they were phoning from or how they'd gotten his number. So, instead of asking Garnet Cobson – an old university friend he had not seen in more than twenty years – what he was doing in his house, Richard asked him to stay for dinner. It was out of his mouth before he could even think of consulting Yvonne. But there was no way to consult Yvonne in any case. *Excuse us, Garn, for a minute, won't you? Yvonne and I need to discuss whether or not we both want you here. You understand.* Here, a single glance, lasting a fraction of a second, could have told him everything. But Yvonne was too fastidiously polite to give anything away in her voice.

It was the little things, like glances, that he missed the most. Not sunsets, or girls' legs, or Jimmy's face, or Rembrandt, or books – just those telling shared glances. He told himself not to be maudlin.

Garnet accepted the invitation without a moment's pause. "Excellent," he said, "I'll cook."

Richard tilted his head back, amused. "You cook?"

*

They did not catch up; they reminisced. Richard was at first delighted, then dismayed, to find Garnet's face perfectly preserved in his memory. It was his face of twenty years ago, but it loomed up before his mind's eye with startling, almost hallucinatory clarity. Sometimes its lips even seemed to move in time with Garnet's words. This dismayed him because he could not remember his own wife's face nearly so well. Indeed, there seemed to be a rule that the more often he saw someone, the more time he spent with them, the more their image faded. Perversely, the faces from long ago, the faces of childhood friends and dead relatives, of people he never met anymore, were the most vivid; the faces of his family and closest friends had almost vanished. It was almost as though the mind wore down the portraits in its gallery through overhandling, the way the hands and lips of pilgrims eroded the features of holy statues.

To his surprise, he found himself thinking of something Garnet had said years ago, in their dorm room. Every man, he said, had a limited number of ejaculations. The exact number was unknown, and anyway different for everyone, but once you'd gone through your stock, that was that, and it was all over. Richard scoffed, but at nineteen he half understood that women had some limitation of that kind; besides, his own experience in that area was confined to what he still, with curdled Catholic guilt, thought of as "self-abuse"; and, though Garnet was certainly no more enlightened on that score than he was, at that moment, in their dark, freezing, tobacco-permeated room, Garnet seemed to speak with the grim authority of the terminally ill when he declared that it was his aim in life to use up all his orgasms before he died.

Richard wondered: had he used up all his memories of his wife's face?

Yvonne had waited a week after the accident to present her case. She laid out her arguments methodically; Richard could hear the bulleted points in her voice. They were both of them very busy; the kids were still too young to be of much help; it wasn't healthy for them to be eating so erratically; the house was too big for them now to keep in order by themselves; they could get someone marvellous, she was certain, for three hundred dollars a week. She said nothing about the burn on his hand. So he could not defend himself, could not remind her that he'd made hundreds of lunches for himself and the kids without a single mishap before, could not say that he was almost certain Jimmy had been fiddling with the pots on the stove while he had been (without mishap) chopping onions. Besides, he knew that any such line of argument would be received by Yvonne with a sigh of solicitous exasperation at his stubborn pride.

Instead he said that he simply didn't like the idea of hiring a maid. Paying someone to cook their meals, to clean up their messes, to wash their dishes and clothes, to scrub their floors, to wait on them hand and foot — that was not the sort of relationship he wanted with another human being. Nor did he want to cultivate the master/servant mentality in the children. Yvonne, with a hint in her voice of feeling insulted, said that she felt the exact same way, which was why she wanted to offer room and board. Of *course* any girl they hired would be treated with scrupulous respect, like a member of the family.

Richard realized that this meant she had in mind one of
her charity cases from work, one of her homeless girls;
but he could see no graceful way to refuse to meet the applicants if she brought them around the house.

What kind of a person was he, Yvonne wanted to know. What
had he been like? What had the two of them had in common?
What did they do together? What did they talk about?

"I don't know," Richard said. "We were twenty."

What could he tell her? That their friendship had been
forged in a hothouse of alcohol, hormonal arrogance, and
enforced proximity? That all they had really shared was a
desperation to get laid, a predilection for drunkenness, and
a dread of being called a fraud that masked itself as all-
encompassing disdain? That they used to piss in bottles to
avoid the frigid trek to the common bathroom? (That
Garnet held the all-time record with one and one-third
litres?) That they had copied one another's essays? That they
had devised an elaborate coded classification and grading
system for breasts?

"It was a long time ago," he said – and could not help
thinking that it seemed a longer time for Garnet than for
himself. There was in his old friend none of the half-aggres-
sive exuberance that he had once feared and admired. This
Garnet was subdued, almost melancholy. Some of this could
be accounted for by his present circumstances, of course.
Richard hadn't needed to read very closely between the lines
of Garnet's patter to discern that his restaurant had fallen
on hard times or that his wife had split up with him; and
now here he was applying for the position of live-in maid.

The contrast was no doubt exaggerated by the sudden-
ness of their reacquaintance. If Richard could somehow see
himself in the mirror today, perhaps the shock would be as
great. Nevertheless, he felt, Garnet had not aged well.

Richard listened to Yvonne undress and get into bed. He
slid a hand over her smooth belly. "You didn't like him?"

She made the sound that had come to stand in for a
shrug. "Oh, he was charming enough."

The irritation she must have been feeling all night finally
surfaced in her voice. He remembered the brusque way
she'd answered Jimmy's "Who are you?" – "This is Daddy's
friend," with the slightest emphasis on *Daddy's*.

"You and he used to be thick as thieves, I suppose."

It was his turn to make the shrug-sound. "We were
kids."

"He seems like he still is."

Richard heard the click of the lamp, listened to the warm,
sweeping sound of her breathing.

"The kids do like him," he said.

She sighed. "The kids like anyone who farts at the table."

But it was no use. Yvonne could feel herself giving in. She
couldn't help it, she supposed. It was the curse of a generous
spirit: you seldom got your own way. Anyway, it was true
what Richard said. Garnet, an old friend, would be treated as
an equal, and not like some servant. Besides, for some
reason, none of the girls from the shelter had come back for
a second interview. She sighed again, ran her hand in reciprocation over his belly.

"You didn't think it was a little strange that he wouldn't
have anything to drink?"

*

On the first night Garnet made a bouillabaisse. The Lapleys had no mortar and pestle, and the leeks were a bit rusty, and there was no laurel to be found in town for any price; but he had found at the little grocery store a beautiful rascasse, head still attached – and the meal was, he felt, on the whole, a success. Unfortunately the children didn't agree. Milly sat down at the table like it was heaped with landmines, then ate only bread. Jimmy asked again and again, "What *is* it?" Yvonne finally had to call it "seafood stew" before he would put any of it in his mouth. Then his verdict was succinct: "It tastes like grunk." Yvonne told him to be polite; his expression and his tone made his opinion all too clear, if his neologism did not.

On the second night Garnet reined himself in and made the lemon pepper pulled-pork baguettes – one of his specialties, even without the smoked apple compote. He called it "sloppy joes." Milly, still broodingly skeptical, again ate a lot of bread, but was at least courteous enough to push things about on her plate a bit, and even went to the trouble of giving an excuse: she'd had a big snack at Patricia's. Jimmy didn't need any cajoling this time; and though he spat a mouthful of pork back onto his plate, his expression remained thoughtful. He had to search for the right word. "It tastes like . . . kreech."

Garnet considered this a modest triumph. But after the dishes were done Yvonne came up to him in that solemn, absentminded way of hers that reminded him of school principals coming back from lunch to find him sitting there, awaiting punishment. Dinner had been excellent, she assured him; but perhaps in the future he could limit himself to more "North American" dishes?

"It's not your fault. It's the kids. They don't have very sophisticated palates, you know."

He was about to ask her whose fault that was, but stopped himself. He could be humble. This wasn't his kitchen. He asked her what sort of things the kids liked. She had a list prepared – a schedule, in fact, with dates and times extending into next month.

So on the third night he made tomato soup and grilled cheese. The kids gorged themselves. "Lee-*kee*-kalee," said Jimmy, kissing his fingers. Everyone joined in the praise – even Richard, who could guess without much difficulty what his wife must have said to Garnet. He smacked his lips and made swooning faces to mask his regret that there would be no more dinners like the first two. It was just as well, he supposed, that he'd refrained from complimenting Garnet as fulsomely as he'd been tempted to. Not only would it have embarrassed them both, but his gushing would have clashed rather conspicuously with Yvonne's quiet edict. It was important, he supposed, with employees as with children, to present a unified front. Besides, these were still the best grilled cheese sandwiches he'd ever had. And he said so.

"Dill havarti," said Garnet, pleased despite himself. The children, of course, preferred the plastic-wrapped processed cheese slices.

"Aren't you having any?" Milly asked.

Garnet, who had finished off the bouillabaisse that afternoon, said that he thought he'd better get a start on the dishes.

After that, he ate most of his meals alone in the kitchen.

The new, less sophisticated menu left Garnet with more time to fill. As Yvonne had told him that the sound of the

television disturbed Richard's work, he took to reading the
newspaper again, as he'd done at Em and Ern's. Richard
and Yvonne had a collection of books large enough to be
called a library, but he found he couldn't concentrate on
novels these days, and non-fiction seemed stubbornly irrelevant. He liked newspapers for their absence of style, their
insistent air of consequence, and, not least, the brevity of
their articles. He read the paper methodically, from front to
back, even the ads and the obituaries. But his favourite
section was the classifieds. Here spare precision reached its
zenith. (If only historians and novelists had to pay for each
of their words, he thought, there would be a lot less
bloated, idiotic, unnecessary books.) He read the classifieds
like haikus; they cleared his mind.

2000 Chev Tahoe Z71 4x4
4 dr leather int, dark blue ext, htd seats
90k km $18,500 obo

$450 some util +cbl
Quiet cul-de-sac nr JC & store. Deck & priv yd
W/D N/S pref. Pet nego

Spouse gone
need to dispose of her jewellery
Reasonable

Carpet cleaning asst F/T no exp nec
$8/hr+comm full ben & 401k. Hard working, clean DMV
transport & ref req

Live-in cook
Prepare meals for busy family of four. Some light housework
Good wage, room and board for right applicant

He hadn't been looking for work, not yet. But something
about this pared-down description of a possible life snagged
his imagination. He could see himself there, cooking and
doing light housework: He could see himself making a home
for himself, by making a home for them, that busy family of
four. And he could see them singing his praises in chorus to
a grudgingly relenting Leah. It was just what he needed. A
chance to rebuild himself, to prove himself – and to
strangers, who would not cut him any slack. It would keep
his hands busy, too, and his mind occupied. There was
nothing to drink at Em and Ern's but there was nothing to
do, either, nothing to think about, and an empty head was a
thirsty head. So he'd left.

Now here he was reading the classifieds again, in a different house – one with, as he'd noticed right away, a
sumptuously stocked liquor cabinet. But that too, he
decided, was just what he needed. Without temptation, the
experiment would be meaningless.

It was odd. Garnet made almost no noise, but somehow the
mere presence of another person in the house, which for so
long Richard had had to himself throughout the day, was dis-
tracting. He could actually feel Garnet's presence, the way he
could sense a wall or a large tree if he came too close.
Sometimes he heard a floor jamb creak, a cabinet door click
shut, a spoon tap against a dish, but that was all. But he could
feel him being quiet, tiptoeing around. He knew Garnet

waited till he came down for lunch or took his tea out on the patio before turning on the dishwasher or running the vacuum. He supposed Yvonne had instilled in him the same fear she'd instilled in the children: the fear of disturbing their father's work.

The fact was that, besides making him feel like an invalid, the artificial silence discomfited him. When on the phone with clients or partners, it positively embarrassed him. *Their* lines were never quiet; there was always some buzz, some commotion going on in the background. True, it wouldn't do to have Jimmy babbling nonsense in the hallway or Milly's car-alarm anti-music blaring up through the floor while he was on an important call. But then again, everyone knew he worked from home. They all knew his situation.

It was part of his image, the idea of him. And it was the idea of him that was responsible for his success. The blind architect. It was almost a punchline: "The guy who designed that must have been blind." But even a joke, he realized – and Donnamer-Clarke-Row realized – could be good publicity. A punchline, after all, had a bigger impact than a shaggy-dog story.

Blindness had not just helped his career; it had launched it. His name and his work were never mentioned without some reference to his condition – but his name and his work were mentioned. Some called his designs controversial, but he knew that it was not the designs but he himself who was controversial. He was more famous than he deserved to be. Several fools had compared him to Beethoven. Another had tried to dub him "The Milton of Monumentality." The notion that blindness had made him better, that the loss of sight had been made up for by greater insight, was in the first place obviously untrue, and in the second inherently idiotic. Architecture was a visual art. He might have thought of himself as an artist once, but not anymore. He was a draughtsman, a plodding, meticulous, necessarily patient technician.

His clients and his colleagues probably realized as much. But they liked the idea of him. He was a homely paradox, like the sound of one hand clapping.

Milly was in love with Garnet. For one thing, he embarrassed her in front of her friends. Her father did this too, like all her friends' fathers: he cracked lame jokes, pretended to like the same kind of music they liked, and pathetically used phrases like "hang out," "right on," and "wicked awesome" – phrases that were *so* overdue. But the difference was that none of her friends made fun of her dad like they did with all the others. They acted like they liked him. They actually pretended he was cool. It was mortifying. It was because he was blind.

But Garnet, they could all agree, was a total lamerod. He actually thought farting was funny!

And she liked the creaking sound his watch-band made when he fiddled with it. She hoped Garnet would stay forever.

Jimmy wished he was a dinosaur. He could bite the head off of anyone who looked at him funny.

He could be a stegosaurus, and Garnet could be a pterodactyl.

Chomp, chomp, chomp.

Those times when he, and sometimes he and Leah, had gone through the house, purging it of all temptation, decanting

entire bottles down the sink or flushing their contents down
the toilet – those were artificial experiments, Garnet now realized. They were empty gestures, pure mummery. The purge
was not, as he might have imagined at the time, an optimistic
act of spring cleaning, the valiant shedding of an old skin.
For one thing, a dry home was a delusion. Alcohol was everywhere – not least of all at the restaurant. But besides that,
the attempt to smash temptation was really nothing but a
crude attempt to straitjacket yourself. You weren't putting
temptation out of reach so much as trying to put your reach
short of temptation. It betrayed your own cowardice, your
weakness, your knowledge that you couldn't be trusted.

The problem with quitting, the real bitch of it, was that it was
never finished. You could never finally, absolutely give something up, once and for all. It was a cliché, he knew, but it was
true: you could only quit a day at a time. You could refrain
today, and you'd still have to refrain all over again tomorrow,
and keep on refraining every day after that. Not-doing was
fundamentally different from doing. With most decisions in
life, you had to choose between A and B, and no matter how
excruciating the decision might be to make, once you'd made
a choice, there was no going back; the first step down path A
rendered path B a what-if dream. But the path back to drinking was never overgrown; it was always there, a single step
away. Temptation was always with you, and with temptation,
deliberation was always possible, and with endless deliberation, succumbing to temptation was, in the long run, almost
inevitable. How could it be otherwise? Only succumbing
could put an end to deliberation. However forcefully you
gave something up, the giving-up could never make the

giving-in impossible. But however feebly you gave in, the giving-in *did* make the alternative – the giving-up, the *not* giving in, the *never* doing it again – impossible. The scales in this dilemma were imbalanced. You were beaten before you began.

And once you were beaten, why not wallow in it? Why not indulge? Giving in twice was hardly any different than giving in once. A bottle was no worse than a swallow, a bender no worse than a bottle. All defeats were equal.

On the thirteenth day Garnet joined Richard on the patio. Garnet drank coffee, Richard sipped tea.

Garnet was about to praise the backyard, the lovely view, then realized how foolish this would sound. And yet Richard must have found it beautiful too, in some way, even if only in memory. Why else would he sit out here every day?

Instead, because it seemed safer, he said, "Beautiful day."

Richard agreed heartily enough. "Though to be honest, I could do with a bit more wind."

Garnet nodded sagely, then grumbled sagely, though in fact he didn't understand at all. Reminding himself that they had once been close friends, he forced himself to say, "I suppose a bit of wind feels nice on the face?"

Richard smiled brightly; his eyes almost opened. (Garnet felt guilty for ogling him, watching his every fluctuating expression, with a voyeuristic directness that would have been impossible with anyone else.) When Richard explained that, in fact, it was the texture that the wind gave to his environment, the way it highlighted everything it touched, filling in the world in rustling colours, he sounded almost apologetic – as if feeling the wind on his face had never occurred to him. "It makes the yard visible," he said.

Garnet hummed appreciatively. "I see what you mean," he said, then bit his tongue. "I mean, I understand. I never thought of it like that before."

"You don't have to do that, you know. Go out of your way to avoid making any reference to sight, or eyes, or light or darkness or colour. Say 'monitor' when what you really mean is 'keep an eye on.' 'Be careful' instead of 'look out!'" Richard laughed in his whistling way, though he was frowning slightly. "It drives me crazy."

Garnet, embarrassed, closed his eyes and tried to hear the breeze.

The house seemed unnaturally silent. Yvonne stalked from room-to room, registering the untidiness. Jimmy's blocks were still scattered all over the den floor. The parlour had not been dusted. In the foyer, the late afternoon sun exposed with forensic clarity the soap-streaks on the cedar floorboards. Upstairs, the clothes hamper was overflowing. The vacuum was not put away – an accident waiting to happen. The dishwasher was full of unwashed dishes. And Garnet was sitting outside with Richard.

She felt a flush of irritation, which she gave time to subside before sliding open the patio door. It was one thing if Richard, after a day's work, wanted to sit moping in the shadows. It was, she felt, quite another matter for Garnet, when the house was still in disarray and supper, by all appearances, was not even begun. She and Richard could both make noble speeches about treating people as equals, but they *were*, after all, paying him to cook and to keep the house clean. That was what it came down to.

Garnet jerked upright in his deck chair when she opened the door – evidence of a guilty conscience, and proof that she was not being unreasonable.

"Hello, hon," said Richard. He seemed bashful too. They were like two teenagers caught smoking. She did not relish the role this cast her in: the taskmaster, the martinet – the adult. She could enjoy a nice cup of hot cocoa and a nice hot footbath at the end of a long day as much as the next person – but it should *be* the end of the day. And why not sit in the sun, while it was still up?

But all she said – all she had to say – was "Hello, dear. Hello, Garnet," and Richard was getting to his feet, mumbling, "I suppose I should go for my walk, while it's still warm." Garnet leapt up too, and went to fetch Richard's walking stick, though he must have known by now that Richard was perfectly capable of getting it himself – as long as it was put back in its proper place.

Yvonne and Garnet stood on the front step and watched as Richard made his way down the path and along the sidewalk.

"It's quite amazing, really," said Garnet softly, when Richard was almost out of sight behind the Tradwells' fat elms.

Yvonne did not disagree – though in fact she often felt that Richard could have expended more energy on keeping his spirits up than on solving little practical problems, like how to get his computer to read books out loud, or how to identify and distinguish between the different colours of his ties.

"He's an inspiration," she said, perhaps a little too pointedly.

"I guess I'd better get started on supper," said Garnet with false enthusiasm.

Yvonne, feeling generous again, said she could hardly wait.

"Retinitis pigmentosa," Richard reminded him.   .

It was the seventeenth day and Garnet had joined him again on the patio. The washer, dryer, and dishwasher were all running; the vacuum was put away; the meatloaf was in the oven. This afternoon there was a breeze.

"No, it wasn't painful. Nothing gradual is really painful. Or even really felt at all. Like watching the hour-hand of a clock. Watching yourself get older in the mirror. When we went to Taiwan a few years ago – well, it was before we had Jimmy – it was the middle of winter here and we told our-selves that we didn't mind the awful cold, that it would make us appreciate the heat over there even more, that the heat over there would feel good because of the contrast. But that's all nonsense. You might feel some relief at stepping out of the cold into the relatively warm airport, and after fifteen hours on a cramped plane of course you feel some relief at stretching your legs again out in the sun. But you don't feel anything at all about the longer, large-grained transitions. And after an hour in the sun you'd kill again for a little air-conditioning . . . . I don't mean I'm unhappy like this. Only that I didn't feel it happen. And that I don't even really feel it anymore – or don't feel, anyway, the difference between this and what I used to be. You only feel the sharpest transitions. I guess that's just another way of saying that you get used to anything."

Richard blushed. These thoughts had all come out extem-poraneously, and only in their articulation did he realize how much time he must have spent going over them in his head; but he was aware of just how prepared this little speech sounded, and he was embarrassed.

"And I suppose it helps," said Garnet, "that you haven't had to completely change your life. You've still got your work, your family. You still go for your walks."

Richard's embarrassment gave way to irritation. Garnet had missed the point; he wanted to turn his detached philosophical meditation into a heartwarming hymn of resilience, a bit of homespun inspirational rhetoric – the same sort of God-only-gives-us-tests-He-knows-we-can-pass treacle that the well-meaning well-wishers at church were always pouring into his ears.

"Oh Christ," he said, "but I hate my walks. Nothing changes, there's nothing to see. A walk for a blind man is like riding in an elevator – only requiring more concentration. I only do it to placate Yvonne, who thinks to not be physically moving is to be feeling sorry for yourself."

Then he felt awful, less for thinking this than for saying it out-loud, and saying it to, of all people, the man who washed his family's underwear. He was angry at himself for having blurted it out, but angrier still at Garnet for having heard it.

"But really I'm very lucky," he added quickly. "She's a saint, of course, to put up with me like this."

And his anger expanded to include Yvonne.

Yvonne decided there was no reason to cancel the Hopnik Family Visit.

"There's plenty of room. We'll just have to move Garnet to the basement for the weekend."

Richard felt uneasy, but did not object. In the end, Garnet suggested the room change himself.

"After all, they're family. I'm . . ." He did not finish the sentence, but smiled self-deprecatingly.

He also had suggestions about what to feed them. But Yvonne demurred. She did not want to give the cousins the impression that she and Richard had employed a private chef. Instead, she thought it would be best if they presented Garnet as an old school friend of Richard's who was staying with them for a while to lend a hand around the house.

"We'll probably just order in. It'll be easier for everyone. KFC, Pizza Hut – it's almost tradition. They're not fancy eaters, you see. And their kids can be really rather fussy. It would just be a waste of your talents, Garnet. And we'll eat out, I'm sure, at least once or twice. Of course you're more than welcome to join us – if you're not too busy."

As the weekend approached, Garnet looked around for things that would keep him busy. He didn't have to look any further than his new room in the basement, which had a funny smell, somewhere between mouldy and pungent, like the smell of something decomposing.

"Aren't you drinking?" they asked.

He smiled and shook his head. "No thanks."

"Aren't you eating?" they asked.

"I think I'll get a start on these dishes," he said.

"What dishes?" they asked.

When Garnet was out of the room, Yvonne surveyed her two families and sighed contentedly, "Now isn't this wonderful?"

*

Lleanne cornered Yvonne in the hallway, on her way to the bathroom.

"Tell me," she said. "Richard's friend."

Yvonne pursed her lips solemnly but said nothing.

"Come clean. He's helping *you*, or you're helping *him*?"

Yvonne shrugged, and twisted her mouth in an expression meant to convey the ineffable complexities of the human heart.

"I *knew* it," said Lleanne triumphantly. "But isn't that typical Yvonne. Even when we were kids you were bringing home limping raccoons, birds with broken wings . . ."

Yvonne, who was made uncomfortable by direct praise, excused herself, and pushed past her cousin into the bathroom. She looked at herself in the mirror, waiting for the blush to fade from her cheeks.

"Ego," she whispered. "Vanity."

Lleanne was still waiting for her when she came out. "What was he, what was it, what did he . . ."

Yvonne shook her head, squeezed her cousin's arm at the elbow. "Let's just say that he's had more than his share of difficulties in this life." This, she felt, was safe enough; it was true of most people. But Lleanne had ideas of her own.

"I knew it," she hissed. "It's *alcohol*, isn't it. I spotted it right away, first thing this afternoon, when he wasn't drinking."

Yvonne was too astonished by this striking echo of her own suspicions to deny or even cast the proper pall of doubt on it.

"You're brave," said Lleanne, with almost accusatory vehemence. "You're almost *too* good, you know that?"

For a moment, as a little warm bubble swelled in her chest – it was a feeling like self-empathy, as though she were seeing into herself from outside – Yvonne felt that her cousin's assessment was fundamentally correct.

Sometimes Garnet caught himself counting the days like some schmuck in AA. But that was just setting yourself up for a fall. It might have been true that the longer you went without a drink the greater the incentive to keep going – or rather, the greater the disincentive to start from scratch, to set the clock back to zero. But this disincentive had limits; its growth followed the drooping arc of diminishing returns. That first week was always a greater victory than the fourth week; the fifth day was more impressive than the entire fifth month. And yet, conversely, the longer you'd been dry, the more cataclysmic the eventual relapse seemed. Two fingers of Glenfiddich after a year of sobriety was ten times the tragedy that a whole bottle after one week was. The longer you'd been on the wagon, the harder you fell off it.

To count the days was like looking down the side of a mountain to see how high you'd climbed; it only made you dizzy.

Yvonne took up the challenge of having a recovering alcoholic under her roof as she took up every challenge: with gusto. She made a weekly search of Garnet's room while he was chauffeuring Jimmy to baseball practice. (Jimmy could be asked quite frankly if Garnet had stayed at the field the whole time.) Aside from the appalling stink of b.o. (she knew all too well from her work how addicts neglected hygiene), she found nothing but an empty flask, which was disappointing only because she was no longer seeking confirmation of her theory. She could hardly confiscate the thing, so she instead took to checking that it stayed empty – sniffing it whenever Garnet was out of the house. But she also prevented, as much as possible, his leaving the house by himself. She had him call in his grocery list to Partridges, and picked up the orders herself on her way home. She and Patricia Hedley's mother arranged to drive the girls to jazz on alternate evenings. She transferred a few of the kids' weekly chores – "upstairs bathroom," "cut grass (summer)," "garbage to curb (Thursday)" – to Garnet's column. (If he had asked her about this, she was prepared to say that it was only temporary, until the kids finished the school year; but he didn't ask.)

Of course, he didn't even need to leave the house to get drunk. She considered a lock for the liquor cabinet, then simply getting rid of the liquor altogether; but this would have gone against her sense of fair play. To remove the temptation completely would be to side-step the issue, to betray the spirit of the challenge. Besides, she subscribed to the hydraulic theory of self-control: if the barriers to one's vice were built too strong, the pressure would build to an explosion. (This was why, she believed, jails only increased sex crimes.)

So instead of locking it away, she monitored the liquor. She could think of no inconspicuous way to mark the bottles' levels or booby-trap their lids to show if they'd been opened: a bit of hair or thread pasted across the cap would not withstand Garnet's dusting. (She still insisted, though without special emphasis, that he dust the bottles.) In the end she had to be satisfied with measuring the levels with a ruler; after a week she knew by heart all forty-two measurements, to the millimetre.

This was not exactly an ideal solution; Garnet could easily replace what he took with water. Accordingly she also kept an eye out for dilution, scrupulously recording the particular hue of each bottle, and always at the same time of-day, so that lighting conditions were consistent. It was less than rigorously scientific, she knew. But between this and the ruler, she felt reasonably sure that she would catch him out eventually.

In a cupboard in the pantry, behind a box of good silverware, Garnet found a stash of junk food: nachos, licorice, chocolate bars – some of them half eaten. He agonized over whether to tell Richard and Yvonne. He knew how serious eating disorders were. On the other hand, aside from her lack of appetite at supper, her frequent "snacks" at her friends' places, there was nothing obviously wrong with Milly. She was thin, perhaps, but not conspicuously so for her age. But he was not a doctor, and the fact remained that she was hiding food – that she was ashamed of her appetite.

The real reason he was hesitant to go to Richard and Yvonne was that he did not want Milly to feel he had betrayed her. She was fond of him, he felt, in her awkward, inexpressive way. They had achieved a kind of playful, teasing, supercilious rapport. When her brother or one of her parents said something unintentionally risible at the table, it was towards Garnet that her eyes rolled. He did not want to put her trust at risk, he supposed; but even more simply, he did not want to rat her out. He could just imagine the sort of grim, patient, "understanding" talk that Yvonne would subject her to. (Richard, as usual, would be present, but would say nothing.) The mere thought made Garnet itch.

So in the end he decided it would be better if it came from him. He was blunt, but affable: "I found your stash."

For a moment she looked at him blankly – or rather, with disdainful incomprehension – then snorted with derisive laughter.

"That's *Mom's*," she said. "She has binge tendencies, if you know what I mean." She spoke dismissively, as though already forgetting what they were talking about; but Garnet could see that she was overjoyed to share this vicious secret. "I don't think she purges, though. Hey, do you want to play chess?"

Garnet twisted his watch. "Are you done all your homework?"

Garnet was not surprised to hear that Jimmy was having a hard time getting the kids in his class to come to his birthday party. He knew how Jimmy asked for anything: with a rising wail of hopelessness – "Can I have a *sandWICH*?" – as though certain in advance of being turned down. So Garnet had a man-to-man with him one evening while they played catch in the backyard. He advised assertiveness. "The other kids, they can smell weakness. Tell them they're coming to your party – or else."

Somehow, it worked. More than a dozen boys and girls showed up, bearing presents. Garnet made a cake. The kids played hide and seek. Jimmy tore into his swag with a joy indistinguishable from gloating: "Look, Garnet! Look what I got!" Everything went well until one of the gifts turned out to be a duplicate and Jimmy punched the giver in the arm. The boy, a quivering little sausage of a drama queen, cried. (Garnet decided his next man-to-man with Jimmy would be on the topic of how to choose your friends.) The boy cried and Yvonne sent everyone home. (Milly rolled her eyes at Garnet with malicious glee.)

After a minute alone with Jimmy, Yvonne confronted Garnet in the kitchen: "I don't believe what my son has been telling me."

Garnet defended himself: "That was a figure of speech – a piece of rhetoric – a joke. I told him to *say*, for example, 'Come to my party or I'll punch you.' I did *not* tell him to actually punch anyone, ever."

Yvonne only glowered. Her gaze – those wet, pitying, beady eyes – somehow had the power to make him feel very small. (That much, at least, was spared Richard, he thought.) Garnet wanted to point out that it had worked: look how many kids had come! But since they had been sent away after forty-five minutes, he didn't think this argument would hold much water.

"I'll have a talk with him, if you want."

"That, Garnet, is just precisely what we don't want. We don't want you having any more talks with either of our children behind our backs. You're not their uncle. You're . . ."

"All right," he said, "I understand."

"Richard and I are in agreement on this. Do you understand?"

So he had to repeat himself, like a child being made to speak up, to echo some moral lesson: "I understand."

As punishment, the birthday cake was thrown out, uneaten.

They took Jimmy into the parlour to talk. It rankled Yvonne that they could not comfortably reprimand their own children in their own house without feeling self-conscious. It was not that they had anything to hide: she knew that she and Richard were better-than-average parents. It was simply that some conversations were properly held in private. There were things you did not say in the grocery store, things you did not say before company, things you did not say in front of the servants. There was a time and a place for everything. Home was supposed to be the place for these things. Home was a place you could raise your voice without thought for who might overhear. Home was a silence in which you could freely express your thoughts.

But it was, she now saw, impossible to have someone in your home and still feel that it was your home. A home could not survive a pair of alien ears.

Richard hated having company. It was as if the more people they brought into their house, the less it was their house; the more people present, the less real his own presence became. He was lost in crowds, forgotten. He could not mingle the way he used to, by affably buttonholing whoever happened to be standing silent or alone, because whoever stood silent was by definition invisible to him. He had to sit back and wait for others to buttonhole him. The enforced passivity was painful enough; but the larger the crowd, it seemed, the more he was left to himself. In small groups, little dinner parties, someone could always be counted on to feel responsible or sorry for him, but with larger groups, the responsibility was diluted. The irony, that his blindness rendered him invisible, was not lost on him. It reminded him of playing "peekaboo" with the kids when they were much younger: by covering their eyes, they had made themselves disappear.

Large gatherings also inevitably centred around the children: at Christmas and birthdays the adults would sit around in a circle and complacently watch the children's antics like it was television. It was at these times, in his role as a father, that he felt his disability most keenly. At the opening of presents he felt especially useless. Jimmy, just turned eight, understood it was no use to cry "Look, Dad!" Instead, he now called for Garnet's attention. Not because Garnet was more fun, or funny, or likeable, or better with children; but simply because he had attention to give. Milly, at twelve, no longer cared if her father came to her dance recitals or not. At the dinner table, he sometimes heard her and Garnet giggling, and had no idea why.

Now, it seemed, his children's attitude towards "Dad's friend" had moved beyond "Look, Garnet!" Now they were going to him to learn how to catch a baseball. Going to him for help with their math homework. Going to him for advice. There was no sense to any of this: Richard could still throw a ball; as an architect his grasp of trigonometry was, he should think, considerably firmer than a cook's; he knew a thing or two about the world, about life, about people and their capacity for cruelty – and besides, wasn't he their father? Only a child could make the connection between being sighted and being someone to confide in.

Thus Richard assured himself that it was not stung pride or hurt feelings that prompted him to agree to Jimmy's grounding, but a calm and fatherly impulse to correct the boy's fuzzy thinking. And, as he made clear, while Yvonne spoke to Garnet in the kitchen, it was not so much because Jimmy had hit another boy. What distressed him, he said, was that Jimmy had gone to Garnet for help.

"Don't you know, sweetheart, that you can come to me for anything? You can always come to your father. Garnet isn't your father. He isn't even family. He isn't even anything. Do you understand?" But the boy only sniffled, and could not be made to understand anything.

On the forty-seventh day, when Garnet found half a packet of cigarettes in Milly's sock drawer, he took them directly to Richard. After dinner, her parents took her into the parlour for a talk. But less than five minutes later she came into the kitchen, seemingly unperturbed, looking for dessert.

"How'd it go?"

She twitched a shoulder: the most economical expression of indifference possible.

She'd made a full confession. The cigarettes were not hers, of course; she was hiding them for Patricia. But Milly Lapley knew her mother well enough to know that innocence was, in her book, the only unforgivable crime: perfect little angels could not be improved, after all; they could never see the error of their ways; they were immune to salvation.

"I just wonder," she said with rich inflection, like someone narrating their own life-story, "how the hell she ever found the damn things."

Then she slammed the fridge and strode ostentatiously out of the kitchen.

His heart, Garnet was alarmed to discover, now beat faster when he heard the garage door open. Somehow, he had begun to dread Yvonne's coming home. She would inevitably find something left undone, or improperly done, or something that, through no fault of her own, she had neglected to tell him to do. The astounding thing, the thing he would not have thought possible, was that he wanted not to disappoint her. From time to time he caught himself wanting actually to please her, to exceed her expectations. He supposed that words of praise, some tangible sign that a job had been done well, was, like privacy, a basic human need. If that praise was scarce, it was only natural that you came to crave all the more powerfully the rare scrap of it thrown your way. It was, at root, a desire for completion, for closure. He could judge a floor well-mopped by its lustre, a load of laundry well-cleaned by its warmth and scent. But most of his duties lacked any such clear-cut conclusion. Only a casual compliment could testify to a garage well-tidied; only a clean plate could testify to a meal well-cooked.

It had been much the same at the restaurant. He could not stay quarantined in the kitchen like the aloof artist. He had to come out and ask his patrons how everything had been. He craved at least that much feedback. It was precisely that interaction, that reckoning, that verdict that had made having his own shop, after all those years of waiting, so satisfying. In other people's kitchens you were chained to your stove, and toiled in a fog of insignificance, a blind cog in a machine you never learned the function of.

It had been no different with his patrons, really, than it was with Yvonne. He had had no more faith in the refinement of their palates than he had in the wisdom of her whims. But when you could not choose your own judge, you could only seek their approval – no matter how fickle, how arbitrary, how worthless their judgement might be.

It was important that he remain honest with himself. The fact was, one drink wouldn't hurt. Indeed, it would probably do him good. There was after all such a thing as underdoing something, which could be just as bad, just as unhealthy as overdoing it. A teetotaller was, in his way, just as despicable as a lush – he'd seen how the Lapleys' guests looked at him. Yvonne herself seemed to be pushing him to drink, and not just in the indirect way of making his life miserable. A drink, one drink, a single drink a week – every Sunday for example, while they were at church, if need be – that wouldn't hurt anyone.

But he knew, too, that he had to be on guard against malleable resolutions. One drink every Sunday was an easy enough resolution to make on Sunday; by Tuesday, it might seem more sensible to take that weekly drink on Tuesday. This was not breaking a resolution, but only fine-tuning one. Thus "never" became "never more than one at a time," or "never before six o'clock," or "never before midnight," or "never when I have an important obligation the next day," or "never in front of the customers," and so on and so forth; and by switching from one of these resolutions to another, depending on the time of day or the day of the week and the needs of the moment, you could effectively change "never" to "whenever" – without ever actually giving in.

Still, he thought, *one* drink wouldn't hurt.

On Sunday, while the Lapleys were at church, Garnet decided to make the call. He was going to call from the

parlour, but then felt self-conscious; the foolish idea entered
his head that Richard and Yvonne had tapped the line. He
went into the kitchen, where he felt less vulnerable, and
lifted the receiver – but hung up when it occurred to him
that maybe he shouldn't make long-distance calls without
first asking permission. It wasn't a matter of the cost: he fully
intended to leave a note and a few dollars after the fact – but
that would be *after* the fact. They had, when he first moved
in, encouraged him to make himself at home; but then they
had also promised him unrestricted access to Richard's old
Ford and every second weekend off. He did not want to take
any privileges for granted. It was a question of policy, not of
permission. They would never actually prohibit him from
using the phone – that would not fit with their idea of themselves as good employers. Nor would they want him to ask
outright. Rather, the correct thing to do, he supposed, would
be to disguise the request as an offhand comment – "I
thought I might make a couple calls later tonight, if no one
needs the phone" – so that Richard and Yvonne could feel
they'd had a chance to refuse, and yet be spared the embarrassment of being treated like the sort of people who might
refuse. Or was he being ridiculous? Let them *be* upset, if his
calling his wife without their permission was the sort of
thing that could upset them.

He picked up the phone again; then, under the momentum of his decision, hung it up and returned defiantly to
the parlour – surely the more comfortable room to make a
call from.

He sat with the phone in his lap and looked around the
room – at the streaky windows, the smudged floorboards,
the bottles he should have been dusting.

No, he couldn't call, not yet. Because what did he have to say? What did he have to show for all these weeks of humbling himself, rebuilding himself, proving himself? He could not even clean a room properly.

He jumped out of his seat at the sound of the garage door. He did not want to be caught in the parlour, of all rooms, when the Lapleys came in.

She no longer hid trash around the house, or put dirt under the throw-rugs, or counted the good silver, or absent-mindedly left money out on the foyer table or stuffed down between the cushions of the chesterfields. Garnet could, it seemed, be counted on to clean a house properly, and without stealing. But so far her campaign to expose his real vice had failed too. The bottles went untouched even in the kitchen, even in the artful disarray they were left in by Doctor Hambridge and his wife (who at least had not disappointed her, more than living up to their reputation around town as a couple of sodden fishes). She could only assume that he felt too vulnerable, too closely watched, with all of them in the house. So she decided to give him some time alone.

Each year, when the kids finished school, they rented a cabin at Penton Lake for a weekend. She told Garnet they would be back Monday, though she planned to contrive some excuse to come back a day early. Her only fear was that he might go out to a pub somewhere to get drunk, and she would never know it. So she told Avery Tradwell that she and Richard were doing a bit of late spring cleaning, and asked her to pop in Saturday morning to get first pick of a few lawn ornaments and yard tools they'd decided to get rid of. She could explain later that she had, at the time of this invitation, quite gotten her weekends mixed up; and Avery, an incorrigible gossip, could be counted on to tell her how the cook had looked when he came to the door – *if* he came to the door – and to know a hangover when she saw one.

In all the excitement of putting her plan into action, Yvonne forgot to make the cabin reservation. All that was left was a musty little two-bedroom cottage half a kilometre away from the lakefront, and hemmed in by giant spruces that blocked out the sunlight completely.

"You don't understand," she assured the officious adolescent who sat behind the counter at the resort office, and who had been hired, no doubt, for his unwillingness to think for himself. "We need to be on the lake. My husband is blind."

After a reluctant call to his manager, they were given a larger cabin overlooking the lake at no extra charge.

Now, thought Yvonne with bitter satisfaction, Richard could sit slumped on the deck all day, reading Dostoevsky in braille, listening to the monotonous splash of the water, and never have to rouse himself for a nice walk down to the beach with his family.

Garnet thought of what Leah had said: "You must really hate your life, the way you keep punching holes in it.".

He was hot and dirty; he was prickly with sweat and covered with grass clippings; he had dog shit on his hands. The neighbourhood dogs used the Lapleys' front yard as their public toilet; just yesterday the Tradwell woman had come around with her mutt, apparently for that express purpose. And Yvonne, of course, had left instructions to scoop up all their droppings before running the lawn mower.

This life, maybe, was one that could do with a few holes punched in it. But his old life, the one he was fighting to get back? A beautiful wife, a business of his own: why would anyone want to escape that? It was true that running a restaurant had involved a certain amount of dealing with shit; but opening his own shop had been the great success of his life – why else would he have kept the old linoleum tile as a memento, a trophy? And if sometimes he and Leah fought, or said nasty things to one another, or had to sleep in separate beds to keep from strangling each other, what they had was still preferable to what a lot of other couples put up with – the Lapleys, for instance. He would rather live hot and cold than a lifetime of tepid. A marriage was not, after all, a business contract. You tied yourself to another person to make the best of both your individual failings. It was like conserving body heat, at night, in the cold, by clinging to another body: their loss was your gain, and vice versa. A married couple was an arch: a strength made of two weaknesses propped up against one another. If you couldn't find anything to hate about your spouse, you'd attached yourself to the wrong person – to a self-supporting structure, to a column.

He stood in the parlour, shit on his hands, and lifted the top from a decanter of Scotch.

It was a diving competition. For this, for once, Richard was the perfect judge: whoever made the least noise entering the water was the winner. He could feel rocks on the bottom and the water here was perhaps a little shallow for diving, but Richard said nothing to the children; he wanted to be the fun dad again for a while, the dad who splashed around in the lake with his kids. Not the dad who was always telling his kids what not to do. Not the frail, disabled, paranoid dad who couldn't trust them not to hurt themselves – because he couldn't trust himself.

"Nine point *two*," Richard cried deliriously, then waited for the sound of Jimmy resurfacing to repeat the score to the new record-holder.

The smell repulsed him. That hadn't changed; he had never cared for the taste. It had never been thirst that drew him to drink, but the promise of drunkenness. He was not after annihilation; he wanted oblivescence. That was what Leah didn't understand. The blackouts – which happened rarely enough anyway – were not empty blanks. They were simply stretches of time inaccessible to memory. He didn't drink to erase his life or to escape it, but to forget it for a while. Forgetfulness was not the absence of consciousness, but the absence of care. You didn't stop enjoying yourself just because you wouldn't remember the joy later. On the contrary, you could enjoy yourself more fully, more freely – like in a dream you knew you would wake from. The dream dissipated, but you were still left in the morning with the sense of having just been someplace else, of having returned from somewhere far away.

As Garnet reached out unhurriedly for a tumbler, he remembered something that Richard had told him one night in their dorm room, during their first few weeks together, when they were still getting to know each other – that is, still impinging themselves on one another by getting drunk and making outrageous, aggressively vulnerable, drunken confessions.

"You know when you wake up in the middle of the night
– in some strange room, maybe, in a hotel or in someone
else's house – and for a few seconds, lying there half-
paralyzed in the dark, you can't remember where you are, or
even who you are?"

"Sure," Garnet said, "I guess so."

"I sometimes think those are the happiest times of my life."

He hadn't heard the garage door.

"Garnet?"

At the sound of Richard's voice he froze. *But they're not
back till tomorrow*, his mind kept insisting like a petulant child.

"Garnet, are you here?"

Richard's steps receded as far as the kitchen, then began
to come closer. His heart flopped in his chest like a fish on
dry land.

Richard came closer, muttering something about an accident, Yvonne at the hospital . . . "Garnet – are you home?"

Then Richard was there, standing in the doorway. Their
eyes met. But Richard, of course, couldn't see him. His eyes
were dead; his pupils vacant holes. If Garnet didn't move, if
he didn't even breathe, Richard could not know he was
there. He might smell the open bottle, but he would never
see him.

Because he was invisible. He wasn't there at all. Garnet
closed his eyes – and disappeared into thin air.

NADESHDA PAVLOVNA

"A machine for converting bread into dung," said Ippolitsky. "What would I do with a dog?"

"But Comrade sir, you wouldn't have to feed it." The peasant implored him with eyes that looked like they were smeared with honey.

"And what use would I have for a starved dog?" muttered the rent collector.

The dog crouched on the table, eyes staring blankly out of its bulging skull, as though ignoring, out of polite embarrassment, the discussion of its fate.

"You wouldn't have to feed it," repeated Petrov slowly, with the slightest emphasis on *you* and *it*.

Ippolitsky looked around the disgusting little room. The Petrovs had already eaten through anything of value, like rats eating through walls. The bare floor seemed bleached, picked clean even of colour. All that remained were a couple of beeswax candles, a pot, the primus stove (useless until another paraffin shipment arrived), the obligatory portrait of the General Secretary, and the filthy clothes the peasant, his wife, and snivelling child stood up in. And the dog.

Ippolitsky had eaten partridge, and fox, and raccoon, and once, in his childhood, he and his sisters had been driven to eat rats. He had never eaten dog.

"You could sell it," coaxed Petrov. "To someone in dire straits . . ."

"And where do you suppose," said Ippolitsky dryly, "I could find someone with money not yet spent on real food?" He bent over to scrutinize the mongrel. Its pelt was as ragged and flea-bitten as the upholstery of an old armchair. Its eyes flicked sideways and met his for a moment; a tremor went through its haunches. "Besides," he said, straightening, "there can't be more than a pound of meat on him."

"*Her*," sobbed the child.

Petrov glared menacingly at his wife, who glared pleadingly at the child, who glared miserably at Ippolitsky, who smiled grimly. Perhaps next month it would be the child cowering on the table.

"You would be surprised, Comrade sir," murmured Petrov's wife, squeezing her dirty little hands into lemon-like fists. "Its breed has a naturally lean look, but we've been feeding it well."

"Which is why you can't make rent," said Ippolitsky. Clasping his hands behind his back, he paced what little of the room there was. The rhythmic sound of his boot heels striking the rough floorboards soothed him.

"Listen, Petrov, if you think the damn thing will be so easy to sell, why don't you do it?"

"But surely, Comrade sir, you can get a better price than I."

In other words, he knew that Ippolitsky would give him

more than the mutt was worth. But to go on discussing the matter only showed weakness.

"One week," he said.

The peasant and his wife fidgeted but said nothing.

"Two weeks' rent," said Ippolitsky in the same firm voice, as though he had not budged and would not budge.

"Thank you, Comrade sir," whispered the wife.

"Grisha," the peasant hissed at his whimpering child. "Bring us a rope – a *short* one."

Madezhkov paid with women's stockings. Tambov paid with pillows. The Zemstovs with charcoal pencils – god in heaven only knew where they'd grubbed them up. And now a dog! Where would he sell a dog? He could never take the thing to Andreyev Grishkovich.

Ippolitsky hated winter. No one paid with ration cards or eggs or extra clothes anymore. During his first months here, before the power plant was sabotaged, the work had been not unlike his work on the *kolkhoz*. On the collective farm, peasants hid grain; in the city, they hid roubles. One had only to find what they'd hidden, or, better yet, persuade them to show you.

But as winter wore on, the peasants had less to conceal – and they became more adept at concealment. Last month, after a thorough search of the Yomjievs's room had turned up nothing but a bucket of dried-up potatoes and a slab of kitchen soap, he had been on his way out the door when the gnarled old grandfather began to cough – he'd almost swallowed one of the coins he'd been holding in his mouth. After that, Ippolitsky made certain that his tenants at least opened their mouths to greet him and to bid him farewell.

If there was one place they could not conceal their money, it was outside the co-operative stores. He had taken to prowling the lineups whenever a new shipment was announced.

"Good morning, Ada Maximova."

"Good morning, Comrade landlord sir."

"You're in a good spot here. Arrived early, eh?"

"Five o'clock, Comrade sir," she said with pride.

"And what are you waiting for?"

"Eh? The store isn't yet open, Comrade."

"I mean, what have they brought in? What is the shipment?"

"Playing cards, I believe, sir – Comrade sir."

"And bowls," someone else in line chimed in eagerly. "I've heard there'll be bowls."

"Tin bowls?" inquired another.

"Clay."

"Oh, it'll never be clay."

"What I heard is what I heard."

"What you heard was the wind whistling through the holes in your head."

"I must confess, Ada Maximova, I'm surprised. Do you have such a great need of playing cards and tin bowls?"

"Oh, but you know how it is, Comrade sir. One snaps up what one can, when one can . . ."

"And just how much are the playing cards and the tin bowls on sale for today?"

There appeared at last on her face a look of dawning anxiety. "Oh, I couldn't say for certain."

"So no doubt you've brought a tidy little sum, just to be safe."

"Oh, a very little sum indeed, sir."

"I wonder, all the same, if your need of playing cards is, after all, greater than your need, and your family's need, of four walls and a roof over your heads?"

"But haven't we paid up already this month?" asked the woman miserably.

"No, not paid. Defrayed some of your debt to the State, perhaps. It's a long time since I've received any *payment* from Unit 317. Besides," he said softly, taking her by the elbow and leading her out of the line, "there is always next month, and times, as you know, are hard . . ."

"Is it the first of the month already?"

"No," he said. "Yes. It will be. In a few days."

Nadeshda Pavlovna Radshova did not invite him in but stood aside with her back to the door, as though defying him to come inside and find anything amiss.

"Is your husband . . . not home?"

"Ivan Pavlovich – no. He is away."

She stared at him for a moment, betraying nothing, then disappeared inside.

He did not go in, though he could have. It was only habit; Radshov had always brought the rent to the door. He had been one of the few who still paid in cash, and paid on time. Old *intelligentsia*. Old aristocrats. One had only to look at the woman, his wife, to see that.

He watched her outline, the brown lustre of her hair, moving in the space between the hinges of the door.

"The rent collector," he heard her say to someone – the grandmother, presumably – without bothering to lower her voice.

Ippolitsky cleared his throat. "And when is he . . . expected back?"

She returned to the door and seemed for a moment surprised to see him still there. But it was only her usual look, her mask of composed disappointment, as though her deepest, most important thoughts had been carelessly disturbed.

"He is on a *komandirovka*."

"Oh yes?" said Ippolitsky casually. "For his organization, I assume?" He was being reckless, toying with her in this manner.

She hesitated, or rather, simply stood silent for a moment.

"For his organization," she repeated.

He laughed at the boldness of her lie. Then, quickly, to conceal the cause of his amusement, he muttered, "Somehow I can't imagine Ivan Pavlovich on a train to Moscow."

"And why not?"

Her brown hair was very brown. Her eyes were all pupil. Her skin was soapstone.

"I always thought he seemed quite . . . comfortable here. Among his many fine things."

Resolutely, without a trace of embarrassment, she said, "Will you return in a day or two? I will have the money then."

Because Radshov had always been polite to him, had never gone out of his way to make Ippolitsky feel stupid or beneath him, because he had always paid on time, and because now he was gone (and not on a *komandirovka*), Ippolitsky said yes.

It had nothing, he told himself, to do with guilt.

Andreyev Grishkovich took the stockings, the pillows, the linen, the pendant, and finally, after a great show of reluctance, the two icons. But he would not touch the pencils.

"Domestically made," was his verdict.

"But there's a shortage," protested Ippolitsky. "In all the offices."

"That is the offices' business, and the government's business. I do not sell to offices." He surveyed his fingernails, which he had chewed down to the flesh, with evident satisfaction. "It would be counter-revolutionary."

"Then sell them to someone else."

Andreyev Grishkovich picked up one of the pencils and looked at it sadly. "My customers wouldn't be interested in such poor quality stuff. You know how it is. The tourists and foreigners are accustomed to lead, and anyone with money to spend on such trifles wants actually *to spend* money."

"Then charge more, for God's sake," Ippolitsky sputtered.

The shopkeeper laid the pencil, as though to rest, on the counter. "Have you tried the bazaar?"

"Don't be ridiculous. Starving peasants don't spend their money on *pencils*."

Andreyev Grishkovich's posture stiffened. "One shouldn't exaggerate, Comrade." He nodded at the other customers in the store.

Ippolitsky bristled. This was the Party co-operative; there should have been no need to speak so carefully behind closed doors. Besides, he did not understand how the mere acknowledgement of shortages could be counter-revolutionary, unless one also took it for granted that the revolution was to blame. To his mind, the real counter-revolutionary act was this mealy-mouthed circumspection; it was this wilful blindness to what was obvious to everyone that betokened the bad conscience.

His own conscience was clean. But he went through with the ritual anyway: "Of course I misspoke. Of course no one is actually *starving*, and if they are it's only the despicable *kulaks* who by resisting collectivization have brought difficulties upon their own heads – of course."

Andreyev Grishkovich shrugged the formality aside. "So you see, your pencils are too good and not good enough." He tittered at his witticism. "Too expensive for the workers, not expensive enough for me. Still, you might try the bazaar." He nibbled at a fingernail and snickered. "You might get lucky. You might find a struggling young Pushkin."

Ippolitsky no longer knew exactly who or what *was* to blame for the present difficulties, but of one thing he was certain: *Things are better now for more than they have ever been before.* Those who denied that or refused to see it, those who cursed the Party for all their hardships, were the real counter-revolutionaries.

The stupid, stubborn recalcitrance of the starving peasants themselves was, of course, partly at fault. He had seen enough horses slaughtered and grain torched by ignorant farmers resisting collectivization – not all of them, by any means, rich *kulaks* – to realize that a large number of the people's wounds were self-inflicted.

But there had to be – he had to believe that there was more at work than stupidity and fear of change. The peasantry could not be their own and only enemy. There had to be forces of oppression still active. How else to explain the shortages, the discontentment, the difficulties on so many fronts? The agents of reaction, the white agitators, the soldiers and spies of the counter-revolution had only gone underground. Most of them, he supposed, were to be found among the old tsarists, the old *intelligentsia*, the old aristocrats . . .

It was every good citizen's duty to sniff out and expose these saboteurs.

Ippolitsky hated the bazaar. It stank of poverty. Although it had been several years since he'd known hunger, as with any old acquaintance banished to exile and consigned to disgrace, he had no desire to meet it face to face in the street. The sight of the peasants – with their bones sticking out of their tattered clothing, their eyes popping out of their swollen faces, and all their junk spread out on the frozen ground, like the steaming innards of a slaughtered horse spilled out onto the snow – the sight of them, not to mention their smell, disgusted him.

The bazaar was chaos. The peasants arrived at the square in the morning, dropped their wares wherever they could find a spot, and hunkered down over their precious filth like brooding hens. They were desperate to sell and loath to relinquish. They knew that what they hawked was rubbish, but desperation and sentimental attachment converted the valueless to the invaluable. Every pair of eyes accused him of theft and at the same time begged him to commit it.

The vendors of anything edible – or semi-edible, or once-edible – did the briskest business. For cups of sour milk, strips of rotten meat, unidentifiable fragments of bone, dirty flour, flyblown pails of grain, and hard crusts of black bread there could always be found willing buyers. Next in saleability were the inedible but needful things: matches, buttons, belts, boots, knives, thread, paraffin, primus needles, scraps of cloth, links of chain, flypaper . . . That the usefulness of most of these things was, in fact, illusory – the matches didn't light, the oil didn't burn, the belts had no buckles, the boots no soles (or the soles no boots), the knives were dull, the thread came in a clump of one-inch lengths, and so on – did not seem to dissuade the buyers. On the contrary, they took the flaws for granted, and seemed even to set store by them. A peasant coming to the bazaar to buy thread might be deterred, even repulsed, by the sight of any-thing so fine as a spool.

Whatever else one might say about them, the difficulties on the harvest-collecting front had at least revealed the inher-ent uselessness of "fine" things. A jewellery box was, in the end, just a fancy box; a china cup was just a brittle receptacle for drink; medals, rings, pins, and pendants were only so much molten metal; portraits, the most useless of all, were even less than so much firewood, so many square inches of oil-speckled canvas: they gave off an unpleasant smell when burned; left unburned, they identified their owners as the off-spring of some feeble inbred aristocrats who had thrived under the old tsarist regime, feeding upon the blood and toil of the serfs, living like gods in rarefied luxury, surrounded by things as fine and useless as themselves. Indeed, *all* the fine old things were tokens of exploitation and cruelty. Ippolitsky could not, even now, look at a jewellery box or handle a leather-bound book without a flare-up of the old anger. How many mouths had to go hungry so that such beautiful trifles could be made? *Quality precludes equality* – for once the slogan had got it right.

The more expensive something had been, the more worth-less it was now. The neat symmetry of this reversal pleased Ippolitsky. But, as a result, only rarely did anything of inter-est turn up here – a clock or book that Ippolitsky might pass along to Andreyev Grishkovich at a profit, a necklace or locket that Maria Smirnova, in her inscrutable discernment, might accept. And, because you could not eat a book, because no one in their right mind would trade so much as a fist-sized lump of rancid cheese for the finest clock in the world, Ippolitsky could usually walk away with these things for a song. Often it did not matter what he offered in exchange; if the peasant had been waiting long enough, if they were hungry enough, any trade was a good trade. The opportunity to sit around not selling something else for a change was, for most of them, an irresistible temptation. He would never be able to sell the pencils outright, but he just might trade them for something he could sell or take to Andreyev Grishkovich.

Sometimes, too, he came across one of his own tenants trying to convert their cherished rubbish into bread. If he caught them late enough in their chain-trading, he could often relieve them of something almost as good as roubles.

Of all his tenants, the last he would have expected to find at the bazaar was Nadeshda Pavlovna.

He couldn't tell whether she was buying or selling. She stood alone, in one spot, as though she owned it. But this might have been an illusion of posture or bearing. She occupied space the way other people occupied their homes. Today, even in the midst of so much squalor, she looked more comfortable – more at home – in her shabby overcoat than he had ever felt in his own skin.

She was holding a box of some sort, and it seemed to Ippolitsky that she held the box in the same way that she held herself: delicately but firmly, as though it were an object of great value. But even at a distance he could see that, whatever it was, it was too fine to be of any value to anyone here. Its dark red wood gleamed in the white sunlight.

She saw him approach, and smiled. It was almost enough to make him check his stride. It was a smile that invited interpretation and simultaneously denied it. Beneath all its self-deprecating frankness there was a thin, hard, reflective crust of defiance: *Whatever you think this smile means, you're wrong.*

"I don't really know what I'm doing here," she said, smiling.

Ippolitsky grimaced. With the white sun smeared out across the sky by a thin gauze of cloud, the day was almost unbearably bright.

"Perhaps," he said lightly, "there is something I can do to help?"

"A gramophone," said Andreyev Grishkovich, contemplatively chewing the red nub of a finger to conceal his excitement. He looked at Ippolitsky shrewdly. "Does it *work*?"

"How the hell should I know?"

Ippolitsky had never before seen such a contraption, not in the homes of even the richest farmers, not in the fanciest hotels requisitioned by his squad during the Revolutionary War. Nadeshda Pavlovna (without quite hiding her amused astonishment at his ignorance) had said simply that it was for playing music. He had seen music boxes before – his sister had had one, once – and assumed this was the same sort of thing. Only larger, and finer.

Andreyev Grishkovich slapped his hands together twice, as though dusting them off, and lifted the lid of the box. He gave the crank at the side one gentle turn, then several more, and the black disc began slowly rotating. Then, reaching out as though from a great distance, he laid the little arm down onto the outer edge of the spinning black plate.

It was not like a music box.

By the time she opened the door, Ippolitsky had already gone through ten or fifteen minutes of the ensuing conversation in his head. Thus it caught him off guard to find himself still standing in the hallway, still holding out the fifteen roubles, when in his imagination she had long ago, with a quick nod expressive of deep gratitude and humility, taken the money and hidden it away somewhere in the plush folds of her gown – when in reality they had not yet spoken a word; nor was she wearing a gown.

She glanced down at the money and lifted a hand to her face. This gesture – two fingers lightly touching her cheek – was somehow, coming from her, more evocative of anguish than another woman pulling out her hair or clawing at her eyes.

"Oh. Is that –"

He stuffed the money back in his pocket, then realized how foolish this must look – like a gloating child flaunting his little hoard of sugared raisins.

"That's not all," said Ippolitsky quickly. And so it was that with the first words out of his mouth he was already repudiating himself, correcting the mistaken impression he had made, instead of calmly and laconically explaining the scenario that he had so carefully formulated. A flare of resentment shot up through his chest, constricting his windpipe. "That's not all." He held out the money again. "That's what was left over."

She just looked at him.

"After rent."

"Oh."

In fact, Andreyev Grishkovich had offered an amount that was one and a half times the Radshovs' rent, and which Ippolitsky could surely have pushed up to two or three. But he had not sold the gramophone. The fifteen roubles – the amount supposedly left over after deducting next month's rent – were to make her think he had. He had thought this detail particularly ingenious, and felt that, in all justice, it should have been all the more convincing for putting him out fifteen roubles – not to mention the month's rent that he would now have to account for somehow. But standing before her, holding out the coins as though anxious to be rid of them, he realized how guilty he must look. Why should she believe that he had deducted only the rent money, and not a kopeck more? Because everyone would skim a little off the top if given the opportunity. It was expected. That's what was done.

She picked the coins, still warm from his own pocket, out of his palm one at a time, like rotten blackberries. He blushed at what she must think of him; and the injustice of her assumption – natural, but incorrect – added to his shame a flush of rage.

He hated her. He hated the way she made him feel.

"Perhaps," she said thoughtfully, turning her head and gaze as far away from him as was possible without actually showing him her back, "perhaps we could find one or two other things for you to sell . . ."

The free-market restaurant was almost empty. Maria Smirnova gave Ippolitsky a look of triumphant reproach, but magnanimously allowed him to take her coat.

One of the girl's most mystifying qualities was the ease with which she turned every situation and circumstance to her advantage – or, rather, his disadvantage. If the restaurant had been crowded, she would certainly have reproached him for exposing her to so many eyes. She had been reluctant to come tonight. When pressed, she'd said something about the difficulties on the food-distribution front, and how would it look? But the free-market places, where they made no bones about serving you in the best international (capi-talist) style, had always been technically illicit. What others might think had never bothered her before. On the contrary, what others might think had always struck him as one of her prime motivations for coming here. Only tourists, Party members, and employees of the better organizations could afford to. Why the sudden scruples? She wouldn't say, and instead trotted out one of her all-purpose Komsomol slogans, something to the effect that one must be vigilant always. Her I-told-you-so look just now was her way of gloating that she had clearly not been alone in those scruples. He might have pointed out that, in any case, with the place empty there was no one here to see them; or that anyone who did show up could hardly throw stones in *their* direction; or that the only other place one could be reasonably sure of getting fed would have been the Party restaurants, and she, he need hardly remind her, was not yet a member. But he did not want to get off to a bad start. It had been weeks since she had last agreed to see him.

She looked more than usually made-up tonight. Not nec-essarily any prettier – he did not think anyone would have called her pretty, exactly – but more meticulously arranged, sculpted, lacquered. He wondered if any of this was for his benefit; and, to forestall any flattery he might have felt, mused that only women lacking natural beauty had to bother, and only those who had, early in life, lacked the means to do so went to such lengths. He thought of Nadeshda Pavlovna's beauty. Perhaps Maria Smirnova's children would be prettier than she. Perhaps all of tomorrow's children would be prettier than today's. This seemed, on the face of it, quite plausible. There might even have been something in the Party line about it.

Maria told him what to order for both of them. He took what she had read from the menu and compressed it to its essence, stripped of all adjectives and secondary ingredients, and told the waiter simply, "The vichyssoise; the stuffed chicken; the caviar to start." This brusqueness was as close as he dared come to stating that he would have preferred a good blood sausage and three or four hard-boiled eggs. Maria thought his tastes hopelessly common; and, though he doubted that she enjoyed actually eating things like red pressed caviar or cold soup as much as she enjoyed ordering or being seen ordering them, she had the power to make him feel ashamed of what he liked with a single disapproving glance. He tried not to embarrass her, though in one way or another it seemed he could not avoid it. The last time they were here he had mortified her by removing his own coat.

They ate in silence, Ippolitsky because he was determined to get as much pleasure and satisfaction out of the food as possible, Maria because she was distracted, her attention drawn to the entrance with every new arrival of diners. Her appetite, as usual, was no match for her imagination.

"Are you really finished, then?" he asked, nodding at her plate.

It galled him to see food left uneaten – though he realized that it would not likely go to waste. If the *maître* did not eat it himself, one of the waiters or cooks surely would, and even if by some amazing oversight Maria's scraps were thrown out, there would be a horde of waifs only too ready to pick through the restaurant's leavings, and more still grazing like cattle on the rotten trash heaps outside town. He supposed, on reflection, that it was better she didn't finish – and he felt a swift pang of guilt at his own appetite, which was as much conscience as it was hunger. It occurred to him that he might take the leftovers back to Nadeshda Pavlovna's grandmother. But Maria Smirnova would never allow that.

She looked prepared to ignore him. Then, dabbing at her lips with her napkin, she changed her attitude, and said calmly, "I'm not hungry."

"You will be," was all he said.

Though not hungry, Maria insisted that they take dessert, a raspberry torte with vanilla syrup and chocolate shavings, and coffee with brandy. Ippolitsky tried not to think that he would have preferred a piece of carrot cake and a cup of beef tea.

"You'll never guess who just came in," she said, leaning over the table in her enthusiastic conspirator's manner.

"Who?"

"You'll never guess," she assured him, but nevertheless wanted him to try. When she realized he wouldn't play, she told him, but with an offhand, slightly wounded air. "Elinskiev and his fat wife," she said, naming the manager of the post office. His wife was supposed to have a position of some influence in the regional division of the State publishing organization. "Can you believe it?" said Maria Smirnova with ominous glee. "After his cousin was deported . . . They must have a death wish."

"Just because someone in the family becomes corrupt doesn't mean –"

She stared at him with blank contempt. "Don't be a fool, please. Reaction runs in the blood." She had a real talent, Ippolitsky had to admit, for delivering slogans: at an even, slightly raised pitch, as though surprised, even in the articulation of it, by the profundity of the thought. "At least everyone acts like it does," she said, moodily now, stirring her coffee in lieu of drinking it. "They should know better." She sounded as though the Elinskievs had quite ruined her evening.

He withdrew from his trousers pocket the necklace that he had been meaning to give her since she first came to her door. There was no occasion for it, and he could not decide how much ceremony to put into the giving. In the end, he simply held the necklace up over the table in the hope that the gesture would draw in its wake the appropriate words, the right tone. But her gaze remained on her coffee cup, and it seemed somehow pompous to begin any speech without her attention. In clearing his throat he set free a little bubbling burp. She looked up then, of course; and the disgust still lingered in her eyes even as she reached out for the necklace – not to take it, like a dog snapping up a scrap of meat, but in an instinctive caress, the way he had seen some women reach out towards babies, as though to get a better look at them with their fingertips.

"Where did you get it?"

"I bargained for it," he said, pitching his voice somewhere between pride and humility; it came out sounding merely deceitful.

A smile slowly broke out on her face. She held the neck-lace up; it glistened blackly in the candlelight.

She murmured, as though to herself, "Beth Yuriovna, you can be sure, doesn't have anything like it."

She leaned over the table to plant a kiss approximately on his cheek. His heart thudded – once, like a cannon – in his ears. He could not shake the foolish feeling that all eyes were on them, crawling over them like spiders.

As usual, Ippolitsky was made to wait half an hour in the anteroom outside Kronstrov's office. A pale young man dressed all in khaki, like a soldier in an American film, went in and out several times while Ippolitsky waited. A messen-ger or secretary, he supposed – though the man was on no obvious errand, carried nothing in and brought nothing out. Each time he passed through the anteroom he had a sly smile for Ippolitsky, who grew annoyed at not knowing what attitude to take towards him. On his third or fourth appear-ance, Ippolitsky got to his feet; the young man did not object. It was the outfit that had decided him: no lowly mes-senger or secretary would dare to dress in such a ridiculous fashion. At last, he left Kronstrov's door open on his way out, and a minute or two later Ippolitsky was mournfully called in.

For being bald, or nearly so, Kronstrov's head was a remarkably variegated surface, crosshatched with scars and wrinkles, spattered with moles, liver spots, and what might have been a birthmark. Ippolitsky found he could scrutinize it indefinitely, which was just as well, since the old man often left him standing there with little else to do, while he stared balefully at the papers on his desk, bobbing and ducking his head as though physically parrying the information that rose up from the page.

"Will you close the door?" Kronstrov said, abstractedly but clearly. Kronstrov never mumbled.

The door was already closed, but Ippolitsky went over and touched the doorknob again.

Eventually Kronstrov's head, for the most part, stopped moving.

"I have been looking over your figures for last month, Comrade."

"Yes, Comrade?"

"They seem to be in order," said Kronstrov, his tone ominously even.

"I should hope so, Comrade."

"You've not encountered any . . . difficulties in your collections?"

"Difficulties?"

Kronstrov looked up. His grey gaze, magnified by his round rimless spectacles, startled Ippolitsky.

"No one . . . refuses to pay?"

"Not everyone is always equally . . . willing." He had almost said *able*. But an inability to pay might be thought to have something to do with a lack of money, and to acknowledge shortages of any kind could conceivably be seen as recklessly counter-revolutionary. "But I know how to persuade them," he added.

"Of course, but perhaps," mused Kronstrov, "you need not persuade quite so diligently."

Kronstrov had removed his glasses and was vigorously rubbing his face, like an old farmwoman scrubbing bloodstains out of a blanket. Ippolitsky waited for him to finish before saying he did not understand.

As though reading from one of the dossiers spread out before him, Kronstrov said, "Of course your building is close to the offices of the People's Water and Electricity Commission."

As he seemed to expect some confirmation – or, more accurately, some violent denial – Ippolitsky said mildly, "I guess it is."

"A Comrade Toblomov is, I am told, being transferred to those offices."

"I see."

"From Moscow."

"Yes."

"I am given to understand that Comrade Toblomov would benefit from a flat close by."

"Of course. But my building – there are no vacancies."

"Comrade Toblomov is coming to aid in the resolution of the difficulties on the electricity front."

Of course Comrade Toblomov, arriving from Moscow, and affiliated with no less an organization than WATCOM, would be a Party member; of course he would be given a flat close to his office. To make up for his momentary obtuseness, Ippolitsky blurted out what had been implicit but should have been immediately obvious: "I should free a room for him."

Kronstrov, perhaps as a reproof, did not bother to confirm the obvious.

"When does Comrade arrive?"

"Soon," said Kronstrov vaguely, then again, more force-fully: "Soon."

"It won't be a problem," said Ippolitsky with some fervour. "I can think of a few tenants who've been more trouble than they're worth, of course."

"Before you go," said Kronstrov, as though he had caught Ippolitsky on his way out the door. "Anything more to report on that Radshova woman?"

Carefully, and with the careful avoidance of brevity that characterized the more official Party discourse, Ippolitsky said that there was not.

"Mmm. Well, keep an eye on them. The grandmother especially." Here, to Ippolitsky's surprise, there escaped from Kronstrov's throat what, coming from another, he would almost have called a laugh. "An old spy, that one."

Ippolitsky, who had been keeping an eye on them well enough to see that the old spy was quite unable to feed or dress herself or defecate unaided, agreed that one must be vigilant always.

The Yomjievs were frying onions; the smell wafted down the staircase. The Zemstovs had been home again all afternoon, smoking *mahorka* and playing cards; he'd heard them trudging back from the employment offices shortly after noon. There was a veritable party going on in the Madezhkovs' room; each day more of the wife's family arrived from around the country; each day there were more names for Ippolitsky to register and more feet clomping across the floor of Unit 224. He would have gone inside, if not for the smell of so many bodies.

From 113 there came neither smells nor sounds. He knocked.

She opened the door wide, like she was on her way out. Ippolitsky had to tell himself to stand his ground.

"Good afternoon, Comrade."

"How are things?" he asked, with a solicitous glance past her, into the flat.

"You've not come for the rent, surely."

He dismissed the very idea with a limp shake of his fingers.

"Would you come in," she said evenly, with neither the rising inflection of a question, which might after all have conveyed a genuine invitation, nor the falling inflection of a command, which might have betrayed the perfunctory familiarity of genuine friendliness. As usual, she gave nothing away. He stepped inside.

As soon as the door clicked shut, she went about her business as if he weren't there, stirring something at the stove, checking on the old woman, whose gobbling cough came from the far side of the curtain that divided the flat.

"The rent collector," he heard her say.

The room was barer than he remembered it. Radshov had invited him in during an écarté game once, and the impression that had stayed with him was one of cramped comfort, luxury softened by shabbiness. But aside from one antique chair and a tottering armoire, Unit 113 was as sparsely furnished as any of the others, and certainly no cleaner or brighter.

He peered inside the armoire and was repelled by the sight of so many books. On another shelf were several records. Towards these he felt an ambivalent distaste, such as a man might feel towards his wife's mother or sister:

whatever charms they might share only stripped his beloved of her uniqueness, and their flaws her perfection.

"I could sell these, perhaps," he said. This reference to the absent gramophone was as close as he could come to acknowledging their secret bond.

She shook her head, the slightest gesture imaginable.

"How are –" No, he had already asked that. "How is your grandmother?"

"Fine."

Fine. That was what she was, all right: "fine." He had once heard someone say at a meeting that, in the future, they would exterminate the old and the infirm, just as soon as the value they contributed to society was exceeded by the burden they placed on it. He never learned if that was in the Party line or not. He'd never heard anything about it again.

"And . . . your husband?"

"Ivan Pavlovich – is fine." He thought maybe she stiffened a little.

"Oh? You've heard from him, then?"

She said nothing.

"But of course he must write from time to time . . . Naturally, if he is on a *komandirovka* . . ."

He felt his face flush red. Had he hoped to bait her, provoke some tearful confession? He was a fool. Her silence said as much.

And who are you? A rent collector?

More than that. Someone who knows what music is . . .

"Here," he said, digging in his pockets for some justification of his visit, "fifty, sixty roubles. For the clock." It was not really enough – Andreyev Grishkovich would have offered at least eighty or ninety – but it was all he had.

From the Petrovs' apartment there came the unmistakable smell of meat.

He felt laid open, exposed. It was like having fingers moving inside him, warm, dry, gloved fingers, palpating his organs with firm expertise.

For the first time he understood how names like Beethoven and Tchaikovsky could be uttered, like the names of saints, with almost superstitious respect, even by ignorant peasants. Indeed, Ippolitsky naturally assumed that the piece of music Nadeshda Pavlovna's gramophone played had been composed by one of these luminaries (Tchaikovsky he thought most likely). It was inconceivable that anyone less than a genius could have produced, out of his own head, such sounds.

The "song" (he felt the word's inadequacy, but knew no other word for it) had taken on for him all the significance of a historical, even a revolutionary event. He wondered how its existence had never been celebrated, or indeed mentioned in the newspapers. The music itself seemed to invite, even demand, a revolutionary interpretation. Not just in the sheer immensity of its sounds, the tremendous, earth-shaking importance asserted in its whispers and crashes, but in its progression, the very arrangement of its notes.

The song began with trilling ups and downs that surely signified the fermenting, but disorganized, dissatisfaction of the pre-revolutionary proletariat; then, as though from afar, there entered for the first time the major melody, the sad but uplifting theme that came in to give sudden coherence, order, and direction to the impotent turmoil; and eventually, after a few unforeseen deviations, interruptions, and delays that could only signify the War itself, the rising and falling turmoil dropped entirely away, and only the theme remained, stronger and clearer than ever.

And it was this recurrent melody – melancholy but always climbing, even when it descended, always pushing forward, despite occasional, inevitable setbacks, setbacks that it magically incorporated into itself, as if these had been planned all along to be used as footholds from which it could spring even higher – it was this melody that seemed the most direct and eloquent evocation of Revolution possible. The feeling that this music was calling him to arms, urging him to action, was, at times, almost insufferably potent. But then came other passages whose placid beauty seemed to say, with the utmost warmth and gratitude, that everything that need ever be done had already been done. By the end of the song he often felt as though he had fought several wars single-handed, had smashed stars and been crushed beneath heels, had slaughtered armies and died many deaths. He felt stretched out and deflated, as though his skin no longer quite fit him.

Such at least were the thoughts that occupied his mind when he was not listening; when the gramophone played, anything that might be called thought was drowned in the tide of emotion that flooded through him. The closest analogy within his experience was extreme illness, when you forgot who you were, even *that* you were. It frightened him.

Down through the ceiling came the sound of Madezhkov's glutinous cough. Disgusted, Ippolitsky lowered the volume on the gramophone and moved his ear closer.

Snow the colour of ash fell in clumps from the eaves. The oily smell of the refineries hung in the air. A thick knot of

factory workers stood waiting for the morning tram, indo-
lently jostling one another for a better position on the curb;
when the overloaded tram came into view, those at the back
of the group would probably not find room to ride, not even
hanging off the running boards. In the mouth of an alley,
two waifs quarrelled, striking at each other viciously but
without much effect. He could tell they were waifs by their
sheer bulk: they wore everything they owned, which
buffered them from one another's blows. The taller one held
something over his head, a hunk of bread, perhaps, which
the other was trying to get at. Ippolitsky watched them for a
moment, debating whether or not to intervene. He had
taken a step towards them when they toppled over into the
gutter. The disputed crust went flying.

The small one got to it first. Good, thought Ippolitsky.
But the victor, instead of fleeing, reached back and threw the
hunk of bread as far as he could; it landed on the roof of a
nearby shop. The tall one tackled him, and they resumed
their thrashing of one another.

Ippolitsky moved on, with ambivalent disgust. Perhaps it
had not been a piece of bread after all.

"Who is *that*?" whispered Maria Smirnova.

Ippolitsky slowly turned his head, then quickly looked
away.

"The Radshova woman," he said, after a pause.

"No, *with* her. I've never seen him before."

"Some engineer or something." He made a sound of pas-
sionate indifference.

"How do *you* know?"

"He's moved into the Petrovs' old flat."

"From Moscow?"

Ippolitsky shrugged.

"What a fool," said Maria with relish. "To be seen *here*, with *her*, when her brother has just been sent away . . ."

"Brother?"

"Oh, they let people think they were married, all right. Probably so they could go on sleeping in the same bed. But then you would know more about that than me."

Was it possible? But Kronstrov would have known, would have said something . . . Nadeshda *Pavlovna* Radshova; Ivan *Pavlovich* Radshov. Yes, it was possible. Ippolitsky tried to remember if she had ever actually called Ivan Pavlovich her husband. Or had she simply never corrected the assumptions of others? Not that it mattered now . . . Nevertheless, for some reason, he felt a spasm of chagrin, as though he had forgotten something, left something undone.

"Is he a Party member?"

"I don't know."

"He's your tenant, but you don't know if he's from Moscow, you don't know if he's a Party member, you don't know anything. What are you *doing*?"

"What does it look like? Inviting them to join us."

Maria Smirnova's discomposure did not last long. Curiosity soon overcame scruples.

"Nikolai tells me, Comrade Toblomov, that you are here about the power plant."

Toblomov lifted his gaze from the menu, smiled as if at some distant music, and gave Ippolitsky a long, playfully reproving glance – one that announced that whatever his role might or might not be, it was in any case a matter of such importance and sensitivity that a man less genial and easy-going than Comrade Toblomov might consider Comrade Ippolitsky's disclosure to be indiscreet.

"Yes," he said at last, "Comrade Ippolitsky is not incorrect."

"You are an engineer, then?"

Toblomov smiled sleepily. "Studied in Vienna and Berlin."

"Oh – you've been to Berlin?"

"You *could* say that; I lived there for four years."

"It must have been *horrible* – yes?" Maria Smirnova asked eagerly.

Toblomov looked momentarily puzzled, or would have, Ippolitsky thought, if his features had not been too elegantly indolent to adopt an expression of puzzlement.

"It was not entirely bereft of charms," he said, smiling now at Nadeshda Pavlovna. She did not smile back, Ippolitsky noted with satisfaction; and Toblomov's heavy gaze slid back down to his menu.

Maria Smirnova tried to look at her own menu, but soon gave up this valiant struggle of self-denial. "How many – tell me, Comrade Toblomov, how many factory workers die each day in Berlin? Is it true that their corpses are piled up in the street?"

Toblomov looked at her with faint curiosity. One of his eyes, Ippolitsky noticed, was lazy.

"I never saw any, my dear."

"I suppose," said Ippolitsky irritably, "it's well known, of course, that the *intelligentsia* in any country would be largely shielded from the more brutal realities . . ."

Grandly ignoring the interruption, Maria Smirnova tried a broader approach. "In your opinion and in your experience, Comrade Toblomov, is *envy* or *hatred* the more prevalent manifestation of foreign capitalist jealousy of our socialist homeland?"

"Oh yes," said the engineer inattentively, "jealousy, definitely . . ."

Nadeshda Pavlovna looked up: first, sympathetically, at Maria Smirnova, then, almost affectionately, at Toblomov.

"Vasiliy, tell them about the confectioners."

Toblomov, with a great show of effort, recalibrated his gaze. "What?"

"Come, you know, the story about the confectioners' shops in Germany. You tell it so well."

The waiter appeared. Toblomov ordered for himself, Nadeshda Pavlovna for herself, and Maria Smirnova, following suit, ordered for herself, which caught Ippolitsky off guard. He pointed at something on the menu and the waiter went away.

He watched Toblomov speak. The man had been in town for less than a week and already she was calling him Vasiliy. Ippolitsky looked contemptuously at Maria Smirnova, who, despite her scruples, was obviously hanging on his every word, was obviously delighted to be seated at the same table with – to be *dining with* – someone as fine as Nadeshda Pavlovna. It gave him a sting of vicious satisfaction to think that she would never be as fine. That kind of beauty, that grace, that confidence, was innate. It could not be mimicked, or donned, or bought. It was not in the clothes or the hairstyle or the elaborate, ritualized mannerisms; it was in the blood. Fineness was for Maria

Smirnova a foreign language, one that she would always speak with a thick accent. She would remain an outsider, a barbarian, all her life. Like him.

"Why Berlin?" he demanded.

Toblomov, like a river in full spate, could not change direction suddenly. His flow of words had to slow to a stream, a brook, a trickle, before they finally dried up. His head was brought to bear on Ippolitsky even more slowly, like artillery rotating on a turret. He said: "What?"

"Why did you go to Berlin? Are there no engineering schools in the country of the future?"

"Assuredly there are, assuredly. But at the time of which we are speaking, they were not, how shall we put it, quite up to the standard of some of their foreign counterparts."

"Schools in Berlin are better than schools in Moscow, is what you're saying."

"*Were*. Yes. Are?" Toblomov rolled this rough proposition around in his skull until it came out a gleaming gem. "Yes, perhaps *are*. But *will be*?" He held up a finger and grinned. "Ah. Indeed. That is the question."

Maria Smirnova, who had been making a sour face since Ippolitsky's interruption, asked if Toblomov's work was at all dangerous, as though she rather hoped it was.

"Dangerous, my dear?"

"There must be *some* cause to fear additional attacks on the plant, once everything is up and operative again."

Toblomov parted his dry lips and looked blankly at Nadeshda Pavlovna. "Attacks?"

"Sabotage," Ippolitsky cut in. "The power plant," he said impatiently, leaving the *as you well know* implicit in his tone, "was sabotaged."

Toblomov half closed his eyes and let out a long, rising grumble, which context alone permitted Ippolitsky to identify not as a death rattle but rather, presumably, laughter. Toblomov laid his hand on Nadeshda Pavlovna's, as though for strength.

"I think," she said softly, "that was just the story. For the . . . newspapers."

By this time Toblomov had recovered enough to say, "Yes." A little later, he was able to add, "No *sabotage*, I'm afraid. No *saboteur*." He pronounced the words in the French manner, as though they were the names of *hors d'oeuvres*. "The whole mess simply stopped working."

"Pre-revolutionary technology, then," said Ippolitsky.

"No," said Nadeshda Pavlovna. "They couldn't have built it more than five, six years ago." She turned to Maria Smirnova. "You remember the fuss they made over it in the local papers."

"I remember it was modelled on the Dnieper."

"Sheer nonsense," said Toblomov gaily. "They're completely different arrangements, completely different."

"So what is your point?" Ippolitsky demanded. "That power plants are better in Berlin? So what if they are. Just because something is better elsewhere is no reason to . . ." He grasped at the thought as it fled. "You only make people dissatisfied with what they have."

"I suppose," said Nadeshda Pavlovna diplomatically, "one has to follow the best example. Learn what you can from them, take what you need, and leave the rest."

Toblomov patted her hand. "Assuredly, my dear, assuredly."

"No," said Ippolitsky. "That's wrong."

You couldn't take from exploiters and oppressors, he wanted to say, without being tainted by what you took. The good and the useful only came at the expense of the bad. You couldn't take a capitalist power plant without, to some extent, taking capitalism. The correct thing to do, the revolutionary act, was not to take, but to *break* what they had. The counter-revolutionary spies, at least, knew that much. Which was precisely why they had sabotaged the power plant . . .

He wanted to say this, or something like it.

Toblomov and Nadeshda Pavlovna were watching him. Maria Smirnova was looking at no one.

He said nothing.

The food came. He'd ordered mussels, it seemed. They glistened in the candlelight like black opals. He wasn't hungry.

A few nights later, Toblomov came to his room. With money.

"I understand," he said languidly, "that Nadeshda Pavlovna is somewhat behind on her rent."

"Not precisely," said Ippolitsky.

Toblomov held out the money as if he could not stand the smell of it. Ippolitsky took it, counted it. Three months' rent, exactly.

"She would also like some of her things back, if possible." He cocked his head to one side, tried to peer past Ippolitsky into the room.

Ippolitsky held the door firm. "I sold them."

Toblomov smiled. "Ah. Yes. But you can get them back?"

"Of course not. I sold them."

"I seem to have gotten the impression that she was particularly interested in a gramophone."

"I don't have it." He began to shut the door.

Toblomov's smile broadened slightly, as though at some pleasant private daydream. "Yes, well, good evening, Comrade . . ."

There was already a long line stretching down the street from the public co-operative store. The newspapers had promised a shipment of onions, and, unbelievably, another of sugar.

He spotted Nadeshda Pavlovna almost instantly. She stood out like the martyr in an old religious painting.

"Good morning," he said.

"Good morning, Comrade."

"Will you come with me?" he said softly, as though to spare her embarrassment. He crossed the street without turning to see if she was following. But then he heard the crunch of her boots hurrying after him.

"What's the matter?" she said. "I'll lose my place in line."

He said nothing. He could think of nothing to say.

"Is it grandmother?" she asked, suddenly anxious.

He shook his head impatiently. "You don't have to wait in line," he said at last.

He could feel her gaze on him, as if it gave off heat.

He took her to the Party store. She would not come in. Still, he was relieved that Andreyev Grishkovich was not working, or was in the back with a customer. Ippolitsky bought a bag of white onions, a pound of the hard yellow sugar.

"What is this for?" she asked when he handed the items to her. She took them as though she were only holding them for him.

"A gift," he said with a tentative grin.

But it did not have the hoped-for effect. She only stared at him with the same mixture of suspicion, puzzlement, and stung pride.

"Pride," he used to think, was one of those strange, contradictory words, like "hubris" and "narcissism," that was uttered derogatively yet rang with positive overtones. One should not be proud (not *too* proud); yet pride implied strength, resilience, self-sufficiency, even a certain will to power.

Looking at Nadeshda Pavlovna's face, he understood for the first time how pride might be despicable. The proud stood straight and held their heads high; this was surely intended to be a sign of strength, a show of resilience. But only the weak needed to advertise their strength. Backed into a corner, a dog bared its teeth. A wolf simply tore out your throat.

Pride was fundamentally defiant; it dared you to attack. In straightening the back one exposed the spine; in holding the head high one gave the executioner a better view of the neck. Pride was the cloak that weakness wore to preserve its dignity.

He was stronger than she was, and she knew it.

"Thank you, Nikolai Ivanovich," she said, "but I do not need your gifts."

She turned and walked stiffly away – still carrying the sack of onions like a messenger, as if it belonged to someone else.

Several days later, Ippolitsky was summoned. This time he did not have to wait, either outside or inside Kronstrov's office. The old man handed him a letter, written in pencil, that he did not need to read. Nevertheless he pretended to study it for a minute or two, though with Kronstrov's eyes on him he found it difficult to concentrate. He caught the phrase "Revolution runs in the blood," and wondered now if this was too much.

He looked up. "I am not surprised," he said weightily.

"You were expecting something of the kind?"

"No . . . No, not expecting, not exactly." He passed the letter back to Kronstrov, who laid it on the desk without looking at it. "All the same . . . I am not entirely surprised, either."

"Your opinion of the Radshova woman, then, I am to understand, has undergone a change?"

Ippolitsky pretended to ponder this, then found himself actually pondering it. He would have to be careful.

"In light of this letter – yes," he said.

"But you just finished saying that the letter did not surprise you. Which implies that its contents, its allegations, could not have been the only decisive factor in your . . . change of heart."

"My suspicions . . ." He paused, cleared his throat, started again. "Recently, in my contact with the Radshova woman, I might have started to entertain certain doubts as to her loyalty to the revolutionary cause. Nothing more than comments, really . . . her general attitude . . . her bearing . . ."

"What sort of comments?"

"Oh, disparaging comments about the backwardness of our technology, for example. That sort of thing." Ippolitsky clasped his hands behind his back and stared fixedly at the wall above Kronstrov's head. "By themselves," he went on, "these probably wouldn't have been sufficient to convince me. And yet . . . On the other hand, without them, I might not have been wholly convinced by the letter you just – the letter you just showed me."

Kronstrov sighed, and looked mournfully down at the letter and the others papers on his desk.

Ippolitsky, who felt somehow that the worst had passed, added, "I admit now that I might also not have properly taken into consideration the full force of background factors: her upbringing, her family . . ."

"You were mistaken, Comrade Ippolitsky?"

"I was," Ippolitsky said, "mistaken."

They came, as they always did, in the morning, when it was still dark.

At the door was the young man from Kronstrov's office, the one with the sly smiles who dressed like an American soldier. He was not dressed like a soldier now, and he did not smile. He was not alone.

"We are searching the premises," he said, his voice ringing down the hallway with pride and self-importance.

"What," said Ippolitsky, "the whole building?" He was still half-asleep.

"We will start here," said the young man indifferently, "with your room."

Ippolitsky stepped aside. "Comrade Kronstrov's orders, I suppose?"

"*Kronstrov*," said the young man with a sneer, "is on his way to Siberia as we speak."

Ippolitsky didn't know what they would find. They would certainly find something. Jewellery, torn-up books, gramophone records . . . It didn't matter. Anything could be used against him. Things were in motion now.

They would find him guilty, he knew, for the wrong reasons, of the wrong crimes. But somehow, he felt, they would not be wrong to find him guilty.

"What is this?" asked one of the men.

"Shut up," said Ippolitsky, "just shut *up* . . ."

The Petrovs' dog would not stop barking. He was afraid it would wake the whole building.

THE MEAN

I hate my life, nothing ever happens to me. There's no one around this summer. Nicky and her family are RVing across the country to Prince Edward Island. Trish is visiting her dad in Victoria for a couple of weeks, then going to camp, not one of those boring camps where they teach you how to fall out of a canoe or what bear crap looks like but an arts and crafts camp. You learn how to make comic books and design magazines and create storyboards for movies and all kinds of cool stuff. I wanted to go too but because you need a reference letter from a teacher Mom said it was elitist. Whenever she says something is elitist she means it's something Jack can't do, so practically everything is elitist according to her.

Lis is still around. We went swimming but all it is is little kids splashing each other and pulling each other's swimsuits off. Not my idea of a real scream.

Lis isn't my best friend. If I had to say who my best friend was I guess it would be Trish. But it's better when it's the four of us, we have more fun.

I hate Snowcap. Sometimes I wish the whole world would just explode.

People don't ski much in summer, the hotels are practically all empty. Last year Lorraine Deverich's brother Tony threw a rock through a third-storey window of the Continental on grad night and nobody working there even noticed until November. According to Nicky, anyway, rain came in through the window and caused almost a thousand dollars in damage to the floor so he had to go to jail. Supposedly if they'd noticed right away he would only have had to pay for the window. Nobody knows why he did it. He was drunk I guess. Drinking turns people into sheer fools. He was going to go to university but they won't matriculate you if you have a criminal record and now he's delivery boy for Grossman's Grosseries and dating Wendy Yarrow who is only like fifteen, barely two years older than me, which is truly Gross-man.

There's no skiers so there's no one to drive anywhere and no one to cook for so even with two jobs Mom is home a lot. She sits outside and smokes and reads. She plows through another one of her Minnie Dobsons practically every day. I'm not supposed to read them, she says they're for grown-ups. I have read them anyway and let me tell you, they're a yawn and a half. They're all about women in the nineteenth century trying to get married or trying to get pregnant. I'd rather read about a rose growing out of a dead horse's nose.

To be honest I sometimes hate reading, especially when it's hot out. I still take Jack to the library because it's cool and she understands that she has to be quiet there. Of all my friends only Trish likes to read but she's practically a lacer.

The biggest lacer in our class is Guen Bertanalby, not

Gwen with a W but Guen with a U. She still rides a bike, I've seen her around town on it. Someone should tell her that she's too old. So-called smart people can be pure stupid sometimes. It's different for boys. If I was a boy I could bike around like Paul Merseger, selling popsicles and ice cream. But I am glad I'm not a boy, they behave ridiculously. I do sometimes wish I had a job though, since I can't even afford an ice cream cone. Mom isn't paying me allowance unless I weed the garden but I'm not about to do it myself. I've tried to teach Jack but she always manages to get thorns under her fingernails, even with gloves on, and anyway it's too hot.

Nobody exactly picks on Guen but she doesn't have any friends either. Sometimes I think I'd rather be picked on than be totally ignored.

We're probably the only family in the whole park that doesn't have a TV. I don't care. It doesn't matter. I hate TV. We watch at Trish's sometimes and there's never anything on. I still wish we had one though.

When Mom is smoking a lot it's easier to lift cigs. I never take more than two and never from an almost full or almost empty pack. In the scrapyard, which used to be the sand lots but now is more junk than sand, there's a pretty decent mattress you can sit on and a pane of transparent blue plastic you can see your reflection in. It makes you look good, sort of smooth and soft, like you're underwater or lit by candlelight. That's where I go to practise, I think I'm getting the hang of it. The trick is to not inhale without looking like you're not inhaling. I don't exactly want black lungs.

Then again, who cares? Sometimes I wish I had cancer, or a broken arm or leg at least. People could sign my cast, they could come from miles around, they could bring gifts and food and tell jokes. Or probably nobody would come at all, I'd die alone in a hospital, surrounded by weeping nurses. Before I died they would let me eat all the green Jell-O with soft vanilla ice cream I wanted. They'd wish I was their daughter. They'd come to the funeral and put lilies on my grave.

But I have never broken any bones and none of my teeth have cavities even though I hardly ever floss.

Guen was at the scrapyard, poking around with a golf club. She didn't see us right away.

I'm not exactly supposed to take Jack to places like the scrapyard, there are too many sharp and rusty things she could hurt herself on. But it's okay, she likes it there. She has a broken hockey stick she plays with and I keep an eye on her. Jack's not exactly as delicate as some people think. Even Mom still treats her like a baby sometimes. I'm the only one who really knows.

I asked Guen if she wanted to share a butt. I showed her my ketchup can with all my butts in it. She said no, she doesn't smoke. I said neither do I, it's a dumb disgusting habit. Which is true. I told her that I was just practising, since I figure it's sort of a good skill to have for if you're ever in movies or anything and the script says you have to smoke in one of your scenes.

So we shared a butt. She was pretty good. She only coughed once.

She was looking for busted typewriters and radios. She is building a computer. She's probably a genius or something.

I like computers, I think they're interesting. I've never used one but Guen says someday they will be smart enough to do everything for us and we will only have to sit on our couches or in floating pods and send them instructions telepathically. She's probably right, if you think about it.

According to Mom, Guen's dad is an elitist. He's a famous chemist or something. He must be famous because he doesn't work. Mom heard that he's writing a book. For someone who reads as much as she does, she doesn't exactly have much respect for writers. She's not so crazy about dads either.

I don't have a dad. I have a father. It sounds worse, *fawther*. It makes him sound stupid. Which he is. I know because I've seen a picture. He looks like somebody who walks around with his mouth hanging open, dribbling chewing tobacco onto his undershirt. He's a truck driver. Well it doesn't exactly take a pound of brains to drive truck, just keep it between the ditches for eighteen hours.

Driving a taxi is totally different. You have to be quick. You work with people and you have to understand them, you have to be able to size them up. When Mom first started she got ripped off three times in a week. Now it almost never happens. She's probably the best taxi driver in town.

My father's name is Don, which is the perfect name for him. In all my life he's sent me maybe three birthday cards. He phoned from Whistler once but I didn't want to talk to him. That was when I was ten. You wouldn't think that for a guy who drives truck for a living it would exactly kill him to visit once in a while. But I'm glad he doesn't. I hate him. The postcards he sends have very bad spelling. I sometimes wonder if maybe he's really only Jack's father. I don't know who my real dad would be but it doesn't matter. There are kinds of bugs in the Amazon that don't have fathers, just mothers. I wish I were in the Amazon right now, I would let a tiger eat me. But I would never go there because I hate snakes, even though I know not all of them are poisonous. But I would still rather be eaten by a tiger than bit by a snake.

I figured it out once. Don left about two months after Jack was born. She doesn't even know that he exists. Which is lucky for her, as far as I'm concerned.

I wish I had a car. I wish I was old enough to drive, I would steal a car and drive to Mexico or the Yukon. In winter it would be easy, everyone leaves their cars running when they go into the drugstore or the bank or the hotel lobby. The police could chase me, I wouldn't care. I'd let them catch up. I wouldn't even care if they shot me full of holes. I hate summer, you can't even steal a car.

Mom's bright idea is that I should learn how to fish. Mom thinks she's pretty hilarious. There aren't any fish in our lake anymore. The snow-machines they installed back in the fifties leaked gallons of oil into it. Even the seaweed looks sick. That's the whole reason why they built the pool. Anyway, I'd rather watch grass grow out of a dead horse's ass than go fishing.

There is a sign outside the pool that says "No Trespassing When Pool Closed," which makes it sound like the only time you should be trespassing is when the pool is open.

Lis called but it's too hot even to go swimming, and anyway we're too old to swim.

Grown-ups either treat my sister like she's just come out of a car crash with seven broken limbs, or else they treat her like she's just won the lottery. The car-crash ones rest their hands on her shoulder and ask her if she would like some candy. They say it like it's medicine, "Would some candy make you feel better?" The lottery ones smile and nod and sometimes even wink at her, like only the two of them share the secret of how great life really is. They give her candy too. Jack prefers the lottery ones. I hate all grown-ups.

Kids treat my sister in one of two ways, they either point and laugh or they avoid looking at her. Nicky and Lis avoid looking. Trish looks but doesn't laugh, she'll probably grow up to be a car-crash type. Jack doesn't care, she pretty much likes everyone.

But she really likes Guen. Guen's about the only person I know other than Mom who doesn't talk to Jack like she's a puppy. And she's the only person, other than teachers, who uses Jack's real name. The teachers only call her Ruby because they don't realize that everybody else calls her Jack. Most of our teachers are sheer fools.

I hate Mrs. Sloban the most. She is always way too cheerful, and she speaks very slowly and repeats just about everything she says three times, and she is always putting her hand on your shoulder or the top of your head as though you were a handrail. Her hair looks like one of those metal scrubs for washing dishes that Mom brings home from the hotel, only it's bright white instead of grey.

Mr. Bearden says you can spell "grey" with an E or with an A. I prefer to spell it with an E because "gray" looks like "day" or "play" or "gay" which are all happy words and I don't think "grey" is an especially happy word. I like the fact that there are words that it is correct to spell more than one way. Another word like that is "traveller," which it is perfectly okay to spell with either one L or two. Unfortunately, according to Mr. Bearden, you must choose one way of spelling the word and stick with it. You can't write "the sky was grey and the kitten was gray," for example, which I think is too bad. Skies are grey and kittens are gray, if you ask me.

Mr. Bearden is the teacher Guen hates most. He is actually my favourite, but I agree with her that he can sometimes be annoying, I guess. For instance, if someone forgets their homework (usually Joann Romplin or Stacey Walsh or Teddy Mollibeau or James Wu) he will pretend to be deeply saddened and say something sarcastic like "With rue my heart is laden." And it is true that all his pantlegs are too short and his socks have holes in them. Of course the most obvious thing about him is the gigantic mole just under his left ear which I admit is pretty gross, but I don't think it is fair of Guen to call him Moleman like a lot of other kids do behind his back, because I have heard some kids call Guen Goon or Goonie behind *her* back. I guess she doesn't know that. I guess no one knows what they're being called behind their back, because otherwise it wouldn't be behind their back. Maybe I'm being called names behind my back. But I doubt it, because I am friends with Nicky and Trish and Lis and nobody ever says anything bad about them, at least as far as I know.

But I like Mr. Bearden because he uses big words and approbates my spelling. And unlike Mrs. Weinraub used to do, he never makes us take turns reading out loud from the text, which I hate, because most kids are not good readers, and they are slow, and if you enjoy the book and want to read ahead you lose track of where the rest of the class is, so when it's your turn the teacher thinks you have been daydreaming or that you are stupid, which is not necessarily true.

*

Guen asked me what my IQ was. I don't know what it is because Mom wouldn't let me take the test at school. According to her, IQ tests are elitist, the whole idea of intelligence is elitist. In fact, she doesn't even believe there really is such a thing as "intelligence." She thinks that the only reason people came up with the IQ test was so that they could find a sneaky way to justify being mean to people who scored worse on it. She doesn't even let me use the words "smart" and "stupid" because they're prejudiced against people (like Jack) who have a harder time learning. When she heard they were giving us IQ tests at school she got super angry and I had to sit with her in Principal Gromby's office while she gave him a piece of her mind. And that's why I never took the IQ test, though everyone else in the school still did.

I guess I agree with her about the word "stupid" but I don't see what's wrong with "smart." Mom says "smart" wouldn't have any meaning if everyone was smart, just like the word "tall" would have no meaning if everyone was the same height, so by calling one person smart you're calling everyone else stupid by comparison, I guess. Just like if you call one person tall you're implying that they are taller than most people, which is another way of calling other people short.

Only it's different because there's nothing wrong with not being tall but for some reason there is something wrong with not being intelligent. You can call someone short without hurting their feelings (unless you're *really* short, like Teddy Mollibeau) but you can't call them stupid without being mean. But the weird thing is there aren't really any words you can use that *aren't* mean. Mom says that Jack is a slow learner or sometimes that she has special challenges but I don't see how it's a whole lot better to be called slow or challenged than to be called stupid. I don't know, maybe that's my mom's point. Because if you compare the intelligences of different people at all you're going to end up with some people who are more and some who are less intelligent, that's just the way it is. But then the less intelligent ones are always going to be made fun of, no matter what, because that's just the way people are. For some reason people are always mean to whoever is different because nobody wants to be different. You'd think they'd be *nicer* to them because they would feel sorry for them but that's not the way it works. And nobody wants to be unintelligent, even though there's nothing exactly wrong with it, and it's not your fault if you're stupid just like it's not your fault if you're short. Unless you cut off your own legs, or have bad posture and slouch, like I sometimes do.

On the other hand, nobody really wants to be too intelligent, either. I don't know. It's all very complicated.

They're not supposed to tell you what your IQ is but they told Guen's dad that hers is 144 and he told her. Not because he was proud but because he said she was not living up to her potential and he thought she should be working harder, which is a laugh and a half because she already gets practically straight A's. Which makes her a lacer and a brainiac. If you are a lacer you are automatically a brainiac, but you can be a brainiac without being a lacer, like Stacey Walsh's brother Trevor Walsh, who is a whiz at math. You can ask him to multiply 153 by 542 (for example) and he can do it in about fifteen seconds, all in his head, and you can check his answer on Mr. Vygotsky's calculator. But he gets bad grades on tests, even though he gets the right answers, because he never shows his work. I don't think that's fair, but on the other hand I don't understand why he doesn't just show his work.

I am bad at math. I've never liked the way numbers fit together. Some go together just fine, like 6 and 6 making 12 or 8 times 8 making 64, but others don't seem to go together at all. For example, you would never guess that 7 times 7 equals 49, and there is something funny about 6 plus 7 equalling 13. It just doesn't look right, I don't know why.

I am better at other subjects. I am a good speller. I know the entire periodic table of the elements by heart. And I know a lot about what happened in World War II and World War I, which used to be called the Great War because before World War II they didn't know there would be another one and it would have been kind of pessimistic to call it the *First* World War. However, I think that "Great War" sounds almost too *optimistic*, because although "great" means "large" it can also mean "wonderful." So sometimes I imagine people in 1920 going around saying to each other, "Wow, wasn't that a *great* war?"

If your IQ is 144 it means that you are almost three standard deviations above the average, which is 100. A standard deviation is 15, and if you are three standard deviations above the average it means that only one in a thousand people is smarter than you. The chances of any *two* people having IQs of 144 is about one in a million. Guen figures my IQ is probably the same as hers or close to it, but I don't know about that. I'm not even sure I would want to be 144. I'd rather be 115 or so. One standard deviation is enough for me.

Still, it's neat to think that the odds of our being friends is one in a million.

*

At night we pretend we are blind. We close our eyes and walk as far as we can down the middle of the street until we bump into something. We would hear a car coming long before it ran us over but it is still kind of frightening.

Jack can't go more than half a block before she has to open her eyes. Guen can never keep moving in a straight line and veers off to one side. I think she does it on purpose.

I once walked all the way from the cemetery to the auto wreckers before I nearly lopped my head off by crashing into a tow truck's side mirror. Guen had to lie down on the road, she was laughing so hard. I sat on top of her and gave her a wet palm. She was screaming and Jack was screaming and a light came on in a nearby house and we ran away, singing in tongues.

We practise our glossolalia when it is really hot. We tried it out on Mrs. Grossman at the grossery store once when we were buying hamburger meat for supper and Mrs. Grossman called my mom because she was worried that I might have come down with heatstroke. She didn't call Guen's dad.

Sometimes I wish I did have heatstroke. Sometimes I wouldn't mind if I was in a coma, because it would be like dreaming all the time. Nobody knows why we dream, not even Sigmund Freud. So maybe dreams are really the real world and this one is really the dream world and we're all just wasting our time here.

We are writing a letter to Mr. Bearden. It was Guen's idea but I am doing most of the work.

Mr. Bearden does not have a wife. He is probably over thirty years old and he has never been married and possibly has never even had a girlfriend. I think this is kind of sad.

When I said that, Guen thought I meant pathetic. But I meant depressing. I think he must be lonely. Even I am sometimes lonely and I'm friends with Nicky Robbins and Trish Warman and Lisa Beddington. And I live with a sister and a mother but Mr. Bearden doesn't live with anyone and I don't think he has many friends. I don't think people should have to be alone if they don't want to be. There are enough people for everyone, it is just a question of bringing together the ones who are by themselves. But I don't know, maybe Mr. Bearden wants to be alone, he often eats his lunch at his desk instead of in the staff room. I guess except for Miss Taylor the girl's gym teacher and Mrs. Williams the teacher's aide most of the teachers are old fogies compared to Mr. Bearden. And I know Miss Taylor has a boyfriend and is kind of a loudmouth, but she is pretty. Maybe Mr. Bearden's mole bothers her. I could never marry Mr. Bearden, not because of the mole, but because I'm too young and I am never getting married or having children, but maybe Miss Taylor is more superficial than I am.

Guen thought we should write a letter to Mr. Bearden, pretending to be a woman that he knew a long time ago who was secretly infatuated with him.

So far we have decided that our name is Léonie McTavish. We are thirty-three years old. We live in a small town called Songbrook, where we teach science. We have no brothers or sisters. Our parents are both dead, though we haven't yet decided how they died. Guen wants a train wreck or plane crash but I would prefer something like cancer or accidental carbon monoxide poisoning. Anyway, they died when we were young, so we were raised by an aunt but she is dead now too. We live alone in a one-bedroom apartment with our

Siamese cat whose name is either Meow (Guen's idea) or Dog's Breakfast (my idea).

We work part-time in a bookstore. We love the smell of books. Our favourite authors are Katherine Anne Porter and Thomas Hardy. Mr. Bearden is teaching *Tess of the D'Urbervilles* to the grade elevens this year, so I checked it out of the library. I am on the third chapter.

We like drinking milky chai tea and putting hot water bottles under our pillow on cold rainy evenings. We enjoy crossword puzzles, swimming, and French films. We have no boyfriend but we are not exactly "a mere vessel of emotion untinctured by experience" either, to quote Mr. Hardy.

We have lustrous dark brown hair which we keep trimmed to chin-length. We have deep hazel-coloured eyes. We have thick, shapely lips. We have pale, faintly freckled skin which sunburns easily. We have long, smooth legs and often wear skirts to show them off. We have a tiny tattoo on the small of our back that is either a dove with an hourglass in its beak or the Mandarin character for "Love." I think Mr. Bearden would admire an interest in foreign languages, and I think Guen's drawing looks like a chicken taking a bite out of an egg timer.

Guen says we should have huge breasts but I disagree. I think they should be small. I think we should be flat as a board.

Sometimes Guen and Jack and I sit in Guen's dad's car and Guen and I make up stories to tell Jack. For example, Guen will say that once upon a time there was a little fox, and I will say that the fox's best friend was a bottlecap, and Guen will say that the bottlecap's name was Monsieur Flubblebum, and I will say that Monsieur Flubblebum was a distinguished theoretical physicist, and Guen will say that all the other theoretical physicists wanted to beat him up because he had come up with all the good ideas first, and so on. It doesn't much matter what we say, Jack loves any kind of story.

The best story we have made up so far is about Windy the Friendly Tornado. We even wrote it down:

Windy was a tornado unlike other tornados. She didn't want to hurt or destroy anything. She just wanted to meet new people and have new experiences. She was really very friendly in fact.

But no one gave her a chance to prove it. As soon as people saw Windy coming, they hid in their basements or ran away screaming, before she could even open her mouth.

And even though she was always very careful, whenever she got too close to where people lived she would accidentally blow apart their homes or knock over their telephone poles.

She couldn't help it. She was clumsy. And the more careful she was, the more clumsy she became.

And Windy thought, "That is why everyone hates and fears me. Because I'm a stupid clumsy tornado." So she went to be by herself in the middle of a field where she couldn't hurt anyone or knock anything over. And she sat down under the rainy grey sky that followed her everywhere she went, and she wept quietly for a long time.

But one day she saw a truck full of people coming towards her. They were heading right for her. They were coming to visit!

She stopped weeping and put on her friendliest smile. The truck came to a stop a few hundred yards away. Two men and a woman got out. They were very excited. The woman pointed a video camera at Windy and one of the men took pictures. Windy felt flattered and a little embarrassed.

Windy said, "Hello. May I ask why you're taking pictures of me?"

The woman said, "We're stormchasers, and we think you're beautiful."

Windy said, "Why thank you."

The man with the camera said, "You are nature's fury unleashed."

Windy said, "I'm actually very friendly."

The man with the camera said bruskly, "Well, we like you, whatever you are."

Windy was so happy to have at last found people who were not afraid of her, who liked her and appreciated her even though she was a tornado, that all of her troubles melted away.

But as everyone knows, troubles are what make tornados spin and blow. Windy was so happy that she stopped spinning. She just disappeared into thin air.

The stormchasers were very disappointed. They drove home slowly, in silence, not even bothering to turn on the radio. The end.

Trish should be back from camp by now. I wonder why Lis hasn't called. I can't believe that school starts again in only ten days.

Guen told me that if you ever don't want to go to school

you can take Vitamin B6, because it turns your skin red and makes it look like you are allergic to something.

Guen told me that she always thought I was a Miriam. I told her that I always thought she was a straight lacer. She said that she has to act like one because you need good grades to get into a good university. When she grows up, she wants to be a) a biologist, b) a mathematician, c) a computer scientist, d) a lawyer, e) an electrical engineer, or f) a theoretical physicist. She does not want to be a chemist.

When I grow up, I want to be a) an actress, b) a police-woman, or c) a taxi driver. I do not want to drive a truck or an ice cream cart or be a maid or a cook or a librarian or a lifeguard or a famous painter or a ski instructor.

Guen told me that her dad has scales on his back like a lizard. I told her that my mom was born without toenails which is why she never goes swimming or wears sandals. I told her that Nicky Robbins can't say SP-words, so instead of "spit" or "spaceship" she says "stit" or "staceship." I told her that Lisa Beddington is such a fool that she thinks that if you get head lice they burrow into your skull and eventually into your brain, which is only true if you never shampoo your hair and if you scratch your head too much, because that pushes them down inside your scalp. And I told her that Trish Warman smells like my granna's basement. It's not a bad smell really, wet and woody and kind of fruity, it's just weird for someone to smell like that. She'll have to marry some boy who works in the canning industry so he won't notice.

I asked Guen what a Miriam is. She said it is someone who is completely average, someone who doesn't deviate at all from the mean.

Miriams stay in Snowcap all their lives and get married to boys who are twice their age and have babies with fetal alcohol syndrome.

Instead of asking us to write about our summers like he's done on the first day back every other year, Mr. Bearden wrote a sentence on the board and told all of us to copy it down, word for word. When we were done he told us to sign our names at the top and hand our papers forward so he could collect them. He put them in the middle drawer of his desk without even looking at them. James Wu asked if we were going to be graded, which people laughed at but I'm not sure he meant it as a joke. He is such a lame rag he probably thought it was a spelling test or something, even though the sentence was written right up there on the blackboard for us. Mr. Bearden muttered something about how only one of us would be graded on it, and people laughed at that too, because they probably thought he meant James.

Then Mr. Bearden made us open our copies of John Steinbeck's *The Pearl* to page one, and Trish pushed her desk next to mine because she's always forgetting her books, and then Mr. Bearden had us take turns reading out loud, starting at the back corner by the door where Josh Tolman always sits so he can carve dragons and werewolves into the desktop without being bothered.

This is the sentence that Mr. Bearden wrote on the board:

I am not exactly, to quote Mr. Hardy, a mere vessel of emotion untinctured by experience.

*

At lunch Guen came poking around the old baseball diamond with her golf club. She didn't see us right away.

Trish whispered, "What the hell is she looking for?"

I said, "Beats the hell out of me."

Lis said, "Maybe she lost a golf ball."

Nicky said, "Probably bugs or something."

I said, "Yeah, maybe she forgot her lunch."

Finally Guen noticed us, but she pretended not to. She kept poking around in the grass for a while, then turned around and headed back in the direction of the school. Jack stood up and watched her go.

"What a goon," I said. I considered telling them that Guen was afraid of the dark, and that she had to sleep with the hall light on and her bedroom door half open. But I didn't, I was afraid they would want to know how I knew that.

Then Jack called Guen's name. Guen ignored her, pretended not to hear, just kept walking, thank God.

Lis said, "A friend of your sister's?"

Again Jack shouted, "Guen!" And again and again, "Guen! Guen!"

I told her to shut up and sit down and stop behaving like a retard.

She sat down and cried a little but she's always crying, she can be such a goddamn baby sometimes.

My cig had gone out, so I lit it again and inhaled the smoke deep into my black lungs.

I hate school, it's the most boring thing on earth. I especially hate gym class. I am not good at sports. There is something wrong with my heart, if I overexert myself it loses its rhythm, some of the beats come too soon. When I was young my mom took me to a doctor and he told me that I was very lucky, I had a precocious heartbeat. But Mom didn't like that, she prefers to call it "premature." It is not really dangerous, it just feels weird, like there is a giant moth flapping around inside my chest.

Miss Taylor is always making us run laps around the gym. She makes us run laps when we don't hustle enough, she makes us run laps when we forget our gym shoes, she makes us run laps when we cheat or play too rough. Her solution to every problem is making us run laps, that's about the limit of her imagination. I hate running laps, it is literally just running in circles. At least if you're running in a straight line you'll eventually end up somewhere different than where you started. Not that I can think of anyplace I want to go, except maybe Honolulu or the Yukon.

I guess driving a cab is like running in circles. At least when you drive a truck the place you end up in is not the exact same place you started from. But I will probably never drive a truck either, because no matter how far you go you'll have to come back someday.

Don sent me a letter from Poughkeepsie, which is in the state of New York in the U.S. My fourteenth birthday is not for three months. I haven't opened it yet, I might never open it, I might put it in the stove or bury it in the scrapyard or eat it one little piece at a time. Once a guy ate an entire airplane by grinding up a little bit of it at a time and sprinkling it on his toast like cinnamon.

Mr. Bearden never did talk to me about the letter from Léonie McTavish. Maybe he didn't recognize my handwriting after all. If he did, he can't be too mad about it because he gave me an A on my last assignment. However, he did circle the word "grey" and write it with an A in the margin, and even though I misspelled the word "brusquely" he didn't circle *that*.

The lights in the gym take a long time to warm up. Sometimes one of us will turn them off while Miss Taylor isn't looking and it takes almost five minutes for them to come back on. And for five minutes we run around in the dark, screaming like crazy and bumping into each other. We used to do it all the time before Shelly Moscovich got knocked over and sliced her forehead open. We never found out whose fault it was, maybe the girl who plowed into Shel never even realized what happened. But it made Miss Taylor and Principal Gromby angry enough that when Joann Romplin shut off the lights a couple weeks later she was suspended for three days.

I don't care if I get suspended. It doesn't seem like such a terrible punishment to make someone stay home. I wonder what happens if you are in jail and you turn out the lights, do they make you leave the prison for three days?

I waited until I saw Miss Taylor kneel down to tie her shoe. I stopped only for a second. Then I was running again, running in circles around the gym and screaming my head off in the dark like all the other girls.

Last summer Guen Bertanalby, who is in my class, told me that if people were radioactive atoms our half-life would be about 52 years. The average person would still live to be about 75 years, like now, but more people would die young and a few people would live to be very very old. One quarter of everybody born would live to be at least 104 years old. One in every sixteen people would make it to

208, and one in 64 would live to 312. A few, about one in 4,000 I think, would even make it to 624. But only about one in a million would live to be 1,000.

That almost doesn't sound too bad, a one in a million chance of living to 1,000. But the odds that you'd die on any given day would always be about 1 in 28,000. That means of course that the odds that you would *live* another day would be about 27,999 in 28,000, but the odds would never change, no matter how long you lived. Even if you were a thousand years old, the odds of you kicking the bucket the next day would still be 1 in 28,000. No matter how old you got, you'd never really be any closer to death, and no matter how young you were, you'd never be any farther from it.

So if people decayed like radioactive atoms, you just might live forever, but you might not want to. Because I think it would probably feel less like living forever than forever not-quite-dying.

Miss Taylor opens one of the gymnasium doors to let some light in, but I just close my eyes and keep on running, keep on racing forward into the darkness. At any moment, at any moment, at any moment I could collide with someone or something. But I might not. I might never stop running, might never open my eyes, time might continue to spill out of the blackness in front of my face forever. The only thing against it is the statistics.

WHITE CROWS

I

"I know what you're thinking," said Joad, chuckling and scratching at his beard. "You're thinking, Hell, it doesn't much look like the epicentre of the next scientific revolution."

Plummer smiled thinly. What he had been thinking was that Carter Joad's office only confirmed the image he'd formed of England's leading parapsychologist from his book, articles, and, most strongly, his series of ripostes to Plummer's piece in the May 1939 issue of *Pseudoscience*.

The shelves were crammed with everything but books; the tables were heaped with papers, none of them clipped or stapled; the walls were as crowded as the horizontal surfaces and plastered with cheap reproductions of portraits of Schopenhauer and William James, hand-drawn diagrams and charts, covers of old issues of *Science* and *Nature*, scraps of newsprint, and everywhere scribbled quotations: fragments of poetry ("There are more things in heaven and earth, Horatio . . ."), hackneyed proverbs ("By filling one's head instead of one's pockets, one cannot be robbed"), inspirational platitudes ("Without rain there can be no rainbows"), and sonorous aphorisms. . . . Plummer could not see a degree or diploma anywhere; instead Joad had framed and hung, in a place of honour above his desk, that famous paragraph of Bacon's:

> It is certain that all bodies whatsoever, though they have no sense, yet they have perception; for when one body is applied to another, there is a kind of election to embrace that which is agreeable, and to exclude or expel that which is ingrate. And sometimes this perception, in some kind of bodies, is far more subtile than sense; so that sense is but a dull thing in comparison of it. . . .

Plummer could quote a few aphorisms himself, but he did not need to hang them on his walls like trophies. He called to mind Darwin: "False facts are highly injurious to the Progress of Science for they often endure long; but false views do little harm, as every-one takes a salutary pleasure in proving their falseness." It was not Joad's views that worried Plummer, but his facts. He had come to prove that they *were* false, not facts at all – but he had begun to doubt whether he would take any pleasure, salutary or otherwise, in the undertaking. . . .

"It's not much to look at," said Joad, wading past boxes that appeared to be full of coat hangers, "but with the Blitz, of course, basements have become rather coveted real estate."

Yes, here was a man, thought Plummer, whose mind was as muddled as his desk; a man who did not pursue truth so much as collect bits of borrowed wisdom and wield them like talismans; a man, above all, who yearned for *meaning* – for a more magical reality, a reality stirred by unseen forces, veined with esoteric significances, peopled with ghosts and sorcerers. His type was familiar to Plummer: smart enough to see the picture that science presented, not strong enough to accept it. And so he had set out on this Children's Crusade to vanquish science, armed with nothing but his talismans and his faith. Epicentre of the next scientific revolution, indeed.

With a pang of homesickness, Plummer thought of his own office: the bookshelves he could have navigated in the dark; the filing cabinets whose locks he oiled monthly; the neat stack of boxes, labelled "University Mail," "Outside Mail," "Assignments Uncorrected," "Articles Needing Review," and "Miscellaneous"; the schedule of his hours posted to the door; the ordered ranks of pencils, pens, and markers lying ready in his centre drawer; the calendar whose days, now, would have no one to cross them out.

He remembered the first time Ev had come to see him in his office, how she had teased him for putting his X's through the day's date before it was finished, as though eager to be done with it.

He clamped down on that – he had not come all this way just to think about Ev.

"Well," burbled Joad, "shall we proceed to the lab?"

As Plummer turned to follow Joad to his laboratory, he was eager, suddenly, to be done with it.

There was, as Plummer knew from his extensive reading, nothing very impressive about the average psychical researcher's laboratory. Indeed, as if to compensate for the outlandishness of their claims, the parapsychologists (as they now preferred to be called) seemed to have designed their experiments to be as boring as possible. In one room, an agent (the sender) looked at an object; in the next, a percipient (or receiver) tried to divine what it was. That was all. There was, of course, the standard array of complications and safeguards in place to prevent both the subjects and the experimenters from cheating; but, in essence, ESP research was nothing more than sophisticated card-guessing.

Joad's experiment was no exception. His only innovation, as far as Plummer could see, was that instead of cards he was using photographs. "We've improved on the Zener paradigm here," he said boastfully. "No boring circles, crosses, and wavy lines for us. *These* targets have real emotional impact." The photos were of an ocean, a forest, a mountain peak, and a desert; Plummer did not feel emotionally impacted.

It was not the experiments that were astonishing; it was the numbers. Some of the results, when analyzed statistically, revealed odds against chance of one thousand to one, 2,500 to one, 50,000 to one – in one famous case in America, several millions to one. Joad himself had reported a series of experiments with one percipient, a "Ms. Meadow," who had made something like 20,500 correct guesses on 80,000 trials – 500 more than would be expected by chance alone. Even this seemed pretty meagre evidence for the existence of telepathy – until you calculated the probability to be 0.000007, or 142,857 to one against chance.

Plummer had no gripe with the numbers; he had checked them himself. What he questioned was not the para-psychologists' math, but their research methods. If their experiments yielded results so contrary to probability, so astronomically unlikely to be due to chance, then Plummer was compelled to conclude that, yes, something other than chance was causing the results. He and Carter Joad were in agreement on this point. Where they parted company was in their belief as to what that "something" was. Joad said ESP, telepathy, clairvoyance. Plummer thought human error the more likely culprit.

"Well, all right," said Plummer, getting down to business with reluctant relish. "The aperture in the screen, for starters. The experimenter – *you* – could get a glimpse of the pictures through it – if not directly, perhaps reflected in the sender's spectacles. Or the pictures themselves – there's nothing stopping the sender from putting them in any order they fancy, or reordering them at any time. As for the little green light – well, isn't that a potential channel of communication between the second experimenter and the sender? And the rooms being next door to one another –"

"The walls are perfectly soundproof," said Joad. "We tested it. Didn't we, Henry?"

Joad's student assistant nodded his little turnip-shaped head. "Even if someone shouts, all you get is *buzz buzz buzz* – you can't make out a single word."

"So it's not *perfectly* soundproof," said Plummer.

"But no one ever shouts, obviously." Joad, flustered, pulled at his beard and grinned fatuously. "None of us shouts. We're not quite *that* wild, Plummer. We're not having *that* much fun, old man."

"Besides, it needn't be words. Inflection, pitch . . . the number of syllables. All these carry information."

"But honestly, Dr. Plummer, you can't hear *anything*."

"No doubt you can't – not consciously. But just because *you* can't, and *I* can't, and Dr. Joad can't, and whoever else can't, doesn't mean no one can."

"Come now, Plummer, *really*. Aren't you being just a little bit captious? Correct me please if I'm wrong, but for all that, any of that, to make a difference, what we're actually talking about is the actual, premeditated, cold-blooded, as it were, intentional intention to commit – let's not mince words, Plummer, old fellow – what you're suggesting is fraud?"

Joad's face crinkled in an impish grin, like someone prompting a child to say a dirty word. Plummer was astounded. What did Joad think all the precautions, all the rigmarole with screens and observers and duplicate copies was *for*, if not to rule out fraud? If he had such faith in the essential honesty and propriety of his fellow creatures, why didn't he simply sit with a friend and a deck of cards in a comfortable parlour and ask his friend what card he was looking at? "Hmm, let's see. Seven of clubs?" "Seven of hearts! Close enough, old man!" Would *that* experiment be scientifically rigorous enough to satisfy him?

"Carter, darling."

Joad's wife had angled herself in between the two men. Next to her burly, red-faced porcupine of a husband, she seemed a mousy, insubstantial wisp of a woman – a sheet flapping in Joad's hot dusty breeze. Yet at the sound of her voice, Joad turned to her instantly, his dilated eyes glistening blackly. What fools women make of us, thought Plummer.

"Darling, I bet you haven't even asked Dr. Plummer if he's eaten since his train."

Joad wiped his hands on his beard in a pantomime of mortification.

Joad's wife sighed, rolled her eyes, and shook her head affectionately. "Would you care to join us for dinner, Dr. Plummer?"

"Yes, Plummer, do join us."

"I appreciate your kindness, Mrs. Joad, but I wouldn't want –"

"I can't promise much, you understand. But we'd be delighted to have you."

"She's being modest, Plummer. There's always too much food. You've got to come. You'd be doing us a favour, really."

"And call me Melanie, please."

Plummer had felt himself weakening, but this presumption of intimacy bolstered his resolve. And yet he could not bring himself to refuse two of her requests at once; so, using her Christian name, he told her that he was not hungry, that he was exhausted from his trip, and that to be quite frank he wanted nothing more than to check into his hotel room and turn out the light.

"Another night, perhaps?"

"I don't honestly know how long I'll be in town."

"Well, that's settled," grinned Joad, as though they'd just shaken hands on it, then went on in his playful, chiding tone: "Now tell us, Plummer. Come clean. Which of us do you suspect, hmm? Which one of us is in on the trick, in your expert opinion? Is it me? Is it Melanie? Henry, perhaps? Or is it our dear Ms. Meadow, after all?"

Plummer only shook his head. That was precisely what he had come to find out.

Back at his hotel room, Plummer unpacked his suitcase immediately. There was just enough room on the single bed to lay out all his shirts and trousers. His pens, he was pleased to see, had not come to any harm on the train (there hadn't been time to wrap them in plastic before leaving). His toiletries he arranged on the bathroom countertop according to size and frequency of usage, so that his toothbrush, for instance, was close to hand, while the bulkier bottle of headache pills was out of harm's way. He unlaced his shoes, dropped his watch into one and his keys into the other, and slid them under the bed.

There was a knock at the door. "Just a minute," he called.

That was when it struck him: he'd forgotten to pack his slippers.

Grumbling, he put his shoes back on to answer the door.

"I'm sorry, sir. The ARP fellow has told me that we've got some light showing through on this floor." The porter's head moved laterally, as though independently of his neck; he peered past Plummer's shoulder. "If you could just double-check, see that you've drawn your curtain properly . . ."

Plummer went to the window, cursing his stupidity. Where was his mind? At home he was always so fastidious about the blackout procedures. Ev had teased him, at first, as she'd teased him about the gas mask tests, but then Aunt Meredith had died in a raid, and the teasing had stopped.

But he was not at home, and not thinking about home.

He could not see past his own dim reflection in the pane. It would not have been much of a view, anyway. Even if the city had been alight, he couldn't have seen much more than the side of the building across the way. The hotel was not renting rooms above the third floor. A sensible precaution; though he had heard – everyone had heard – stories of bombs with delay mechanisms punching through several floors before going off . . .

Ev was right, of course: it was a pointless nuisance. Did anyone really believe that one little chink of light could be seen from the air? Did anyone really think that one glowing window out of millions was enough to bring the entire city, the entire nation, to its knees?

He frowned and shook his head in apology at the ARP fellow down there in the street somewhere, then drew the heavy cloth across the window and fastened it tight.

"Look," said Plummer, clutching the ring of keys in his pocket in one hand and the stem of his wineglass in the other, "to hold that there is a soul in addition to the body, or some immaterial mind-stuff above and beyond brain-stuff, is like Dorothy in that silly movie drawing aside the curtain, finding the little man at the controls, and explaining him away as a mere coincidence. We have in the first place the most staggeringly complex three pounds of matter in the known universe, and in the second – lying right on top of the first, as it were – we have consciousness. Considering their intimate proximity, their demonstrable interrelatedness, that these are two facets of the same miracle seems a reasonable enough hypothesis."

"Maybe consciousness," said Melanie cautiously, "is not something that is produced by the brain. Maybe it's shaped, or restricted, or limited by the brain. Maybe the brain acts as a sort of valve that allows certain things to seep through, while keeping others out – most of the time."

At this there were a few sly nods and shared half-smiles. All eyes in the room were on Plummer. He felt like some exotic bird that Carter, plumped with pride, had acquired for his menagerie. "Alan Plummer, the famous skeptic," as Carter had introduced him. For not the first time that night, Plummer regretted having come. Melanie and Carter had promised a quiet evening: "a few friends, a few drinks, some good conversation"; but Plummer should have foreseen that the Joads' friends would all be believers of one stripe or another, and that he, as not only the newcomer, but also that great rarity, the dyed-in-the-wool doubter, would naturally arouse their polite but hungry curiosity. They kept asking him idiotic questions: But don't you believe in *free will*? But surely you believe in *a soul*?

Perhaps Plummer would have turned down the Joads' third invitation, as he had done their first two, if not for the fact that, after nearly a week in London, he had rather begun to lose sight of the purpose of his presence in the basement of the Academic Complex (a building in which little seemed to be going on that Plummer would have called either academic or complex). Once he'd registered his initial criticisms of the experiment's "imperfections" – which he'd only done out of a nebulous sense of duty, and not in any real belief that they were responsible for Carter's results – there seemed little for him to do but stand by and observe. One fact about psychical research that had been insufficiently impressed upon him by his reading of the journals and books was its shocking tedium. Carter said he'd found that most percipients were only good for about three or four hours a day before their powers waned; though inclined to be dubious, Plummer had to admit that his own powers, such as they were, waned even sooner. He could watch Carter flashing cards or Henry staring at pictures or, in the next room,

Melanie silently writing or Ms. Meadow the great mystic sitting and doing her impersonation of someone concentrating for only so long before his patience utterly left him. For the first few days he had taken copious notes, pages brimming with the most irrelevant of minutiae, in the optimistic belief that, as in detective stories, it was always one little thing, some *prima facie* innocent detail, that provided the key to the entire mystery. But on looking back over what he had written he could not imagine that even the great Father Brown could find a needle in such a mountainous haystack. He continued jotting in his notebook only to appear attentive, and then finally to prevent his mind from wandering. But soon even this expedient failed, and during the long hours in the lab he'd found his thoughts turning, despite all his efforts, to Ev. . . . And in the evenings, of course, alone in his hotel room or sitting at the dusty counter of the basement *"café"* (more accurately a refectory) down the bombed-out street, there was even less to distract him. And so this evening he had come to the Joads'.

Having seen Carter's office, Plummer had come prepared for chaos and squalor. It was much worse than he had expected. The Joads' flat existed on a separate plane of filth, one for which Plummer had no point of reference. Like a backyard botanist dropped into a teeming rain forest, he felt overwhelmed, utterly unequal to his task; he couldn't even begin to categorize, let alone label, the alien species of rubbish and disorder that flourished in such suffocating profusion all around him. Ev had always found exposition tedious; when pressed to describe some scene or person or event to someone who'd lacked the foresight or courtesy to have been present in the first place, she most often limited

herself to one salient and, to her mind, sufficiently illustra-
tive detail: "You know the kind of chap I mean – he parted
his hair down the middle." "You know the sort of restaurant
I mean – French onion soup with every meal." If pressed to
describe Carter and Melanie's living space, Plummer supposed he could have done worse than to say, "You know the
kind of place I mean – there were charred cigarette butts
stamped into the carpet."

Most of these had apparently been deposited there by Ms.
Meadow, the putative psychic, who chain-smoked as though
conducting an experiment of potentially global humanitarian
significance. Over the last few days, Plummer's suspicions
had gradually lifted from Carter and settled in a flock upon
the head and shoulders of this unbearable woman. Carter
may have had the off-putting intensity of the proselytizer, the
bloodied-but-unbowed smugness of the precocious visionary,
but Plummer no longer thought him quite capable of outright fraud. He was, it seemed, at worst, tragically misguided.
It was, indeed, almost a shame; he might have made a com-
petent researcher. But this parapsychology stuff was a dead
end, both scientifically and, *a fortiori*, academically. They
had let it into the universities in America, which was not
such a surprise; now, like a black mould, it was beginning to
infiltrate the musty basements of England. But it could
hardly last. Carter, in his misplaced enthusiasm, had backed
the wrong horse. It was Melanie, however, that Plummer felt
sorry for. Could she know what her husband was getting
them into? What if, when the war was over, she wanted to
start a family? You could hardly support a child as a dis-
graced former professor. It did not make Plummer's task any
easier, either; for wasn't he the one who'd come to drive

Joad and his colleagues out of the academy and into disgrace? But the truth must out.

"Who was it at the door, darling?" asked Melanie.

Carter had at some point returned to the cramped, stuffy little room, and now stood behind his wife, holding in one hand a fresh bottle of the only moderately vile merlot and three or four glasses, and balancing on the other a plate heaped with cubes of cheese, pale sausages, hunks of black bread, dollops of what could only be called "spread," and other bite-sized boluses speared with toothpicks. (Where had the fool managed to find *toothpicks*?) Plummer's stomach, rather unnecessarily, clenched in protest.

"Oh, just the ARP bloke being a bother again."

"He's just doing his job," said Plummer, clutching his keys.

Ms. Meadow, exhaling twin trails of cigarette smoke from her nostrils, said, "Tell me, Professor. It must really be terrible to not believe in *anything*."

Plummer could not suppress an impatient sigh. "Of course I believe in things. Many things. Mathematics, for instance. Evolution. The special theory of relativity – though I don't profess to entirely understand it, mind you."

"Ah-*ha*," said Carter. "So you admit to having faith."

Plummer shook his head sadly. "If belief in the special theory of relativity is a kind of faith, then it is a faith in great minds, minds greater than my own. And it is a faith in the scientific method, in man's ability to test ideas by subjecting them to analysis and rigorous testing. I believe in truth, and I believe fundamentally in man's ability to discover truth – through science, not intuition or inspiration."

"Man and woman's ability, you mean," added Ms. Meadow.

"What bothers me," said Carter mildly, splashing wine less into the glasses than over them, "is the way so many scientists – myself included, old boy – have used the progressive, self-correcting nature of science to justify our refusal to progress or to correct ourselves. 'Science is superior to all other methods of inquiry,' we say, 'because of its empiricism, its divine adaptability, its willingness to test theories in the crucible of the universe and jettison outmoded ideas,' and so forth and so on. But that's just what makes us so unwilling to jettison outmoded ideas or countenance new ideas. We're willing to change – until we've got it right. And, hmph, perhaps we've got it right already. Who are *you* to say we haven't? It's our very nondogmatism that makes us dogmatists."

With a sigh and a wink, Carter held out towards Plummer a very full glass of wine. Plummer had to stand to take it. The room pitched and rolled like the deck of an ocean liner, but for a moment only. Did this make four, or five? He had lost count.

Ms. Meadow leaned forward to tap the ash from her cigarette. She did this in what Ev called the feminine manner: by extending her slim index finger and bringing it down near the ash end.

There were, as Ev liked to say, two kinds of people in the world: lumpers and splitters. Lumpers said, "There is only one kind of person in the world: splumpers." Splitters said, "There are two kinds of people in the world: lumpers and splitters; but there are also two kinds of lumpers, and, of course, two kinds of splitters . . ."

Ev was always a splitter. "There are two kinds of people in the world" was one of her favourite sayings. One of her favourite equators was the one that separated the male and female hemispheres. She wondered why, for example, in French, an arm was male but a leg female, or a footpath male but a lawn female, or, in German, morning, afternoon, and evening were male but night, only night, was female. Sometimes she detected chauvinism behind these distinctions. But for the most part she simply relished the anthropomorphization. That the word "pencil" was masculine lent each pencil a boyish mischievousness. That "flower" was feminine endowed flowers with a maternal dignity.

She went further than most languages, however. She ascribed a gender to not only nouns but also prepositions, adjectives, colours, smells, days of the week, months of the year, numbers and mathematical concepts. Verbs, too, had sexes – and not just those simple human activities that could be summed up in a single feminine word like "climb" or a masculine word like "jog," but complex actions, elaborate behaviours. To look at your fingernails by extending your fingers was feminine; pressing them against your palm was masculine. Checking the sole of your shoe by bending your leg back and looking over your shoulder was feminine; lifting your foot sideways, in front of the other leg, masculine. Tapping the ash from your cigarette with your index finger was feminine; flicking the filter-end with your thumb was masculine. Blowing out a match was feminine; shaking it out, with a flick of the wrist, masculine.

"Tell me, Professor," said Ms. Meadow. "Do you believe in an *afterlife?*"

Yes, if there was a fraud here, it was Clara Meadow. She certainly had all the outward markings of the professional charlatan. She waved her arms and flapped her hands when she spoke; even platitudes about the weather she uttered with oracular flamboyance. Her eyes were too large for her skull, so that her merely impudent gaze appeared carnivorous, engulfing. She seemed always to be watching him, but her gaze never met his. Her short blonde hair was cut into strata and made her head look like an onion. She wore lipstick and trousers. She smoked like a wood stove but seemed to never eat. She wore more scarves than any coat rack, yet was always shivering. Indeed, she was, like all impostors, a brittle bundle of contradictions. She tapped ash in the feminine manner, but extinguished her matches in the masculine manner. She checked the soles of her boots in the feminine manner, checked her long unpainted fingernails in the masculine manner.

"I have no reason to believe in anything like an afterlife," said Plummer at length.

"But doesn't that sadden you?" Ms. Meadow's eyes grew cloudy and she grasped his elbow, as one might grasp the elbow of the recently bereaved.

A jolt went up his arm, but he did not pull away.

Perhaps it was not wrong, after all, to think about Ev in this way – that is, to remember her, to reminisce about their life together. Because the past still belonged to him; in the past, *she* still belonged to him. Memory did not have to be a mausoleum, he decided. It could be a kind of shrine.

"I've had some time," he said, "to grow accustomed to the idea."

11

She had been told not to use the elevator.

Normally she wouldn't have needed to be told. She hated elevators. All of her nightmares were of being trapped in small spaces.

She'd assumed they didn't want the regular guests to see the girls going in and out, and she'd assumed that during an air raid such rules were suspended. Anyway, it didn't matter. Once she heard the siren, she didn't need to be dreaming: all she had to do was close her eyes to see walls collapsing, glass shattering, bricks and mortar tumbling down on top of her.

Now, she didn't even need to close her eyes. She was trapped in the elevator in the dark. They had told her not to use it.

It was just like this. This was how she'd pictured it. The darkness, heavy as packed soil, closing in on her, squeezing her in its fist, turning her inside out.

Clara pulled at the grille but, as she'd known, it would not budge when the car was between floors. There must have been a latch or switch that would release the mechanism but she was blind and her fingers were clumsy.

Someone would come. There were procedures, procedures that would require someone to come check the elevators. Someone would probably come within thirty seconds. Well, she could count to thirty.

How fast should she count? Simple. She would count her breaths.

The only problem with this plan was that she could not hear herself breathing over the seashell roar of blood in her head; nor, when she felt her diaphragm with her fingers, could she feel anything but the erratic, fidgety stirrings of panic. With the swift, inexorable logic of nightmares, it occurred to her that she had already stopped breathing.

The fact that she could hear herself muttering did not disprove anything. One could speak without air in one's lungs. It happened all the time in her dreams. One could even scream.

Voices. Clara held her breath and listened. In holding her breath she was able to regain some control, some reason: holding her breath meant that she had breath to hold. And now that her eyes had begun to adjust she could see that the blackness was not absolute. She could make out the argyle crosshatching of the grille against the panel behind it.

The voice came again, surprisingly close. "Can you hear me?"

"Yes," she called, "I can hear you! I'm in here! Hello?"

"Are you . . . all right?"

"I can't open the gate."

"Yes, but are you . . . You're not hurt?"

He'd heard her screaming. Clara was not embarrassed but, rather, annoyed. She felt that he had trespassed on her momentary anguish. She had not exactly been calling for help.

"I'm afraid of the dark," she said – then *was* embarrassed. Because that wasn't it at all. She was ashamed of her childish lie, her childish simplification.

He said something she couldn't hear. A moment later, he was tugging at the outside grille.

"Can you . . . ?"

"It won't –"

The power came back on. As the light returned it seemed to bring with it a draught of oxygen.

"Oh, thank God."

"There," he said, as though taking credit. "Will it open now?"

The lever was still in the down position. She pushed it back to the upright STOP position and tried the OPEN button. The gate purred but would not disengage.

"I'm still between floors," she cried.

"Which floors?"

"I don't know." Irritated by this irrelevance, she looked at the indicator, which showed the bottom half of a "4." "Three and four."

"Well, come down to three."

She did, and the gate opened.

"Oh," she said, pleased but not exactly surprised. "So it was you."

Before the professor could say anything, she strode past him, intent on the stairs.

He followed her out into the street, one hand, as always, in his trouser pocket, the other dangling uncertainly at the end of its arm. She gulped air for a minute or two, then smiled at his silhouette.

"I feel much better now. Thank you."

But he did not go back inside. "Should you be out here?" he asked.

She laughed bitterly. "Better than being trapped indoors. Half these buildings collapse if you sneeze on them."

"I meant, rather, in the dark."

She could see now that he had been as upset as she by the ordeal, perhaps more. He had heard her screaming, after all. She had cast him, she supposed, in the role of rescuer, but had given him no real opportunity to discharge his duty. The fingers of his free hand fluttered, like those of a pianist before a recital. He seemed to need something to do.

"Where are we, anyway?" Under the pretense of getting her bearings, she looked around, watching him with the edge of her vision. In the blacked-out street, she could not make out his features, but she could see his flicker. Tonight it was clear and stable, as reliable as a metronome. It soothed her. How he would have laughed, or scoffed, if she'd told him that she felt safe in his presence. She did not want him to leave her yet.

"I understand there's a public shelter in the park, next block but one."

"No," she said softly, pulling her scarves around her and shivering. "I can't stay in those filthy things."

She smiled at the tremor of frustration that appeared in his flicker; the impression was of a child pouting impotently. What a strange bird he was.

Perhaps she had gotten on that horrible elevator for a reason, after all. If Mr. Empson had not missed his appointment; if she had not lingered in the room, unwilling to go back to the club so late to arrange another appointment; if the air-raid siren had not sounded just then; if the elevator had not come as soon as she'd called it – if all of this had not unfolded in precisely such a way, she would not be here, alone in the street with Professor Plummer, the famous skeptic. How marvellously odd that he had come into her life, at this moment, in this fabulously roundabout way.

Didn't everything happen for a reason? Like all coincidences, this one was surely significant; but what was it telling her? No, she did not want him to leave yet.

"Come, I know where there's an Anderson," she said – perhaps too imperiously. He hesitated, so she tried to sound less sure of herself. "Won't you come? It *is* rather dark."

She took his arm to guide them, while letting him seem to lead the way.

They walked down the black streets, shadows navigating among shadows. The sky was clear, as always on air-raid nights, but there was no hint of a moon. The stars stood out more distinctly, without appearing any brighter. Occasionally, a searchlight's beam scraped across them like a dragnet, leaving them looking washed out and ashamed. One could discern the buildings they passed only by contrast: they were the starless patches of darkness.

Every second street lamp was lit, and these were covered, so that only narrow cones of light fell down from them. You could just about read your watch if you stood directly beneath one. Lorries occasionally trundled past, their headlights smeared daubs of blue. Otherwise they seemed to have the street to themselves.

The night was far from silent, but the sound of the attack came from a distance, and in its impersonal persistence only strengthened the impression of solitude. The rumble of explosions, the susurrating crackle of fires burning, the deceptive buzz of the circling planes carried by the fickle winds, sounding near, then far, now near, now far, like darting insects – this ongoing cacophony seemed no more threatening or purposeful than the mindless churning of the ocean or the respiration of some forest.

Now that they were safely out of doors, she felt almost exuberant. She loved the city like this. Under blackout it was an alien planet. She was brimming over; she had to speak. But she doubted whether the professor would understand her enthusiasm. She did not want him to think her frivolous.

"I didn't realize you were staying in the hotel," he said, his voice strained, as though from effort or embarrassment.

"Yes – that is, no, I'm not," she gushed in gratitude; he had needed to break the silence as much as she. "I was visiting a friend, you could say."

"I thought they'd closed the upper floors. What with the . . ." He shook his fingers vaguely at the sky.

"My friend wasn't in, anyway. How lucky for me that you just happened to come along."

"Someone else would have, I dare say. Even if the power hadn't –"

"But it wasn't someone else. It was you. Tell me, Professor, what are the odds of that?"

"They could never be calculated," he muttered.

"That's what I mean. A million to one!"

He grumbled but did not object. She felt almost drunk with triumph. They walked another block in silence.

"I suppose I should apologize for the other night," she said.

"Eh? Apologize?"

"I felt like we sort of raked you over the coals a bit."

"Nonsense," he said, then clicked his tongue thoughtfully a few times and again fell silent.

Closer now, there came the distinctive snoring whistle of falling incendiary bombs; instinctively, though quite use-lessly, they stopped in their tracks and ducked their heads down between their shoulders – much as they would have done if someone had crept up behind them and blown a birthday-party noisemaker in their ears. How pathetic the war had made everyone.

She counted as the bombs fell, measuring their distance, as she'd measured the distance of lightning as a girl by counting until the thunder came.

The whistling ceased at "four." There followed no hissing explosion. More duds. She almost hated these more than the effective ones. Like the fellow in the radio joke, she kept waiting for the other shoe to drop. And she was possessed by the idea that these undetonated shells could go off at any time, at the slightest provocation. She could not bear even to pass by a cordoned-off street, and could not imagine what it must be like for the men whose job it was to drive around each morning and collect the horrid things like oversized Easter eggs.

"I suppose," said the professor kindly, "if they've fallen from planes and punched through the roofs of buildings and whatnot, they're rather unlikely to be set off by some poor chap picking them up with his hands."

She clutched his arm more tightly. "You aren't frightened?"

There blossomed in his flicker a little whirlpool of self-satisfaction; it lasted only a moment.

"It's fatalism, I suppose. I will be hit or I won't be hit. But the odds, I think," and here he paused, perhaps in ironic acknowledgement of their different interpretations of that concept, "are in my favour."

It was hard not to hear in this admirably philosophical detachment a critique of her own comportment. "I know," she said, accepting the unstated indictment. "A million to one. But I can't help thinking that the odds drop with the number of bombs. The longer I go unscathed, the worse my chances – like steam pressure building up in a pipe."

That, he said gently, as though dispelling some illusory bogeyman by turning on a lamp, was just the Gambler's Fallacy: the idea that if a number hasn't come up for a while, it's "due." The roulette wheel in Monte Carlo had once hit black twenty-six times in a row. "After about the fifteenth time, people began rushing to put all their money on red. A lot of people lost a lot of money."

"But sometimes," she said, gripping his elbow urgently, "I feel the exact opposite. As though the longer I survive, the more of this war I live through, the more invincible I become. It can't be any more sensible to keep playing black, can it?"

"Black or red, odd or even – you can't predict what comes next from what's come before. Which is why I don't gamble," he said, with a glimmer of that same self-satisfaction.

"Coming here wasn't a gamble?"

"They drop bombs in Liverpool too."

"But all it takes is one. That's what gets me. No matter how good your luck, for no matter how long, no matter how smart you play it, all it takes is that one time being in the wrong place . . ."

"To disprove the law that all crows are black, one white crow is enough. Yes."

She watched with the edge of her vision as a complex turbulence, rich in overtones and patterns within patterns, swelled in his thoughts, then slowly subsided.

Memories. Unhappy ones?

"There," she pointed. "Isn't that the old Commerce building?"

"I don't know how you can see a damned thing."

"It's not far now."

She steered them around the corner and into the narrow alleyway that would take them to the courtyard behind Patrice's place. The blocks of flats here towered over them, further stifling the distant noise of the air raid.

"What did bring you here, Professor? And please, don't say the train."

"Eh? Well, Carter invited me. That is, it was his idea. He seemed to think he needed a skeptical observer to come in and poke his nose about, as it were, presumably to bestow an air of legitimacy or rectitude to the whole . . . business."

"No no no. *That's* what I mean by the train. I mean, how did you come to be sort of caught up in all this business, as you call it, when obviously you're so, if you don't mind my saying . . ."

"Skeptical?"

"Yes."

"I suppose it began last year. I wrote an article, you see, rather polemical in its way, I suppose, which our friend Carter, for obvious reasons, rather took exception to. Well, there followed something of a duel in print over the next few months –"

"No, that's still the train. I mean, what brought you around to ESP in the first place?"

"You mean, I suppose, why am I a skeptic?"

"Of course not. I *am* quite able to grasp the arguments against mind-reading or telepathy or whatever your universities prefer to call it these days, Professor. I've used most of them myself. I know perfectly well why people disbelieve in things that shouldn't be possible. Skepticism is not such a great rarity as perhaps you believe. What *is* unusual, in my experience, is the skeptic who dedicates himself so passionately to studying the very thing he doesn't believe. What I *mean* is – if you don't mind my asking – what possessed you to become such a *professional* skeptic?"

He made the sound – a sort of drawn-out snort with falling inflection – that she took to signify annoyance or uncertainty.

"Marvin Vlastnikczy," he said at last.

"*Gesundheit.*"

"Marvin Vlastnikczy was one of the most highly respected, most brilliant mathematicians of his day. Laid much of the groundwork for what is today modern statistics. Formalized and shed a great deal of light on what is meant exactly by words like 'probability' and 'chance' and 'randomness' – revolutionary work without which men like de Broglie and Heisenberg could never have built their theories. A giant, in other words, on whose shoulders many giants have stood.

"A couple of years ago I came across a rather obscure paper, published posthumously, called 'Notes On the Statistical Challenges Peculiar to Psychical Research.' Well. It was a short paper, rather densely technical, and as far as I could tell it had gone largely unnoticed by either statisticians or parapsychologists." The professor paused. "But it had an effect on me. This man – one of the great minds of our century, one of the grandees of mathematics, one of my heroes, you might even say – had written his little paper as though he quite took it for granted that this ESP business had already been established . . . And I remember thinking: Wouldn't it be awful. Wouldn't it be awful if it were true. Because it would change everything. The entire edifice would crumble. It would mean starting over from scratch."

It seemed to her that she knew exactly what he meant. But there was no time just then to investigate the sense of recognition: the strip of sky overhead had suddenly turned pale green; the entire street was bathed in a uniform, sickly sheen, so that everything – buildings, doorways, lampposts, dustbins – appeared to be made of, or carved from, the same chalky, sulphurous material. It gave her the overwhelming sensation of having entered some giant set or Hollywood sound-stage, where nothing was real – a beautiful, master-fully constructed, hermetically sealed illusion. She felt almost light-headed with excitement.

"Parachute flares," she said, her voice trembling. "So they can see what they're bombing."

"Makes the blackout nonsense all rather pointless, doesn't it."

"Come on," she said, tugging on his arm affectionately. "They'll be dropping here soon."

The courtyard had once been a rock garden. There had been a fountain, statuary, benches, and, because no flora would reliably grow where the sun never quite reached, all manner of burnished rocks and stones. Now, all of that had been torn up and pushed to one side, so that a new kind of garden could take its place. The courtyard had been replanted with Anderson shelters.

As they crept through the shantytown of corrugated sheet metal and dirt, they could hear voices and even what might have been the plucking of a ukulele. The Andersons, of course, were notoriously ineffective when it came to keeping sound out, or in.

Clara picked up a brick and bashed at the door of Patrice's Anderson. The professor looked horror-stricken.

She laughed. "She's a heavy sleeper." She listened for a few seconds, then said, "She's not in."

Some of the shelters had locks on the doors, but Patrice thought it immoral to lock up an empty shelter. You never knew who might need it.

And, indeed, there was someone inside after all. Sitting up, stiff as a plank, in the lower bunk on the right side. She could just discern the whites of his eyes, and could smell the candle he'd just blown out – which meant he would not be able to see her.

"Hello there," she said from the threshold in her most neighbourly voice.

His flicker was faint, but she recognized in it the heat-haze shimmer of fear. Ridiculous that he should be afraid of her, with the Nazis that very moment dropping fire down on both their heads. What fools the war made of them all.

Then she saw the second set of eyes in the bunk above, and understood.

"Daddy?" said the girl.

"It's all right," said Clara. "Are you friends of Patrice's too?"

"Hold on a minute," said the man. His flicker grew stronger, steadier. "I'll light a candle for us."

*

Before, the man had been a veterinarian. Clara was delighted.

"I love animals. I wanted to be a vet myself, for a while." She spoke openly, to dispel the lingering tension, addressing the daughter as much as the father in her bright, clear voice. "I've always thought: What a noble cause. Helping animals. When we tend to forget that we're not the only creatures on the planet." She smiled at the professor. How ridiculous he looked in this cramped place, folded up like the starched napkins at the club, his bony knees almost in his face. "Maybe someday we'll get our priorities straight, and instead of shooting each other we'll try talking to each other. And then maybe we'll try talking to the animals. God knows there's a lot we could learn from them. They're right to be wary of us, of course, with the way we've treated them in the past. But we did it with horses, and dogs and cats, didn't we? Wouldn't it be wonderful to have a pet fox, or a pet bear? It's been years since I've had a pet. Maybe when all this nonsense is over . . . A little doggie, I think. Something to take care of." She leaned towards the little girl, who had come down to join her father on the bottom bunk. "Do you have a pet? A little puppy or kitty?"

The child buried her face in her father's side.

"We . . . lost our pet." The man looked meaningfully at her, then the professor. "She ran away," he said slowly, emphasizing each word, so that even the child must have understood that he was speaking in code. "Many pets had to run away because of the war."

The man sighed; his eyes, filled with candlelight, went blank. Forgetting his daughter, he murmured, "So many, they were piling up outside my clinic."

"Dear God," said Clara, making no attempt to hide her disgust.

"So you see," said the man, wrinkling his lips as though delivering a punchline, "it's not such a noble occupation these days."

She pulled her scarves around her and pursed her lips. She did not believe that a veterinarian could do such things, in wartime or not. People were never what you expected.

The bombing did not come closer. This, too, drove her mad, this absence of rhyme or reason. How could you ever hope to go about your life if you never knew what to expect? She felt flushed, anxious, restless. She took the cards out of her purse to give her hands something to do. She shuffled the deck a few times, then noticed the girl watching her.

"Would you like me to read your cards, darling?"

The girl said nothing, but her eyes remained fixed on the deck. The father glanced at the professor; Clara ignored him and spoke to the girl.

"They're tarot cards. See the pictures? They help me to see people's futures. Do you want to look at your future with me? Do you want to know what you will be when you grow up?"

The father bristled. "She's not interested in any of that occult eyewash."

"Oh for God's sake," said the professor in his cold, blaring voice. "It's only a harmless card game."

"She's not interested," said the former vet, holding his arm in front of the girl protectively, as though Clara or the professor might lunge at her.

"Here," said Clara, "the professor and I will demonstrate. Won't we, Professor?"

She began to lay down cards in the foot or so of space between them on the mattress.

The professor looked aggrieved. Then he glanced at the girl, who was clinging to her father, afraid of the sounds coming out of the sky as well as those coming out of the grown-ups around her. His expression softened.

"Of course," he said.

"Now, as everyone knows, before you can read the future, you must read the present, and before you can read the present, you have to read the past. Right? So, what I need the professor to do is pick his past card."

"What, any card?"

"Oh ho no," she cried. "Not just *any* card. You must choose *very* carefully. Concentrate, my dear sir. Think *only* of the past – of your life leading up to this moment in time. Then, with the past firmly in your mind, choose the card – or, rather, let the card choose itself."

She smiled at the girl, but her attention was on the professor's flicker at the edge of her vision. For several seconds the pattern seemed unchanged; then, slowly, faint ripples began to appear.

"This one? Very good."

Turning over the card, she allowed a gasp to escape her lips. She held the card up so the girl could see, and so that she herself could continue to watch the professor's reaction.

"The Fool," she intoned. "A very interesting card. You can see that he is carrying a rose in one hand – a symbol of life, and also of love – and in the other, a long traveller's staff. His head is up in the air – perhaps deep in contemplation of the finer things? – and he is blissfully unaware that he's about to walk over a cliff. There, you can see in the bottom corner his little doggie trying to warn him. But he is oblivious."

The professor's flicker had grown turbulent; she had struck a chord. So, the professor had stepped over some cliff – as who hadn't? Something had happened that he had not anticipated; and because he had not anticipated it, he felt that it had been his fault. Regret. Loss.

She instructed him to select his second card. This time there was no need to gasp. She could not have chosen a better card if she had chosen for him.

"Don't worry," she said. "It's not a bad card. An end, remember, is also a beginning. And a beginning is also necessarily the end of what came before. I know what you're thinking – but it's not as foolish as it sounds. It's fundamental. What *is* death? The end of life. And what is life? Movement, change, creation. But the end of change is permanence, eternity, life everlasting. Birth is novelty, newness, invention, but nothing can be new unless you measure it against the old – that is, what it's replacing, what it has killed. Death and birth, movement and stasis, habit and change – they're just the imaginary poles of an infinite spectrum."

His flicker was reverberating in response to her words. She could make out the shape of his loss – a woman, of course. She could almost discern her name. She proceeded softly, with light step, pausing for confirmation.

"You've lost something. Someone." Yes. "And you miss them. You miss her." Yes. "That's natural. We all lose things. It's the condition of our existence. Life didn't begin in the Garden of Eden. It began with the expulsion, with the flaming sword. Without loss, there can be no progress, no forward movement. Adam and Eve only came to life with the Fall."

Again, something had struck a chord. Eve? Could it be that easy?

"She isn't dead, your wife – your Eve. She isn't gone. She's only undergone a change."

At the name, his flicker suddenly went rigid, becoming claustrophobically involuted, like the hothouse hallucinations of fever-dreams. He hadn't been prepared for this.

"Don't be alarmed. It's natural. The names of loved ones often leave behind an echo, you know, 'clanging on the heart like a hammer on an anvil . . .'"

His thoughts went silent. He'd clamped down, shut her out. All that remained was the calm, reliable metronome.

"All right. That's enough."

But it was not the professor who'd spoken.

"We've heard enough," said the man, propping his daughter up on her feet. "We're good Anglicans."

Clara was too bemused, and the professor, it seemed, too stunned, to object; before either could think of a word to say to stop them, the pair had gone out into the night.

Amazing. He'd rather risk both their lives than risk seeing something his faith wouldn't allow him to understand.

"All right," said the professor, grinning with false mirth and false confidence, like a boy asking a bully for his lunch money back. "You can tell me now. How do you do it? What's the trick?"

What should she tell him? What did he want to know? She gathered the cards and handed him the deck.

She didn't read the cards, she explained; she read the person. He'd been to the cinema, she assumed; he knew how film projectors worked? They flashed a lot of pictures on the screen, twenty or thirty pictures every second – fast enough that you couldn't tell it was a series of still pictures at all, fast enough that the image looked like it was moving. But if you looked at the screen indirectly, out of the corner of your eye, you *could* see the flash of the individual pictures, the flicker of light and dark.

That was sort of how it was for her. She could see people flickering.

"In other words, you read people's thoughts," he said blandly.

"But it's not like watching a film. I don't see the thoughts so much as the spaces between the thoughts – the speed or movement or pattern of thoughts."

"Even if they're in the next room, hmm?" He spoke with so little emphasis, so little surprise, that he must surely be mocking her.

"No." She sighed. "It's different in the lab. I don't know how it works – *if* it works. All I know is I try to clear my mind and let impressions come to me. Sometimes they do. Mostly they don't."

He stood up, seemingly without any conscious intention of doing so, then, as though formulating a plausible motive, said that he thought it was time he was getting back to the hotel.

Just then, as if his words had invoked it, the all-clear signal sounded.

Seeing that he was embarrassed, even unnerved by his prescience, she let him go, without even reassuring him that it was, after all, only a coincidence.

"By the way," he said on his way out, almost smiling. "Her name isn't Eve. And she isn't dead."

She smoked two cigarettes, then made her way back to the club. With the air raid over, the streets had lost their menace, but also their magic. The blackout struck her now as nothing but an idiotic inconvenience, a childish conspiracy, a monumental game of dress-up or make-believe. She stumbled in the dark, and twice lost her way.

Wouldn't it be awful if it were true? It would mean starting over from scratch.

Because the truth was black or white: Either the universe was predictable, or it wasn't. Either nature was governed by laws, or it wasn't. Either science could provide an adequate description of the way things worked, or it simply could not. Either everything was right, or everything was wrong.

She had been the same way with Gordon: *Either he is good for me, or he is not.* And the thought of starting over from scratch had been too much for her to bear.

She now saw that the problem with black or white was that it made you inflexible. And inflexibility also made you brittle. Unable to bend, you could only break. To disprove the law that all crows are black, one white crow was enough.

And when the balance finally tipped in the other direction, you were condemned, by your premises, to a total renunciation. If one crow was not black, no crows could be black! *I thought he was good for me but he was bad for me; whoever might seem good for me can only be bad for me; no one can ever be good for me.*

Only now that she had seen it reflected in the professor could she recognize her own muddled thinking. Not that she had been wrong to leave Gordon; she'd been wrong to stay with him as long as she did, wrong to go on sweeping the grey under the rug, wrong to stick around until the one sure indisputable demonstration came – and lucky that when it did, it had not been worse. But she had been just as wrong to give up, to conclude that all men were Gordons. She'd behaved as though an exception to a rule *reversed* the rule – and, indeed, so great was the compulsion to make laws, one reversed rule reversed *all* rules. Because if laws weren't *laws*, what good were they?

She understood now why she'd been attracted to the professor. At first, perhaps, the metronome-like calm she'd seen in his flicker had tantalized her with its promise of reliability, of stability. But, in fact, the reason he had come into her life was to show her that nothing was reliable, nothing was stable – not even her wounded conviction that nothing was reliable, nothing stable. That was what the professor had been sent by fate to teach her. That was the significance of this episode in her life.

All she could say for certain was that not all men were good for her; at least some men were bad for her. Whether or not *any* man was good for her remained, for the time being, an open question.

If she'd hoped to be left alone with her drink and her thoughts, she should have known better than to come to the club. There weren't many other girls around this late, and she was soon joined at the bar by a fidgety bloke in a bowler who seemed to mean business. In lieu of introductions, and without first asking if she'd like one, he bought her a second drink; in lieu of small talk, he asked abruptly, and quite guilelessly, if she wanted his company.

Normally she would have given him the same answer she gave any of the men in whose flickers she read desperation, or anger, or hate, or pain. With this one, though, she could get no read at all. Hiding something? If so, it was hidden even from himself. There was nothing coming off him, not a glimmer. This was surely a first. It was bewildering.

She decided to make an exception, to play it by ear, to see how things went. Stepping back out into the black street with his hand at the small of her back, she felt quite reckless; the feeling of not knowing what to expect was intoxicating. Nor was it even really so reckless. There was no danger in waiting and seeing what happened next. After all, she had been doing this for years, and had never had a problem.

III

She fumbled for the phone in the dark. She knew it was him before she picked up.

But that wasn't so extraordinary. Only a coincidence. She'd been thinking about him, and the phone had rung. Not even such a coincidence, really. He hadn't called all week, and the longer he was away, the more she thought about him, naturally – about why he'd left so suddenly, about when he would be back. All he'd deigned to tell her was that something had come up in London. But he hated London, even in peacetime. And it was altogether unlike him to do anything on the spur of the moment. He'd been running away, then, she supposed – from her, from what she'd done, or what he thought she'd done.

"Ev," he said, "do you remember that Joyce poem? The one we memorized together?"

"Who *is* this," she found herself teasing from force of habit – it was the greeting she reserved for him when he bypassed his greetings.

"You know: 'They come shaking in triumph their long, green hair,'" he quoted. "'They come out of the sea and run shouting by the shore.'"

"Yes." She thought back. "'My heart, have you no wisdom thus to despair?'"

He said nothing, allowing her to finish. She went on with reluctant relish:

"'My love, my love, my love, why have you left me alone?'"

"You remember."

"I *had* forgotten all about it."

The effortlessness with which they'd slipped into the old modes of talking to each other made her feel both guilty and hopeful. Guilty, because it failed to acknowledge all that had happened – the accusation, the argument, his sudden departure, the week of silence; hopeful, because it conjured a future as ignorant of such things as their past. But hope was premature, and made her feel guilty all over again. She heard herself say, in the loud, brassy voice of someone trying to conceal from the greengrocer that he has given her too much change, "What on earth made you think of that?"

"Did you ever tell anyone else about it?"

"What, about James Joyce?"

"Never mind. It's a popular enough poem, I suppose."

She said nothing. She was afraid to ask for clarification, afraid to scrape at the surface of his words. Anything might lie beneath them.

She was limited by the length of the phone cord to the chair or the window. She stood and looked out the window. With Alan away, she'd stopped bothering with the black-outs, and simply never turned on the lights after dark.

The rain had stopped. The Henkley boy was still out there. Like a caged moth, his torch cast fluttering wings of shadow across the dome of the tent. She was surprised his mother didn't consider this a breach of national security.

A part of her remembered what it felt like listening to the sound of rain pattering on canvas. The memory made her throat ache.

The telephone line sputtered and hissed – the sound of distance compressed into time – then suddenly went quiet.

"Alan?"

He was gone; the connection had been severed.

Then: "Ev?"

She said nothing.

"Ev?"

"Yes?"

She remembered the dog, but not its name. Alan had had it since he was a boy. And as a boy, he'd believed it was a mark of distinction, a gesture of respect and affection, to give a pet a human name, a grown-up name. Pets were named silly things like Rex, Spot, Killer, Shadow. Friends were named Arthur.

She remembered, but only as she remembered the tat-tered armchair or the finicky radiator in that gloomy old

house where her mother had sent her to learn French with
Mrs. Plummer the summer after Alan's father had died. The
warm, snoring, flatulent rug called Arthur had disappeared
from the floor of the library by the time Ev returned, several
summers later, to visit not Mrs. Plummer, whose French had
been significantly less advanced than her own, but Alan.

"He was old," said Alan. "It was painless, I suppose."

Among the things that his father had left behind was a big
orange toolbox. Alan emptied it out and placed Arthur
inside. Then he dug a grave at the edge of a small clearing
where he had taken Arthur to chase squirrels, though he'd
never caught a single one. He put the toolbox in the hole
and put the dirt back on top. He covered the mound with
branches and leaves and moss. Feeling stupid, he muttered a
promise to visit often, then walked home.

He did return, a few times, before the visits began to seem
pointless. A week after he stopped going, he had a dream.
Not a dream, really. A hallucination.

It terrified him. He didn't know why it should have. But
then, even as a boy he'd never understood why the people
in the Bible should have been afraid of the angels that came
to visit them, either. Weren't they *angels*?

She realized now that he was speaking with a slight lisp
and, as though to make up for this, he was taking more than
his usual care to enunciate. So he had been drinking. This
frightened her, though she could not say why. It felt like he
was armed, or driving them down a dark road; she thought
he should have his wits about him.

What he had seen that night was Arthur. He didn't know
if his eyes had been open or closed, whether he had been

awake or asleep or someplace in-between, but he saw the dog's shape, his form, standing in the shadows of the far corner of his bedroom. Mixed in with this illusion, overlaid with it, in the palimpsest fashion of dreams, was the knowledge that Arthur was there, had come to *him*, because *he* had decided to stop going to Arthur.

There was a pause. Then Alan said, "I've never been so scared in all my life."

This was not how she had wanted the conversation to go. She had expected bitterness and reproach, and had prepared emollients for these; she had expected direct attack, and had prepared defences; she had expected indictment, and had prepared justification. She had prepared for a discussion, cold, perhaps, but rational, even mechanical, ratcheting them by degrees closer to mutual understanding, closer to some truce. She had not expected this formless, murky stream of association and remembrance, beneath which she could but faintly detect a riverbed of threat, and in whose sludge, in any case, she could find no purchase. She had been prepared to dig in her heels. She did so now.

"Alan, why are you telling me all this?"

"Because," he said, "this is something I've never told anyone before."

There was a pause.

"Don't you think we should always tell each other everything?"

Here it was at last. The direct attack. She closed her eyes.

"It was more than just fear, though," he went on. "It was disgust. *Repulsion*. Like I'd been poisoned. Like my mind was retching. Now, does that make sense? That dog was the first thing I ever loved, and the thought that he had come back to me, back from the dead, made me *sick* with fear. Does that make any sense?"

She did not know what to say. She supposed that now he would demand his *quid pro quo*. Now that he'd told her something, it was time for her to tell him something.

And she'd intended to. She'd had all week to build her resolve. She had planned to tell him everything, as much as there was to tell. But now, at the critical moment, her courage left her. Now that the direct attack was coming, she was unable to meet it as she'd planned, and could only take cover, could only flee. It was instinctive, like ducking and hunching one's shoulders at any loud noise.

She could *not* tell him the truth. She knew that she would only deny, all over again, that anything had happened, that she had done anything wrong.

And as soon as her resolution had faded and this counter-resolution had sprung up in its place, she recognized immediately that it was the right thing to do – indeed, the only thing. Because Alan would never understand. He would hear the words, but not grasp their significance. He would jam the square peg of truth into one of his preconceived round holes. The one labelled "unfaithful," perhaps. The one labelled "betrayal." The one labelled "the end."

Let the attack come now. Please, let it come now. Now she was ready.

"Ev?"

"Yes."

"The next day . . . I dug him up. Stupid . . . But I had to know. I had to make sure. Didn't I?"

The smell, when he'd opened the toolbox, had made him vomit.

Arthur was crawling with bugs. They'd eaten away his eyelids.

"Ev."

"Yes?"

"I don't want you ever to die."

IV

In the empty lot across the road, Nat Henkley turned off his torch, gently unzipped the tent's flap, and watched as the lights in his neighbour's house came on, one by one.

He closed his eyes and listened for raised voices, crying, breaking glass, gunshots – any of the noises his imagination associated with domestic distress.

But the only sound was rain pattering on canvas.

He tied his boots and ran up to the house in search of his mother, who had become, since the war, good friends with Standish, the blackout warden.

IN THE DARK

Here's what happened: I arrived at the Sandstone at about a quarter to seven and, after a quick look around upstairs, settled down to a pint at a table near the entrance. At five to, I experienced the first perfunctory pang of worry that you wouldn't show. Then my imagination, which seems to have something against me, suggested that perhaps you'd thought I meant the Sandstone on Iverness, which is after all just a block and a half off Eighth *Street* – an almost conceivable mistake, given that all I'd asked was whether you knew the Sandstone on Eighth.

So I waited until exactly one minute to seven before slamming down the remains of my beer and dashing out into the street like a drunk fleeing the onset of DTs. By eight minutes past seven I was satisfied that you were not at the other Sandstone either. So I dashed back out into the street. With a little less gusto I returned to the original rendezvous point by about a quarter after seven. There I drank another beer and watched the door, and drank another beer and watched the door. Then I went home.

Did you perhaps turn up at one minute past seven and leave disappointed thirteen or less minutes later?

I'd like to think it was just a misunderstanding.

A few weeks ago I was making french fries. I was cutting potatoes and one of them got away from me, rolled off the table and onto the floor. I finished chopping the others before pushing my chair back and bending over to look for the errant spud. It wasn't under the table. It wasn't under my chair. It was nowhere to be seen. I got down on my hands and knees and searched every square inch of the kitchen floor. The potato had been too big to roll under the stove or the fridge, but I pulled both appliances away from the wall anyway. I carried all the chairs into the living room. I shifted the table to one side of the kitchen, then the other. I even looked under the sink – as though a potato could, if properly motivated, open a cupboard door and slip inside. But it was not hiding out among the detergent bottles either.

A potato disappeared in my kitchen. But potatoes don't just disappear.

I can't explain it. It still bewilders me. I would probably pay a great price to learn the fate of that vegetable. It's not what I might learn; the explanation would be sure to be mundane. It's just that not-knowing is maddening.

I don't know what to think. Or rather, I don't know what *not* to think. Every possibility, every interpretation, every story I come up with seems utterly plausible at the moment it occurs to me. But they're all built on sand.

Why won't you pick up the phone?

Maybe you thought the more compassionate act was to break it off clean, to amputate the limb at the joint. Or maybe you thought it gentler, less injurious to my fragile self-respect, to permit me to cherish a glimmer of hope that I had not been stood up, had not been rejected.

In fact, I'm perfectly capable of handling rejection. My self-respect is quite robust.

I don't really need or want to know why I'm wrong for you. After all, I could never put words to what I felt was missing in any of my exes (those times when there was something missing) and would hardly have expected them to be any more eloquent about my own flaws and failings. What good would a critique do, anyway? We can change ourselves only superficially, can improve ourselves, I sometimes think, not at all. By my age, and perhaps even your age, each of us has been incarcerated within her personality, has been left to forever pace the narrow cell of his character.

I don't need you to tell me what was lacking. I only need to know that something was.

Maybe you're on holiday. Or maybe there's been an illness. A death.

I don't know what to think. Your phone has been disconnected.

This can't be about me.

*

Do you know how many used bookstores there are in this city?

Twenty-seven. Four have someone named Angela working for them.

Naturally, you never told me your last name.

To be honest, I'm a little afraid to visit these shops. I'm a little afraid of what expression you might have on your face when you look up from the till or the shelving cart and see me standing there, dipping into Hardy or Bergson, nodding my head appreciatively, pretending to be transported by Hardy's divine prose or humbled by Bergson's perspicacity.

So I walk by, glance in windows, and do not see you.

I'm not pining for you. I liked what we had, I think, what there was of it. But now, to be honest, I hardly recall what you look like.

I am sick of being alone, though that's not what this is about. I don't know you well enough to know if you'd be a cure for solitude.

I'm only curious. I have an inquisitive mind. I am a scientist, after all. Science strives to shed light on those parts of the universe that remain veiled in darkness. Science pursues truth impersonally, dispassionately, disinterestedly.

"The aim of science," wrote Hegel, "is to divest the objective world of its strangeness and to make us more at home in it."

I'm not really lonely. I'm homesick.

I called one of the stores and asked, "Do you have an Angela who works there?"

"Yes," said the voice on the line, "this is she."

It didn't sound like you but nevertheless I panicked.

"Sorry, I think I must have the wrong number."

Brilliant.

It's an unofficial tradition in computer science that the first output of any new program should be the two words: "Hello, world."

I remember the first program I ever wrote, it must be nearly twenty years ago now, in an antiquated programming language aptly named BASIC. It was two lines long and ran as follows:

```
10 print "Hello, world!"
20 goto 10
```

This innocuous-looking program caused a cataract of "Hello, world!"s to spill down the left edge of the screen, ad infinitum, effectively crashing the computer.

At the time I thought it was funny. Now I think there's something depressing about a dumb machine stubbornly blurting out an endless stream of cheerful salutations to an oblivious, utterly indifferent world.

There are cafés across the street from two of the bookstores and a little parklet across from another. That left one shop uncongenial to surreptitious surveillance. I finally worked up the courage to go inside.

In an old jean jacket Chuck left behind one Christmas, a baseball cap that I paid too much for at a Sportmart, and with contact lenses on behind cheap aviator sunglasses, I don't look much like the man you met twice.

I'm incapable of walking out after half an hour of browsing without buying anything. Already I've spent almost seventy dollars on books I'll probably never read. Seventy dollars I can ill afford, now that I've used up the last of my paid sick leave for this year.

Christmas gifts. Do you like Thomas Hardy?

This Bergson chap isn't half bad in spots. My favourite lines so far:

> Our freedom, in the very movements by which it is affirmed, creates the growing habits that will stifle it if it fails to renew itself by a constant effort. It is dogged by automatism. The most living thought becomes frigid in the formula that expresses it. The word turns against the idea.

Though it contradicts itself. Here, at least, for once, the word serves the idea.

Besides, what alternative do we have?

I think I found you. Or maybe I should say that you found me.

I was puttering around Bob's Book Nook in my undercover outfit when I received a sharp tap on the shoulder.

"Can I help you with anything?"

The way he (Bob?) asked made it clear that he already knew the answer and could give it to me if I didn't.

"No thanks, just browsing really."

"Are you looking for anyone in particular?"

That "anyone" sent my heart clattering.

"I don't know. I'm really just looking around."

"I noticed. What's your name?"

"Jim," I said, before the strangeness of the question could occur to me. "Say, do you know what time it is?"

He raised the wristwatch arm automatically but overrode the reflex by keeping his eyes fixed on me.

"I have an appointment at two," I said. I could feel my own watch dangling just below the left cuff of my brother's jacket.

"It's well past three," he said, without having to look.

"Oh Christ," I muttered without much feeling, "thanks, sorry, I have to – excuse me."

Why would you tell your boss about me? You should have just talked to *me*.

"Listen, I work at Bob's Book Nook, but please don't come around. I'm sorry I didn't respond, but [circle one] (a) I was called out of town suddenly; (b) I've been in the hospital; (c) my computer crashed and I forgot my voice mail password and then the phone company cut off my service; (d) I was trying to let you down gently; (e) I wasn't really attracted to you physically; (f) my ex and I have decided to get back together; (g) aren't I a little too young for you?"

He did say "anyone" and not "anything," didn't he?

I spent most of this weekend sitting in coffee shops or walking along the river. Thinking. Making up stories.

I hate not being master of my own thoughts. There's nowhere I can go to get away from them.

I know that if I were to see you or talk to you it would probably only make matters worse.

But I would make it worse. I don't care. I'd make everything worse if I could.

*

"Bob's Book Nook," said someone other than Bob.

"Hi, I was wondering if Angela Roberts is working today."

"You mean Angela Hastings?"

"I don't think so. No. It can't be. I have the wrong number."

There's a "HASTINGS, A" in the book. The phone number's not your old disconnected one. There's an address too.

I sent you a letter.

I regret now the tortuous wording and the overly formal tone. But naturally I wanted to impress you with my calm, my reasonableness, my imperturbable sanity.

I didn't put my name or return address on the envelope. Not that I'm hiding anything. I was afraid you might toss it in the garbage, unopened. Of course I can't think of anything preventing you from tossing the thing after one quick glance at my name, lying there so vulnerably at the bottom of the third page. I have no way of knowing if you read a single word. You can't make someone listen and you can never know if they hear. All speech is prayer.

I got your machine. Your voice on the outgoing message sounded different. Maybe I just don't remember what you sound like.

I didn't leave a message. I didn't know what, short of everything, to say.

I would like to tell you everything. I would like to open myself up. I would like to show you my organs.

*

Where should I begin? You didn't read my letter. It's sitting here beside me on my desk, unopened. I can't understand that. The lack of curiosity.

I came by. You weren't home, at first.

I only stepped into the vestibule out of an obscure desire to see your name listed in the directory. There it was, two thirds of the way down the first column, for all the world to see. "Hastings Angela." I found it strangely touching, if also faintly obscene, the unguarded nonchalance of this little exposure, contrasting so strongly with the paranoid secrecy you apparently reserve for me.

Someone else entered the lobby. Reflexively, my fingers flew to the number pad. Because I had just been staring at it, I entered your code in a sort of delirious panic. (What if that was you who had just come in and now stood fumbling with her keys three feet behind me?) The intercom had just begun to ring when the woman behind me pulled open the door unnecessarily wide and, as a common gesture of politeness, held it open for a fraction of a second longer than necessary. Casually I reached out and caught the door before it swung shut. The intercom stopped ringing. I watched the woman, your buildingmate (it is appropriate that we have no word for these strangers, our accidental neighbours), stride purposefully into an elevator, jab a button, then stand glaring out at me. Still holding the door, I entered your code again, looked at my watch, bounced up and down in place a little, just like a man who'd come to visit someone he would be disappointed to find not at home. The elevator doors slid slowly shut like hands brought together in prayer. The intercom clicked off unapologetically, mid-purr.

I looked outside. The wet sky was fading from weak gold to grey above the leaf-strewn street. I went inside.

I wouldn't have entered if that woman had not, however briefly, held the door open for me. I was only being civil, only acknowledging her courtesy. Don't you feel obliged to put a little extra hurry in your step when someone lingers to hold a door for you, even though it's actually less trouble to pull the door open yourself when, in your own good time, you reach it?

I would never have climbed the stairs to your floor if you had answered the intercom. And I wouldn't have knocked if I'd heard any sound, even that of a television, coming from inside your apartment. And I would never have tried the doorknob if there'd been any response to the knock. In fact, I'd probably have sprinted away down the hall if I'd heard so much as approaching footsteps or the sound of your cat rubbing herself against the door. But there was nothing.

People don't leave their doors unlocked. It was so unexpected, so very odd, that I felt a visceral premonition that something was wrong. The thought occurred to me that you might be hurt. In one suffocatingly vivid flash I even saw you dead inside your apartment. You'd been lying there on the linoleum (I saw you in the bathroom, for some reason), lying there for weeks. Since the night we were supposed to meet, in fact. And wouldn't that have explained everything?

Pushing your door open and stepping inside, I half expected to be repulsed by the nauseating odour of decaying human flesh. Instead, I got roast chicken. I took this to be the memory of a meal, not the promise of one. If I'd turned right, gone into the kitchen first, I might have noticed the light on the stove.

I turned left, into the living room. Your cat was curled up on the sofa. She (to me, all cats are female until proven male; dogs the opposite) began humming like a radiator when I petted her but didn't crack an eyelid. I took this as a sort of welcome, I guess. I started looking around.

Where I grew up, we had one movie theatre. They screened exactly two movies a month. One show on a Friday, the same show the following Saturday, then a different flick the next Friday, and so on. There was no money in it. Everything was run by volunteers. Half a dozen men took turns threading scuffed-up reels into the projector and half a dozen women took turns watching the cashbox and supervising the couple dozen kids who took turns running the concession stand. My parents, I guess, were among the civic-minded. My dad was among the half-dozen men, my mom among the half-dozen women. And I, despite my limp protestations, was among the couple dozen kids. That meant we had a key to the theatre.

I borrowed it a few times. Mostly I just sat in the darkened theatre (I didn't know how to turn on the lights) and dreamed up my own movies. Sometimes I helped myself to stale popcorn. A couple of times I relieved the concession stand's change-drawer of its dimes. Once I filled my coat with Snickers, Oh Henry!s, wine gums, jawbreakers, and chocolate-covered cherries (which I didn't even like, and threw away rather than give them to my brother).

These little misdeeds gave me a thrill of a particular kind. When I unlocked the theatre door, after glancing casually up and down the street, I always felt a warm tingling in my belly that at first I confused with fear. Later, however, when I dumped my loot onto my bed and sat down to admire it, the pleasurable twinge I'd felt revealed its true nature. I discovered I had an erection.

I felt the same dimly erotic tug when I started looking around your apartment. Not an erection or the prelude to one, but a brief, not unpleasant prickly feeling in the gonads.

Why should going where one's not supposed to go be so exciting?

You scared the living hell out of me when you came back. And you can be sure the *frisson* vanished, just as it would have if my mom had walked in on me revelling in my plunder all those years ago. There's nothing sexy about getting caught.

My reconnaissance hadn't progressed beyond the living room. I'd only had time to stroke your cat, dreamily admire your furnishings, and discover my letter on the back of your sofa. Face up, unopened, like a piece of evidence being preserved for trial.

Then the sound of the doorknob turning, the hinges creaking, brought a scream up my throat like a bubble of blood. I must have swallowed it.

I ducked into a room, what turned out to be your bedroom, and, with all the inspired resourcefulness of the mortally petrified, hid myself behind the door. My lungs were labouring loudly in their effort to bring extra oxygen to my thundering heart. I battled with them and won, but only ended up more out of breath. For what felt like an hour, I could hear nothing but the thudding and wheezing of my own body. I was self-deafened and self-blinded. You could have walked in on me at any moment.

Slowly the clangour subsided, slowly the innocent domestic sounds of you preparing a meal – tap tap tap, clink clink, chop chop chop, snick snick – began to reach me through the fog of terror in my brain. You were whistling. The tune, which I've still got in my head, was maddeningly familiar. The odd thing about recognition is that it's felt most acutely when incomplete. No sense of familiarity, no *déjà vu* washes over me at the sight of my mother. But that woman on the bus . . . *Where* have I seen her? It's enough to drive a person crazy. I've spent hours trying to recall names or bring to mind specific words. It seems appropriate that it is the *tip of the tongue* that burrows so compulsively into all the unfamiliar nooks and grottoes of the mouth, no matter how tender those pockets, no matter how painful the probing. What were you whistling? Mozart, maybe, or one of Mendelssohn's string symphonies. Maybe this will be the first thing I ask you. The second.

I didn't know what to do. I couldn't stand there all night, but neither could I slip out unnoticed. Unless you took a shower . . . But your bathrobe was hanging on the back of the bedroom door, three inches from my face.

As for the blue bottle, the vase, the one on top of your armoire, the one filled with the pink plastic flowers and the unplastic pussy willows (my mother used to pick those too; I can still see them in their jam jar, on the table between us as we ate) – I can only plead fear, fuzzy thinking, self-defence. At the time, it seemed prudent and rational to arm myself. What if you came at me with a knife? I didn't know what you might be capable of. After all, I hardly know you.

I thought you were still in the kitchen. You surprised me. There you were, there we both were, facing each other in the doorway.

I don't think I would have done it if you hadn't screamed like that.

I can understand it, of course. Suddenly face to face, in your own home, with . . . who? A thief? Stalker? Abductor?

Tell me – *this* will be the first thing I ask – did you recognize me? Did you have time to, before you screamed? Because I don't think so. I don't think you could have. I hardly recognized *you*. We'd met in dark bars, weeks ago. You'd done something to your hair.

I think I can understand how you must have felt. But that scream! To scream like that – what good does it do? What does it *say*?

Was it a cry for help? A cry for help is something, at least. An attempt at communication of a sort. At the time, though, it sounded less like language than a yelp of pain. As though I'd already hit you.

As a cry for help it wasn't wasted. Almost immediately there was a knock at the door. This time it was perhaps good that I wasn't thinking straight, that I called out: "Come in, come in, the door's not locked," because your neighbour helped me carry you down to my car. I couldn't have done it alone. I wouldn't have tried.

I told him, your buildingmate, that you'd tripped over the cat, hit your head, smashed the vase, screamed and passed out when you saw the blood. I don't think he completely believed me. But I was obviously distressed, lunging about your apartment like a lunatic. I kept insisting that we had to do something, had to get you help, take you to a hospital. So don't blame him. What would you have done in his shoes, ask to see my ID?

None of this was an act. I really did, at that moment, have every intention of rushing you to the hospital. In fact, it was the only thought in my head. I'd checked that you were breathing, that your heart was beating, but I had no idea what kind of damage I might have done. What if I'd cracked your skull or something?

What if I hadn't?

The only thing that terrified me more than the thought that you might not come to was the thought that you would, there in the back seat of my car, while I was driving.

When you started mumbling I almost veered off the road. I was relieved, of course, that you were okay or were going to be. But I was soon overwhelmed by alarm. You were about to wake up. What if you started screaming again? Hurt, bleeding, in the back of some strange car. How you would have screamed!

I'd never given much thought to how difficult it is to make someone who doesn't want to be unconscious unconscious. There had been times when I'd been ill and exhausted and wanted nothing more than to be nothing for a few hours. And I'd been unable to knock myself out. The body fails us, hurts us, falls apart on us. But when we want it to just go to sleep, the body has ideas of its own.

Pretty soon you were forming words and half sentences. Then, quite clearly, you asked, "Where are we going?"

I didn't know what else to do.

I would have cleaned you up a bit and brought something down for you to eat if you'd only stayed blacked out a little longer. If you hadn't started trying to stand up. If you hadn't given me that sad, hateful, bewildered look and asked, "Why are you doing this?"

I'm sorry about the rope and the gag. It seems cartoonish, I know – something out of a gangster movie. But I didn't know what else to do. I needed time. Time to explain myself.

I just looked at the clock. Almost eleven. You really will be hungry by now. I could order something. I'm not much of a cook. I guess I don't understand what people see in food. Eating bores me. I make whatever's fast and easy. Bacon and eggs, grilled cheese, soup, french fries. I take a lot of empty cans to the recycling depot.

"Why are you doing this?" That's what you asked me.

Why am I doing this? Why am I doing what? What am I doing?

I'm trying to explain. Trying to tell you everything. Trying to make you understand.

Haven't you been paying attention?

Maybe it's my fault. Maybe I should start again. From the beginning. Tell you everything. I'll be clear. I'll choose my words with care. I'll get it right. The word shall not turn against the idea.

But where do I start? How far back should I go? This morning? That day in Bob's Book Nook? The night you stood me up? (*Did* you stand me up? I still don't know. After all this, I'm still in the dark.) The night we met?

The last time I was really drawn to a woman? The last time I was on a date?

The day I met my wife? The day I proposed to her? The day she left?

The delirious afternoon I lost my virginity to Eloise Parker, who was supposed to be my brother's girl?

The moment I discovered that there was, after all, nothing wrong with me – that I too was capable of loving and of being loved?

THE BLACK GANG

I

Geoffrey would never understand the rapturous sighs that escaped his sisters' lips as they stood pressed against the promenade railing, as though they could not imagine a fate more romantic than tumbling down into the tumbling waves below. He had needed no more than a single glance to see the ocean for what it was: a cold expanse of grey water, a collection of drool in the gaping maw of the idiot earth. His father was a bridge builder – or, rather, the financier of bridge builders, the owner and exploiter of men who built bridges – and, though Geoffrey despised his father's work, he nevertheless felt that here was a spot that could use a few Stanislee Steel bridges: that, at least, would be one way to divest the sea of its cheap romance. The Atlantic Ocean was a river that did not go anywhere. He refused even to look at it.

After three days out his stomach continued to lurch in response to the incessant roll and pitch of the ship; and no matter how calm the waves, how still the deck beneath him, he seemed always to be stumbling and swaying across some invisible rugged terrain.

My knees, to which I have never wittingly done any injustice, have betrayed me and become like butter. My feet and my head do not seem to be attached to the same torso. As everyone is only too overjoyed to inform me, I have yet to get my "sea legs."

On second thought, he would not include this in his letter to Daniels, nor in the article to which it would serve as preface. He was afraid such a disclosure, so unrelievedly personal, might strike the wrong note. He did not want Daniels or Higgins or anyone else at the *Tribune* to be able to accuse him of aristocratic self-absorption.

Perhaps he could somehow incorporate that bit about his torso into a letter to Meredith Quigley. But he would not write to Meredith Quigley.

As the impromptu tour group made their halting way along the promenade deck, Mr. Harbrow drew their attention, quite unnecessarily, to the sunning chairs (empty, of course: the weather had been unremittingly vile since they had put out), to the boys playing quoits, and to the lifeboats in their davits, of which Harbrow seemed rather proud. He went into some detail about their construction, their weight, size, capacity, and number (more than enough to accommodate all the passengers and crew, he assured them), but none of the party displayed any interest: Mrs. Galston, the wife of the factory owner, looked at Harbrow as though he had spit something out onto her plate; Geoffrey's mother said that it

was "a pity" the boats took up so much deckspace; his father
and the other men passed by without even a glance, mur-
muring and puffing at their wet cigars. Geoffrey remained
behind, staring with stubborn appreciation at the boats,
lashed down and wrapped up in white canvas like mummies
or madmen.

"Don't worry, they are perfectly seaworthy."

The Galston girl, who had been given some such ridiculous name as Lily or April or Summer, stood at his elbow,
suppressing the perpetual giggle of the bourgeoisie.

"We had to take one into shore in Liverpool last winter,
if you can believe it. Some fool had spilled coal all over the
dock and in the harbour."

"That is not," said Geoffrey evenly, "what I was thinking
about."

He shifted his feet as the deck tilted beneath them. The
girl, however, behaved as though he had fully stumbled, and
quite needlessly reached out a hand to steady him. He did
not thank her.

"First time at sea?" she giggled.

Behind her, his sisters Maisie and Lucasta looked on in
exquisite amusement, their shoulders shaking, their eyes
moist.

"We are vacationing," he muttered, because it was the sim-
plest thing to say. But he was ill content with this bourgeois
word, and struggled to explain himself. "That is, my family is
vacationing. I am here in order to do what I suppose you
might call research."

In truth, he did not know why exactly he had come
(unless it had something to do with the fact that not coming
had not been on offer). His father and mother were pleased

to describe the trip as an educational adventure, an overdue lesson in history, culture, and geography for their unworldly children – by which they could only mean Geoffrey, who was due to matriculate to the university next year.

But Geoffrey had no intention of going to his father's university; and besides, he was certain that the real motive for the voyage had nothing to do with him: Walter Stanislee was, in fact, going abroad for his health. The air, his parents had been told, was more salubrious in the Old World.

Geoffrey took satisfaction in the irony that his father was, despite his outward pretension of vitality, despite all his blustering activity, in actuality a weak and frail man, a man who, though he exploited the wage-labour of a force in excess of four hundred men, had not the physical where-withal to lift a hammer or drive a single spike.

Only under capitalism, with its systematic inequalities, can such a state of affairs obtain. Only under capitalism can the weak thus thrive. Is this outrageous imbalance not a decisive illustration of the inevitability of the proletarian revolution? In the end, as Darwin has felicitously demonstrated, it is the fittest that survive.

With his balding pate, flabby belly, and girlish wrists, Walter Stanislee reminded his son more of the aging apes he had seen pulling out their own hair in the Zoological Gardens in Boston than of a real man. "Nervous exhaustion" and "neurasthenia" were the terms the doctors used; but Geoffrey preferred another word: obsolescence.

At the edge of Geoffrey's vision a black shadow passed. Up ahead there seemed to be some commotion among the men. He pulled away from the Galston girl with an air of grim alertness, like a doctor called to dress a wound.

"Now now," Harbrow was crooning. "Nothing broken, I hope and trust?"

Walter Stanislee shook his big bald head. "I was not watching my way."

"Nor, it seemed, was your dancing partner," said Stebbins, his man.

"Not even a 'beg your pardon,'" said Lucasta, with unsurprised disgust.

"He looked just like a gorilla," squealed the child.

"Constance," said Geoffrey's mother in vague admonition.

"Well now, ma'am," said Harbrow, with factitious good humour, striving to give the impression of still leading the party on its tour. "They tell me we are one and all descended from the gorillas, every mother's son of us."

Geoffrey made a scoffing noise.

"I should rather have a gorilla for an uncle," chortled Mr. Galston, "than something like *that*," he said, nodding in the direction the black shadow had gone.

Nothing irritated Geoffrey more than a superficial understanding of Darwin. Men like his father, Harbrow, and this Galston fool, who spoke so lightly of the origin of species and the descent of man, were worse than the church officials who had stubbornly refused to look through Galileo's telescope. *Those* old ostriches had at least appreciated the enormity of the debate; they had realized, if nothing else, what was at stake. With his father's friends it was quite otherwise: they had looked, and they had laughed.

What they none of them understood was that, simply put, the line between Man and Animal had been erased – or revealed, rather, to have been artificial all along. It was not enough to say, as porters and publicans and factory owners were so tickled to say, that Man had descended from Gorilla; one had to go further: Man *was* a Gorilla. Man was a beast; his claim to demigodhood had been repealed. There remained standing nothing between him and the jungle. His bones had been found in the swamps and forests; the swamp and the forest were in his bones.

This it was that the intelligent critics, like Soapy Sam Wilberforce, feared and fled from. The unintelligent, like Galston, spoke glibly of the forest as of a thicket, and never looked properly into it; or, if they looked, did not see.

"What was that . . . *man* doing on the promenade deck at all?" Mrs. Galston wailed.

"He was very, very dirty," said Constance scoldingly.

"That was not dirt, young miss," said Harbrow, arching his eyebrows enigmatically.

Maisie groaned. "It was coal dust," she said, in the wearily omniscient tone that she had affected since her debut. She added through a grimace, like one passing a stone, "Steamships run on coal, you know."

"Now that is a fact, miss," said Harbrow, rediscovering his tour guide's tone. "Nine hundred tons of coal, to be exact. Fourteen bunkers above, twenty-six below, filled to the brim. That is where our dusty old friend must have been headed – the bunker hatch."

"All the same," said Mrs. Galston, by no means mollified. "They should be kept belowdecks."

"Out of sight," Mr. Galston agreed, sucking aggrievedly on the stub of his cigar. "Where they belong."

Here, Geoffrey sensed with excited scorn, was more

material for the article – the "piece," as he supposed Daniels would call it – that was slowly taking shape, like a daguerreotype plate in its developing box, in the dim but fertile recesses of his mind. Here was yet another concrete illustration of what he sensed might become a running theme in the piece, perhaps indeed the very keynote of the entire work: the wilful blindness of the bourgeoisie.

> Just as the controller of capital turns a blind eye to the deplorable conditions of the labourers he exploits, so do the so-called upper classes, in their never-ending hunt for greater ease and luxury, wilfully blind themselves to the distasteful conditions that make their leisure possible.

He turned phrases over in his head like a jeweller appraising fine gems, regretting only that there had not been time after lunch to return to his cabin for his notebook and pencil.

It would be his first piece published in *The Worker's Tribune*, though not the first he had penned. He had, a few months ago, spent several hours interviewing and observing Mrs. Gretl, the woman to whom the Stanislees sent their dirty linen, and whose long hours of back-breaking labour under deplorable conditions of sweltering squalor he had described at some length and detail, and with not a little ferocious (but restrained) indignation. Higgins – Geoffrey had no doubt that it had been Higgins – had summarily rejected the article, ostensibly because Mrs. Gretl controlled her own means of production (the laundry, it turned out, belonged to her) and was thus to be classified as *petit* bourgeoisie. Daniels, to his credit, had, in a handwritten post-script, praised Geoffrey for his manifest passion and for the vividness of his prose, paying particular tribute to the harrowing description of the woman's carbolic-ravaged hands – a detail whose rich symbolic import might have been missed by a lesser editor, and which Geoffrey himself believed he had brought off rather well. Geoffrey still had the rejection letter, locked in his *escritoire* back in Boston. He had, once the sting of disappointment had faded, decided to start a collection of such letters (they were sure to be rarities), and perhaps someday, with ironic humility, he would have them framed and hung in his study. (The article itself, returned by Daniels by post, Geoffrey had, with an artistic impulsiveness he now regretted, set aflame.)

"He looked just like our *negro*," Constance babbled happily.

"Well now, that is just precisely why we call them the Black Gang, young miss."

The grey sky descended, squeezing out a gust of wind. The deck beneath them lurched; Geoffrey stumbled.

"Oh Walter," cried his mother, "your *suit*."

Meanwhile Poll, Constance's fat negro nurse, went on grumbling and dabbing at the black smudge that had been left, like a giant thumbprint, on his father's lapel.

The man did not look well.

Harbrow showed them the swimming pool, half filled to avoid spillage in rough weather; the racquets room, newly installed this autumn past; the gymnasium, crowded with all manner of equipment designed to exercise the inactive muscles during long days at sea; the little library, lacking, of course, any edition in any language of the *Communist Manifesto*; the saloon (which they had all seen already), with its gaudy domed ceiling, anemic-looking piano player, and crisp waiters, tucked inside their uniforms like Japanese *origami* and dashing about like battlefield medics with tinkling carafes of ice-water; and finally the ladies' *boudoir*, or lounge, with its quaint little hearth, which burned smokelessly and (in case of the unthinkable) was framed on either side by two gleaming steam annihilators, looking more like clumsy flower-pots than devices for fighting fire.

"Where does that go?" asked Constance, pointing to a door on which were inscribed the words NO PASSENGERS BEYOND THIS POINT PLEASE.

"Down to steerage," Lucasta said with a smirk.

His sister was, in fact, not far from correct. Geoffrey had been through just such a door the previous day, when he had paid Lacklin, his steward, to take him down and show him his quarters. These had, like the steward himself, rather proved a disappointment. Though it was true that the boy was required to share his room with three others, there was in this room none of the claustrophobic sordor, none of the fetid desperation and subdued rage that Geoffrey had been given to understand typified cramped workers' accommodations the world over. The bunks were bigger, the mattresses softer, the blankets heavier, the electric lights brighter than Geoffrey had imagined they would be. There was a shaving sink and a rather surprisingly capacious clothes locker. On the whole, the room was larger and cleaner and altogether much less oppressive than Geoffrey had expected. The crew, it seemed, were "making do" in conditions not far removed from those of the steerage passengers. This was good news for the crew, Geoffrey supposed, but bad news for his article.

As for Lacklin himself, Geoffrey soon saw that he would be of next to no use to him, either. The steward had obstinately refused to countenance the possibility that the work he was being paid (by the hour!) to do was in any way demeaning. Geoffrey recognized that this proud stance was only a defensive reflex, an instinct of self-preservation, but that did not make it any less exasperating. Nor did the steward endear himself to his would-be advocate, comrade, and liberator by extorting from Geoffrey a "gratuity" for every service or favour rendered that fell outside the strict corpus of his duties.

It was not, he supposed, Lacklin's fault. He recalled the words of Marx: *The bourgeoisie has left remaining no other nexus between man and man than naked self-interest, than callous "cash payment."* Nevertheless, Geoffrey vowed to waste no more time on stewards.

"Where does it go?" the child persisted.

Harbrow, ignored by his audience, ignored the question. Instead he put his hand to his face as though contemplating a plan of unutterable daring and audacity.

"I wonder," he mumbled, "I wonder . . . Would anyone like to meet the Captain?"

Captain Stegnan was bowed, as though from pain, over the chart table when the tour party silently entered the wheelhouse. Harbrow smiled uncertainly at his group and, drawing himself to his full height, loudly cleared his throat. The Captain popped up like a cork from a champagne bottle.

"O-hoy," he cried. "What have we here? Are these the new seamen you have brought me at last?" The Captain cupped a hand to one side of his mouth and lowered his voice to a bellow. "I must say, Mr. Harbrow, they are a rather hobbledehoy-looking lot."

Harbrow, with noticeably less alacrity than he had evinced half an hour earlier, introduced the men – giving their name, their company, their industry, a brief ode to their preeminence therein (less, it seemed to Geoffrey, for the Captain's ears, than for their own). Of this man's wife or that man's children, Harbrow made only glancing mention, thus reducing two thirds of his audience to the status of chattels or *accoutrements*. (The servants – Stebbins, Poll, and Galston's man – were not even conferred this much existence.)

Grinning and nodding oafishly, Captain Stegnan clapped his hands together and extended them like an offering. "I welcome you all aboard the *S.S. Vanguard*."

His sisters and the Galston girl were charmed; but Geoffrey was cynically sure that, like Harbrow's sudden whim to "drop in on" him, the Captain's reception was all a performance – one with all the subtlety of a pantomime or Punch and Judy show. The celerity with which Stegnan launched into his speech only reinforced this impression.

"Four hundred forty-four feet in length," began his rumbling litany, ominous as distant thunder; "four thousand nine-hundred ninety-two tons unencumbered; room and strength enough for up to five thousand tons more in her eleven cargo holds. Her speed a stunning seventeen knots in weather favourable, fifteen without fail in any other; eight days thirteen hours, reliably and regularly, from continent to continent. Her keel was laid in 1872, the tip of her topmast completed in February 1873. Aye, twenty-two stupendous years plunging through the waves, come typhoon, come high water, come the devil himself."

His sisters, of course, were near swooning, but Geoffrey felt obscurely disappointed by the bridge. There seemed to be less equipment and gadgetry in evidence than he would have imagined necessary to pilot a five-thousand-ton steamship across the ocean. No doubt he had been under an exaggerated (even romantic) impression of the difficulty of that task; apparently crossing the Atlantic, which he could not help but notice lay before them like a tatty blanket of dirty wool, required no more vigour or finesse than conducting a train down the railroad's tracks.

The wheel was really just a big wheel, and the wheelman's only duty, apparently, was to prevent it from turning. The compass, chronometer, and sextant were clever devices that had been invented years ago by clever men, and passed down, with careful instructions, to men who need never ponder why or how they worked. The Chadburn telegraph, in particular, incited Geoffrey's disdain: with its big gilded handle and its simple commands in big black letters – FULL, HALF, and SLOW, AHEAD or ASTERN – it looked like a toy, a child's idea of what a ship's controls should look like.

Stegnan, catching his glance, perhaps, and mistaking disdain for puzzlement, explained – as though it were not self-explanatory – that the telegraph transmitted his or the first mate's order to the engine room, where the chief engineer, alerted by a ringing bell, received the order on a Chadburn of his own – which *he* then put into action.

"Can we see the engine room?" asked Constance.

"Well, now," said Harbrow, "the engine room, you see, is a very hot, very loud, very dark and dirty, very *dangerous* place."

The child pouted. The Captain crossed his arms over his chest and eyed her appraisingly.

"Perhaps that does not dissuade you? Perhaps you are made of sterner stuff?"

The men chuckled; the women smiled indulgently. Constance scowled at everyone, uncomprehending, certain only that the wheels of injustice had been set inexorably in motion.

In the end, it was decided that the ladies had seen enough. The women and children would return to the lounge, while the men – Galston and his man Holroyd, Aitkin and his brother, Stebbins and Geoffrey's father – would complete their tour with a descent into the ship's "netherregions" (a phrase of Captain Stegnan's that caused Mrs. Galston visible distress).

"Will you go?" the Galston girl asked Geoffrey.

"Oh, I don't know." He had no real desire to see more of the ship, nor to spend more time in the odious company of the likes of Galston or the Captain; he was, however, distinctly keen not to be left behind with the women and children.

"Oh, but you *should.*"

Thinking of his cabin, with its little steam-pipe stove, his slippers and his dressing-robe, his trunk of books, his note-papers arranged neatly upon the desk, he said, "I thought I *might* do a spot of work . . ."

He felt his father, whose gaze he had been avoiding, place a hand on his shoulder.

"I am not . . . feeling well at the moment. Geoffrey will go."

Harbrow cast a quick inquisitive glance in Walter Stanislee's direction; the hand on Geoffrey's shoulder tightened in a limp squeeze, then fell away; and Harbrow's gaze slid sideways and settled on him.

Constance sneered, her eyes ablaze with miserable envy.

Geoffrey sneered back. God, what a perfect little fool she was.

After descending another staircase they reached at last an elaborate hatchway. The Captain was explaining the role of this door in the event ("Quite unthinkable event," Harbrow hastened to reassure them) that the ship were to take on water. It had something to do with automatic mechanisms and sealed bulkheads and Geoffrey, though in some obscure way he felt expected, even required, to pay attention, found none of it very interesting.

"A hundred to one are the odds," Captain Stegnan was saying, "that you'll die of thirst at sea as against drowning. Scarce indeed is the ship afloat today that won't outlive her most stalwart passenger or steeliest mate; the captain given the chance to go down with his charge is a dying breed. A brig like the *Vanguard* can lap up no less than three thousand tons of briny deep and keep her head above water for weeks, months. Do what you will to her," he growled, "she will not sink. Be she swamped, flooded, turned turtle, or set afire, she'll stay afloat. Aye, and more's the danger to her sister ships."

Geoffrey was more intrigued by the Captain himself than his disquisition. He seemed to have undergone a change since their descent belowdecks: his voice was deeper, his movements slower yet more assured, his demeanour more grave, as though the bulk of the ship or the sea weighed more heavily upon him down here. Perhaps it was only the absence of the women and children that had wrought this transformation (if transformation was not too lofty a word for it); Geoffrey had seen many men – real men, men's men, not like his father – drained of all *savoir-faire* and dignity in the presence of children.

"Each year I meet men who ask me why today's steamer needs a captain, men whose idea of pushing across the Atlantic is to take aim at the horizon and throttle her full steam ahead. Each year what these men look out upon from their Portknockie or their Coney Island and see as but a wide and vacant void, no more treacherous than a snow-covered meadow, becomes more and more like a churning trash heap, a dancing graveyard, a roiling black inferno littered with lost ships, lost cargo, lost souls. Flotsam clogs her valleys and jetsam crowns her peaks. Everywhere dross, detritus, and dead ships lie in wait, with murderous intent, for the blind and unwary. At fifteen knots a steamer collides with the capsized hull of a derelict schooner like a keg of dynamite. *There's* the peril of your indomitable buoyancy: today's ship *will not sink*. Her skeleton, unburied, unmourned, drifts endlessly like one of Hades' shades."

Whatever the reason, Stegnan had shed his clownishness; and in its place Geoffrey thought he detected a sort of battered worldliness or beleaguered cynicism that he could almost (with self-conscious largesse) recognize as kindred. As the Captain went on with his exposition, Geoffrey began to form a fresh impression of the man as a sort of regal caged animal: a circus bear, perhaps, balancing upon a bright red ball for his dinner. But beneath the fur there beat, at the rate of the tides, a sailor's salt-encrusted heart.

Was the man proletarian or bourgeois? he wondered.

The Captain shouldered open another portal, but paused in the passageway.

"There are ships lost at sea still. You'll have heard, I suppose, of *The Brunswick*? No? A 280-foot freighter she was, 2,485 tons, capable of twelve knots with the wind at her chin. Left Liverpool for New York November 19, 1869. Not seen again till February – of 1874."

"Five years!" gasped Aitkin's brother, his moustache trembling.

"Aye, nearly five years the interim. It was *The May Parade*, under Captain William Roscoe (whom I knew), that came upon her, drifting like a phantom, showing nary a sign of life, nor evidence of any stripe or species that she was aught but, as they say of the body after the soul has departed, an empty shell."

"The ship was deserted?" queried Aitkin's brother.

The Captain pursed his lips, as though at some unpleasant taste remembered. "An empty shell."

"But whatever became of them?" asked Stebbins. "The passengers, the crew? What happened to –"

"All that can be said with certainty is that they were none of them ever seen or heard from again."

"And what of the lifeboats?" said Galston querulously. "Surely they did not every man Jack of them sit cozy as cottage pie in their sun chairs till –"

A hiccuping bleat rose from Captain Stegnan's throat and lifted his head as though it were on a hinge.

"Did they not *have* lifeboats?" demanded Galston.

The Captain slowly lowered his head. "A lifeboat is a fancy bit of wreckage that one clings to," he said contemptuously. "A lifeboat is but a gulp of air in your lungs before you go under."

Aitkin came softly to Galston's aid. "But Mr. Harbrow

said that a good lifeboat is as sturdy as a little island. He showed us –"

"An island indeed," said Stegnan. "You can no more paddle a lifeboat out of the middle of the Old Atlantic than you could an island." His gaze flashed pityingly in Harbrow's direction. "Nay, no matter how many push-ups or chin-lifts you do of a morn."

The narrow tunnel they stood in tilted madly as the ship slid sidelong into a trough; but in the absence of any relative cues it appeared as though they had all leaned over in almost perfectly choreographed unison. Aitkin and Galston's man quite lost their footing.

"But what *happened* to them all?" moaned Aitkin's brother.

"None know. Some say fire. Some say disease. Others say pirates. Still others say mutiny – foul play."

Geoffrey sucked in his breath. "What do *you* say?"

Stegnan peered, unseeing, in Geoffrey's direction. "I? I suppose I say hurricane. There are waves the likes of which'll convince even the saltiest seaman that his vessel is sinking fast."

Geoffrey frowned but said nothing. He did not, by any means, think this the most plausible explanation – nor the most satisfying – at all. A hurricane! Indeed!

The engine room, after the drab and silent austerity of the corridors they had passed down to arrive at it, was overwhelming. There had been in those corridors no fore-warning, no presentiment: on the instant they were upon it, inside it, looking down on it from a platform above. To Geoffrey the sight was a cloudburst, a *coup de foudre*, a visceral blow.

There was more to see, more going on, than he could process, yet he was dizzyingly aware of his eyes registering every detail, like mean little meticulous clerks recording debts in a vast ledger. For the longest time he could form no idea of what he was looking at. Naturally, as a writer and thinker, his propensity was to view the things that composed the world as elaborate index cards, of varying perspicuity, for the words of which they were instantiations. But here the woeful inadequacy of his catalogue was at last revealed. He could not get a handhold on this world or its things. Such labels as he had collected – pipe, gear, duct, flue, bolt, piston, belt, screw, chamber, and the like – seemed to have no application to the gallimaufry before him. He felt as Adam on the day of his creation.

The thought occurred to him that he might be sick. He closed his eyes at the absurdity of this possibility (only after a few moments bethinking himself to put a hand over his eyes in a gesture that might pass for deep or difficult meditation).

The Captain's voice reached him again above the din, and though he paid no attention to what was being said, the words, the mere flow of human speech, calmed and soothed him, like the reassuring gurgle of an eavestrough in a rainstorm.

"Feeling quite all right, sir?" inquired Harbrow.

Geoffrey wondered what this man would be doing after the revolution. Laundry, perhaps.

"Fine," he said. "Quite."

"Some of her," Stegnan was crowing, "is, in truth, as young as she looks. This beauty, the heart of her heart, as you might say, was put in sometime near on towards the end of the great slump, might have been '88 I reckon" – Stegnan eyed Harbrow superciliously, as a pupil might eye his doubting teacher – "when more and more gentlemen renewed their interest in getting things from the wrong end of the ocean to the right."

"The boilers," added Harbrow, "were also replaced at that time. The new 'scotch' or 'fire-tube' boilers burn much more efficiently than the 'water-tube' style that preceded them. We used to burn through nearly three tons an hour; now it has dropped almost to half that."

"*And* a new propeller. Don't forget the propeller and shaft, which bumped no less than two full knots onto her gallop."

Galston took off his spectacles, looked through them at arm's length, and returned them to his nose. "So you," he said, "or she – the ship – the engine – it uses, what did you say, about one and a half tons of coal an hour?"

"Oh, more than that," assured the Captain, who was clearly not much impressed by Harbrow's efficiency. "Two is what I should wager. Why, on our last crossing alone we fired up more than six hundred –"

"That was an anomaly," said Harbrow. "You put in at extra ports. And the quality of coal was substandard."

"Coal's coal," said the Captain. "Carried us across the drink, didn't it?"

"The Captain does not always read the reports. Nor does the Captain often see the inside of a furnace or communicate with our stokers. Nor is he expected to. But Llewellyn – our chief engineer – was quite unequivocal. Uneven combustion, high percentage of clinkers – bad coal. Not our usual supplier. Test mine. We are being reimbursed. An altogether untypical trip, you see. Over the last dozen voyages prior the *Vanguard* averaged only 471 tons per crossing."

"Still comes out to more than two an hour," mused Galston.

"Aye, two tons, as I said," said Stegnan gleefully. "She's a hungry ship. Two tons an hour, that's her feed. Two tons of coal shovelled into her fiery belly every hour of the live long day."

"Two on average, only on average." Harbrow touched his kerchief to the side of his brow and inspected it. "Much of that is spent in manoeuvring. In and out of port, around bad weather, that kind of thing. Out at sea, under a constant heading, that will drop significantly."

Galston turned his head and looked thoughtfully at Geoffrey. "I'm surprised," he said, like one confiding a secret. "But hell – coal's cheap."

"Come," said Stegnan, lifting one arm above his head in a rabble-rousing gesture. "Let's all go together, shall we, and see the inside of a furnace."

II

The engine room had surprised him, but it was the sight of the boiler room that remained in his head, like a painting hung on one of its walls, over the next two days. It was this image that he sat for hours at his desk trying to recreate in prose, a *duvet* wrapped around his frame to buffer him from the bitter draught that had begun to slither in through his cabin window no matter how tightly he latched it. How he wished he were belowdecks, in one of the cozy little steerage rooms, with their proximity to the boilers and their portholes that could not in any weather be opened. It was impossible to get any work done in such surroundings as these, with the child next door bickering pettishly with Poll, shadows darkening his drape every five minutes as another pair of layabout saloon passengers took yet another *faute-de-mieux* stroll along the same old promenade, and all about him there pulsed the chit-chattering thrum of hysterical idiots feigning gaiety at sea.

The Black Gang is the quintessential exemplar of the dehumanizing exploitation of the proletariat by the bourgeoisie.

He stared at this sentence for several minutes. At last he dipped his pen and in one confident slash crossed out *quintessential*, eventually writing beneath it, after another minute, and with less bravado, *ultimate*. Fifteen minutes later he had crossed this out and replaced it with *perfect*, crossed out *perfect*, replaced *exemplar* with *symbol* and then *apotheosis*, and finally blotted out *is* in preferment of *represents*. Then he rewrote the sentence in its entirety.

The Black Gang represents the apotheosis of the dehumanizing exploitation of the proletariat by the bourgeoisie.

He was not displeased. At the same time, he was keenly aware of not yet having provided his readers any tangible evocation of the image that so haunted him. It would be necessary, he realized, to ply his pen like a painter's brush if he was to limn that scene in the boiler room. In his mind, in fact, he saw it as a woodcut, its lines stark, tortuous, precise, its dark figures locked like Sisyphuses in a frieze of

eternal gloom and toil. The ovens clanking and creaking dys-
peptically; the glowing coals as bright and hard and round
as orange cakes of paint; the blue fires blazing steadily,
almost soundlessly; the trimmers and passers, shovels aloft,
moving like mercury around one another, their skin soft and
supple as burnt and blistered wax, their sleek and gnarled
bodies glistening blackly with sweat and steam . . . The con-
founded lines of Blake kept ringing in his head, and in an
effort to exorcize them he wrote them down.

> *What immortal hand or eye*
> *Could frame thy fearful symmetry?*

As he dotted the question mark with a purgative flourish
of finality there was to be heard a sound like chthonic
thunder, a low yawning groan as of a mountain pulling up its
roots, that arose from deep within the bowels of the ship and
sent shudders up through its frame, causing the floor beneath
his chair to tremble for a moment before it subsided.

Then came silence.

Then came the dinner bugle, shattering the silence.

He swore, threw down his pen, and tossed off the *duvet*.
It was impossible to think, let alone to write, in these conditions. He might as well get dressed for dinner.

After some deliberation, he sat down next to Maisie, who
could be trusted not to speak to him, spread his book – *The
Expression of the Emotions in Man and Animals* – on the table,
and planted his elbows like posts on either side. But it was
soon apparent that he would not be able to concentrate.

Across the table, his mother and Mrs. Galston were gibbering excitedly.

"It sounded to *me* as though we had run aground of something."

"Are there islands this far out?"

"Perhaps we have hit an iceberg."

"It *is* that time of year, I suppose?"

"I do hope it's nothing *too* serious."

"But it cannot be. We're due in London Friday."

"What do *you* think it was?"

April Galston had somehow materialized in the seat next to his. She had not been there when he had chosen his seat, he was certain of that.

He blinked at her. "What do I think *what* was?"

She treated this as a jolly good jest. "They have stopped the engines, too," she whispered happily.

"That's nonsense," he said. But, in fact, he *had* felt some change come over the ship since the groaning sound; not till now had he been able to put his finger on it. There was less noise. He had not been consciously aware of any sound or vibrations emanating from the engines but he was aware now of their absence.

He became aware too, as he lifted his head, of the general buzz of suppressed elation. All around him passengers were clucking and cooing and smacking their mouths with relish at their own delicious bewilderment as the speculations passed their lips.

"Why do they not put on the lights," he murmured, noticing for the first time the rows of candles burning at every table. The vast domed room was refulgent and, if not for the continuous rolling of the ship as it was buffeted by the wind and waves, would almost have seemed festive.

Maisie snorted. "The electricity is *out*, you fool."

"They have stopped the engines," April Galston repeated.

They all looked up as a man came clattering through the saloon entrance, then stopped and stood there wild-eyed and panting, like an animal having burst out of the forest onto a road milling with humans. Heads rotated silently in his direction. The *maître*, without seeming to move his feet, approached the interloper and, leaning in towards him with a sort of menacing servility, uttered some pointed query or command.

"The Captain," the man was at last able to gasp. "Where's the Captain? We've got to tell the Captain –"

But the *maître* and two other stewards were already guiding the dishevelled man back through the door.

"Steerage," was Mrs. Galston's curt diagnosis.

There had, Geoffrey thought, been something peculiar about the man's trousers. They had appeared to be wet.

"I *hope* it's not an iceberg," said April, like one expressing a hope that she might shake hands with the Queen. "Would that not be just too utterly devastating?"

"I imagine, my dear," said Mr. Galston from the far end of the table, "that it was nothing more 'devastating' than some of the cargo coming loose and tipping over in one of the holds."

"But didn't you *hear* that sound, Father? It was . . . smashing, crashing –"

"A large drum of oil," said Galston, unfolding his napkin one corner at a time, "or a crate of sheet metal, improperly secured with dunnage. Nothing to be alarmed about."

"But, were that so, why would we have stopped the engines?" asked Geoffrey's mother.

"In order to sort things out a bit down there, I should suppose."

Captain Stegnan, Geoffrey saw, was not at his table.

"But why," persisted his mother, "should we need to completely cut the engines, unless we –"

"Lois, please," said Geoffrey's father. "Really. All this clapwaddle is giving me a splintering pain in my head. You heard what Harbrow said. There's nothing whatever the matter with the ship."

At that, the table fell to silent perusal of their meal cards.

"Harbrow was here?" Geoffrey asked.

April Galston lifted one shoulder.

"What did he say?"

"That nothing was wrong, I guess."

"What exactly did he say?"

"Oh, I don't remember *exactly*. You know: that there was nothing for any of us to worry about, that it was all being taken care of, that sort of thing."

"Attended to," Maisie corrected. "'Being attended to,' he said."

"But did he not say what's happened, what has actually occurred?"

"Geoffrey." His mother uttered his name like a reproof. "You heard your father."

He was negotiating again that invisible terrain; his head was not attached to the same torso as his feet. "Did none of you *ask*?"

"I suppose we did not think it any of our business," chirped Mrs. Galston.

"The important thing," said Walter Stanislee, "is that everything is under control."

An anomalous clearing appeared in the heavens and, as the ship plunged into a deep gutter, a pale shaft of dying sunlight spilled down through the saloon's dome windows and rolled sideways like a drunken spotlight over the tables and ballroom floor, before being extinguished again by the churning stormclouds. Those walking stood still, those standing steadied themselves against a table or passing cart.

"Geoffrey?"

"My room," he said. "I left my notebook in my room."

"But Mr. Harbrow said for all of us to stay –"

Geoffrey, with a sudden giddy clarity, felt certain that they were all going to drown.

Everything was being attended to: that was what they had been told. That had satisfied them. It was enough that *someone* – one of their employees, one of their wage-earners – had the matter well in hand. Their complacent indifference was due in part, of course, to their utter ignorance and incompetence; there was nothing they could do to help if they had had a mind to. But that they did not even want to know what had occurred, wanted only to be reassured that the situation, whatever it might be, was on its way to being remedied, could only be the result of fear. They were like Galileo's persecutors after all: if they did not look, if they turned away, the problem would not exist.

He had not turned away. He was proud of that. He had stood there longer than any of the others. He had stood there, baking and sweating, and watched the Black Gang feed the fires. He had remained behind till his discomfort became acute, till he felt as if he would burst into bright blue flame himself, and still he stood there, watching; and still those men bent and lifted and thrust without rest, without respite.

It was horrible, intolerable. And yet he had withstood it. He had forced himself to look.

"Quite the sight, isn't it?"

He and the Captain were the last two in the boiler room. The tour was ended; the rest of the party had already gone on ahead, following after Harbrow like wide-eyed baby ducklings.

"It is . . . staggering," was all he could say.

"A shame your father could not be here to see it."

Geoffrey felt dizzy; there was on Stegnan's grizzled face a look, not of sickened pity, but of glowing admiration.

"Harbrow's a fool, of course," said the Captain. "But for God's sake, don't let his monkey antics, all his bright shiny facts and statistical baubles, dissuade you. The Blue Line is as stable, as unsinkable a concern as any one of her ships. And she's due for an upswell. She's got the pedigree, she's got the backbone, and you can see for yourself that she's got the strength. All she's lacking is the funds – the capital."

One of the firemen was bent double before his boiler's hatch, screaming with red-faced fury at his counterpart on the other side, who had opened the opposite hatch at the same time and allowed a gust of cold – that is, slightly less scorching – air to pour over his precious coals. The man looked capable of murder.

Geoffrey felt ill, but he did not look away.

"My father and I will discuss it, I'm sure."

Stegnan grinned at him slyly, as though twitting him for some unwarranted modesty.

*

But Geoffrey and his father had not discussed it. Indeed, in the two intervening days, they had not exchanged a single word. Granted, his father spent most of his time resting in his stateroom; but Geoffrey, for his part, was quite content to avoid him. There was, anyway, nothing to say – just as there had been nothing to say about his coming on this trip, and nothing to say about his presumptive attendance at the university. He could no more talk about the fate of the Blue Line with his father than he could tell him what he really thought of Stanislee Steel.

Something shook him. He thought at first it was the ocean rocking the ship, but then he felt the aching aftershock of the collision, and the hands slapping at his lapels, brushing him off.

"I am sorry, sir. All right? Nothing busted? No harm no foul?"

"What happened?"

The steward chuckled. "Asked myself the same thing. Trimming along I am, you come out of nowhere, and pitch as night's guts it is with the blooming electrics out, and – *pof.* No fault, no flaw, far as I can make it. Bit of hamburger grease on your lapel'll come right out in the wash."

"Oh, God," groaned Geoffrey. "Lacklin."

The hands ceased their slapping. "Mr. Geoffrey? Christ, I thought I knocked me over some blooming saloon passenger."

"I am a saloon passenger," he muttered.

"Never fails. Every time there's a blow-up, out they come crawling, get underfoot and in your way. Sniff a spot of trouble and there they are, tripping you up, slowing you down, and not a nickel of thank-you for your bother."

Where a moment before he had sounded relieved, he now sounded angry. He was already hurrying on; Geoffrey dogged after him.

"Lacklin, you must tell me: What has happened?"

The back of the boy's throat rattled. "You all right then, are you?" He spat it back over his shoulder like an accusation.

"Are we in any danger? Is the ship –"

"Naw, you ain't in no danger. Not the *saloon* passengers ain't."

"Lacklin – where is the Captain? He was not at his –"

"That old log-lump? Like as not cowering in his cabin under his down-feather mattress. What you want the like of him for?"

Geoffrey did not know why. Because he was in command; because he would know what to do. Because . . .

"Something has happened. To the ship. There was a man, he came into the . . . His trousers –"

"Something happened?" jeered Lacklin. "You want to save this ship, you be wiser help bring this fried hamburger to the lifetubs like me."

"Lifeboats?"

But Lacklin was already out of sight.

The wheelhouse was empty. It looked less forlorn than simply vacant, as though the Captain and wheelman had just stepped out for a minute. This was, he supposed, because it had never been but nominally occupied; you could not abandon that which had no importance. That the bridge had been evacuated did not prove the severity of the emergency, but the inconsequence of the bridge. Whatever might be happening was happening belowdecks. What had Stegnan called the engine room? The heart of her heart. The bridge was, at most, the ship's eyes; and in times of trouble, in times of darkness, there was nothing to see.

The wind up here was a ceaseless and ubiquitous screech. The deck plunged; he grasped the wheel and looked out at the sea.

Though the view was smeared and pitted by rain, the rolling clouds still harboured enough of a charcoal glow for him to see that what had been a tatty blanket two days ago had been transformed into a mountain range of tumbling pitch. The black waves rose up with swift malevolent purpose, as though summoned each by name, before crashing down upon one another in a gulping frenzy of spume. The rain was visible only as a wavering diagonal streak clogging the air like a heat mirage, but down below he could see where it chewed and churned the surface of the water into a pebbled froth. In the distance, patches of pale lightning skittered across the ribbed underbelly of the storm.

He imagined, for a moment, that he was guiding the ship to safety. But the wheel would not budge, no matter how hard he pulled.

He turned for the stairs and saw that the A and B Deck promenades were teeming with people – crew members, he surmised, stocking and readying the lifeboats. There appeared to be hundreds of them down there, battered by rain, crawling over one another, running in every direction – not *en masse*, like a mob, but with individual purpose, like ants stirred by some threat to their hill.

He had not imagined there could be so many. They must have all of them been called up from their bunks, their tables, their parlours, wherever they had been resting or recuperating. He wanted to scream down at them: Why are you doing this? Why do you sacrifice yourselves to save *their* lives, when they do not even lift a finger to aid themselves – no, do not even bestir themselves enough to wonder what disaster imperils them?

But, of course, if the crew did not save the ship, no one would.

He had come to the wrong place. It was belowdecks that the real work was done, the real problems solved. It was, he felt sure, in the engine room that he would find the captain of this ship. He descended the stairs at speed.

He paused before the first of the bulkhead doors. At the top of the corridor some light from the lamps of the deck above had still filtered down to him; now he no longer knew if the darkness was total or not. Phantom forms hovered before his eyes, but these might have been due to nothing more than strain coupled with imagination. His hand found the hatch wheel; the hard cold metal seemed to drain his fingers of all their substance, all their strength.

The scene from the boiler room, the image of those blackened figures toiling over their fires, rose afresh in his mind.

Like the importance of the bridge, the strength of men like his father was only apparent. In calm weather they appeared to be in control of the world's ships, but with rough seas the superfluousness and superficiality of their reign was revealed – and they sat munching post-prandial cigars while the crew fought off shipwreck.

But if the crew, the workers, the proletariat possessed the true power, could one speak of them as oppressed? Or was it, in the end, their oppression that gave them their power? After all, was it not by enduring hardship that one acquired strength?

One became hard by doing what was hard.

He gripped the hatch wheel with both hands and twisted it loose.

He did not close the doors behind him – to allow whatever light there might be to pass through, and because he could not countenance the thought of sealing himself in down here.

Meanwhile, to steady himself, he let his mind turn back to abstract reflection: Who used whom? Could it be that the proletariat used the opposition of the bourgeoisie to make themselves strong? Did the brain use the body to get around, or did the body use the brain to get itself around?

He did not remember the floor sloping downwards in this way. Perhaps he was in a different corridor altogether. But at least he knew for certain that he was moving in the correct direction.

Was the brain more dispensable than the body? Was the bridge less important than the engine room? Direction without propulsion was immobility; but propulsion without direction was shipwreck.

He fumbled, fingers now almost numb, with another hatch. This one was harder to release than its predecessors. He had to stand to one side and heave downwards with all his might. He held his breath and tugged.

There was a hard hollow sound like a sledge's runners scraping across ice. He felt a constellation of pinpricks all along the left side of his body and believed for a moment that he had ruptured something, torn some sensitive nervous tissue. Reflexively he gasped and jumped back into the wall, which rang under the impact like a struck anvil. In the two or three seconds before he grasped the nature of this sudden barrage of noise and pain, his mind reeled vertiginously – seemed actually to spin about, as though his head had swallowed something nauseating – in an abject disorientation and alarm that was a hundredfold worse than what he had experienced two days earlier in the engine room. For two or three seconds, all he knew was that he was alone in a dark and confined space, some distance below the surface of the ocean, that he was being attacked by some unseen menace and was utterly defenceless, utterly powerless.

Then he understood: water. A stream of water was blasting in through the door he had partially opened, ricocheting off the opposite wall of the corridor, and drenching and freezing him.

His terror – elementary, without object, absolute – was extinguished by an inrush of fear: he would be drowned.

He turned and fled, one hand skimming the wall to guide him, the other extended before him in anticipation of the inevitable collision.

He was in the dark; his shoes were wet; the floor was slick as though with oil; the invisible corridor continued to tilt and plunge all around him – and still he did not stumble, still he ran. He had his sea legs now, he thought bitterly.

But he miscalculated the distance, the number of portals remaining; the faint lamplight from the deck above reached his eyes only a fraction of a second before the stair smashed into his shin and sent him careening forward in a crashing purler. His chin hit first; he took the brunt of the fall in his teeth and jaw. The pain was immense; it felt as though his face had exploded. He blacked out, and awoke in water.

It gripped him with long sharp claws and shook him. He was floating in a void of cold pain. He could no longer see the light. Up, he reasoned laboriously, had to be in the direction of air. He found the edge of the water by waving his arms: one of them seemed to move more freely. He pushed his head in that direction and sucked breath down into his lungs, as though his throat were a straw. He could not swim.

He realized he was still on the floor: the water had only come up to his knees. He found the bottom step and pulled himself onto it, then the next, and the next. His legs were half frozen; they paddled him up the stairs like a riverboat.

He came out onto C deck. He had not intended to go out into the storm, but he had to warn the passengers that the ship was taking on water. He had to tell his family, had to tell his father, that they were sinking.

Where was everyone? He could not see anything for the rain. The lancing drops fell on his numbed skin like little pressing fingertips. The sky was now almost completely black; there was not even lightning. Where was the crew? Where were the lifeboats?

With lethargic ease, as though shrugging one of its giant shoulders, the ship tilted; Geoffrey stumbled and was sent sliding into the railing. At the same time, a corkscrewing gust of wind came sweeping in to fill a freak vacuum in the ship's lee – and Geoffrey was blown overboard.

He could but thrash wildly as the waves tossed him about. He was in the ocean in the middle of a tempest and he could not swim, but the magnitude of his predicament did not enter his awareness. His only thought, his only instinct, was to fight the waves until something changed, until the next thing happened. There was only this moment of struggle. The worst never occurred to him.

Then he went under. With an abrupt shocking completeness that seemed almost gentle, the dark viscous water lifted the storm and the rain and the crashing spray over his head, closed around him like a protecting fist, and pierced his lungs.

He was coughing, choking on black ice.

Then, with an effort of will, he was able to suppress the spasms in his chest, and with them much of the fear. It was just like holding one's breath, except that one no longer had any breath to hold.

Then came a moment, almost a respite, in which he could do nothing more.

He thought of his piece for the *Worker's Tribune*. He thought of Meredith Quigley, and the letter he would write her. He thought of the shade-dappled road leading down the hill from his grandparents' acreage. He thought of his father, and wished him health.

The cold turned to pain and infiltrated his bones. That was good, he thought. That was where it belonged. This way, he would carry it with him always. This way, he would never forget.

BLACK·INK

I

The study was in disarray. Papers and cards, bills and folders, were scattered across the floor. The drawers of the filing cabinet – which my father had never seen unlocked – were hanging open. Books, which he'd never been allowed to touch, were splayed on every surface. And at the centre of the room, the trash can lay on its side, spilling charred debris onto my grandmother's Persian rug.

No one had been in here since the night of the accident. It looked like a crime scene. At this thought my father felt a spasm of what he supposed was grief – as though Lloyd, my grandfather, were already dead.

The tang of ash and whatever chemical snow the fire-fighters had doused the curtains with still hung in the air. This, at least, gave him some place to begin. Almost grate-fully he crossed to the window and, pulling the sleeve of his sweater over his hand, tugged on the bladelike lever until it moved. A nearly visible current of cold autumn air came pouring in, like a leak sprung in the hull of a ship.

He brushed some white dust from one curtain, then realized they'd all have to be taken down and replaced anyway. He picked up a pen from the blotter and returned it to the mug that held the others. He returned the phone receiver to its cradle. He righted Lloyd's chair. Then he bent down, reached for the trash can, and paused.

Photographs. Lloyd had been burning photographs.

Most of them had been destroyed. Those not consumed by flame had been wilted by heat or tarnished by smoke. But they had clearly been photographs. My father got down on his knees, upturned the can, and began raking through the detritus with his fingers.

There were only two survivors. In the first photo was a man with a round, puppy-dog head, black beady eyes scowling out from beneath bristling eyebrows. He looked surprised but scornful, like a nocturnal predator encountered at midday. My father didn't recognize him.

He did recognize the woman in the other photograph – or at least he recognized her features. The hexagonal face like a faceted stone. The lips pressed together in suppressed amusement. The impatient eyes.

It was his mother. In the photo she must have been no more than twenty years old.

He slipped the singed photograph into his pocket.

Then he swept the blackened fragments into a garbage bag and, with belated guilt, delicately rolled up my grandmother's rug and carried it out into the backyard. He shook it out and hung it over one of the espaliers marking the entrance to her garden.

The garden had once been lush enough – or he small enough – that he could hide indefinitely, undetected, undetectable, among its maze of roots and branches. Now it was gone to seed, overgrown with brown weeds, like a living midden, a self-refreshing compost heap.

When had he last been out here? When had anyone? The funeral?

The morning sun was diluted, smeared across the sky by a haze of cloud. He went back inside.

My grandfather was asleep in front of the television. His face had gone slack and stupid – like an insolent teenager's, thought my father.

Neil gathered up the papers without looking at them, like a student snatching up his notes before the wind could carry them away, and shoved them inside the top drawer of the filing cabinet. He would help tidy, but it was not, he decided, his responsibility to put all this back in order. Let his father clean up the mess he'd made. Or Deanna.

I'm here every day, she'd said at the hospital. I'm here every day while you're off somewhere living your own life.

Off in Winnipeg living my life. I live in Winnipeg.

You know what I mean.

But he didn't. What did she mean by *here*? Not the house, obviously. If she came every day, the house could never have gotten like this. There would not be garbage bags piling up on the curb. The mail would not have gone unopened. Their father's bedsheets would not reek of urine. His pills would not be mixed together in a pickle jar in the fridge. The study would not look like it had been ransacked, the drawers of the filing cabinet left hanging open . . .

The second drawer, he saw, was full of books. Little hard-cover books, all sizes and colours, none of them labelled. His first thought was that they were ledgers or bankbooks, memorabilia of Pembroke (later, briefly, Pembroke & Son) Signage Co. But inside there were no columns, no numbers or figures, only line after line and page after page of loose, slanted handwriting. He riffled through the notebooks impatiently, almost resentfully, his eyes conscientiously unfocused, sensing but reluctant to confirm that here was something else he would have to take care of, another mess he would have to set in order.

Gradually, inevitably, his eyes began to catch on isolated words and phrases –

. . . qualitatively . . .
. . . bloody awful . . .
. . . show up till 7:30 . . .
. . . troop of morons . . .
. . . LOVE HER or anything . . .

– and the nature of what he was looking at began to sink in.

II

My mother was the light sleeper but my father's side of the bed was closer to the phone.

What's happened? my mother whispered. A disaster film was playing on the screen behind her eyes, images of disease and dismemberment flickering one after another at merci-fully subliminal speed. It was past 3 a.m.

Who is it? she asked.

Irritated, my father frowned and shook his head. My mother, taking this as confirmation of her worst fears, leaped out of bed and hurried downstairs.

On the phone my aunt Deanna said: I can't deal with him.

What's happened? What's he done now?

Downstairs, my mother knocked on my door, then let herself in. But I was not in my room.

She picked up the phone in the kitchen and said, Is he all right?

He's in the hospital, said my aunt.

Oh God.

Peggy, said my father, it's not Andy. It's my dad.

She began to say Oh thank God, but stopped herself.

Lloyd? she asked. Is he . . . all right?

Neil, said my aunt, it's you he wants to see.

In one bed, a man was chewing and sucking on his lips like they were beef jerky. In another, a patient was pulling at his ear as though trying to bring it into his field of view. Only Lloyd seemed indifferent to the state of his body, and indeed everything else. He lay on his back, scowling at the ceiling, his lips moving silently.

Hi, Dad.

Lloyd's lips stopped moving. What did she tell you?

The nurse?

Lloyd glared at him for a moment, as though unable to grasp the extent of his ignorance. Your sister.

I haven't seen her yet. I just got in. I came from the airport.

Did she tell you this was all Mossbank's fault? She didn't, did she. Of course she didn't. She wouldn't.

There was a chair at the foot of the bed. Neil dropped into it. Hospitals always made him feel sick.

All I heard was there was a fire. I heard you hurt your knee. I came to see you. How are you feeling?

Lloyd dismissed this question with a shudder of his shoulders. The lights were out again, you know. The power. These municipal . . . He lifted a hand as though searching for something in the air. After a moment he let it drop, not, apparently, in frustration, but disgust, as though casting away what he'd found. That Mossbank woman watches windows like they're television sets. Sees a little flame in my study and thinks the bloody house is on fire. Calls the goddamn fire department.

And what about your knee?

You have to speak up. He said it like a jail sentence, a memento mori: *there will come a day when you will have to speak up*. I'm not a bloody lip-reader.

WHY WERE THERE FLAMES IN YOUR STUDY? Neil half-shouted.

Lloyd grimaced. All a sudden there's a goddamn midway carnival flashing outside my window, then a dozen men in my house, shouting and thumping up the stairs. Christ, I thought I was being robbed. He narrowed his eyes at Neil as though in anticipation of some rebuttal. You read about these things, you know. Looting during blackouts. It's not at all uncommon. They should lock that woman up. Menace to society. Put her in a place like this. They wouldn't even give me my own room, he said loudly, as though accusing his roommates of conspiring against his privacy.

What was – WHAT WAS BURNING?

Having to shout made Neil feel self-conscious – blustering,

clumsy, insincere, like a robot or a bureaucrat, a billboard or a warning label. It was impossible to have a genuine conversation at maximum volume.

Lloyd shook his head, but distractedly, as though addressing his own thoughts. Didn't even ring the doorbell. Didn't even knock. No better than Mossbank, going off half-cocked like some kind of . . . bloody . . . He lifted his hand, dropped it, shook his head. Scared the hell out of me, he muttered. Fell out of my goddamn chair. Bashed the holy bejesus out of my knee. Knocked over the trash can. That's why the curtains caught. He made a sound in his throat almost like a drawn-out chuckle. They went up like a, like a, like a . . . He faded to silence, then shouted: I should sue the bastards. Scaring the hell . . . Barging in like . . . Didn't even ring the doorbell. Didn't even *knock*. No bloody better than Mossbank. Coming into my home. What did *she* tell you?

Neil looked up. Who – Deanna?

Lloyd shook his head. I want to go home. I have work to do. I have to get my affairs in order.

He sounds, thought my father, *just like Andrew.*

He found Deanna in the cafeteria. She was the only person he knew, besides their mother, who sat facing the wall when alone at a table.

Well? She was too large to cross her arms, but in her voice they were crossed.

I don't know. In a tone almost of apology, he said, He seems much the same.

Well, yes, Deanna said, he'd do that for you. Pull himself together. Wouldn't he.

Neil tried a conciliatory tack. His hearing does seem worse.

That's ninety per cent not wanting to listen. Ignoring you. Forgetting you're there. No, not even that. Not wanting to remember you're there. Not being able to be bothered. Believe me.

On the phone, the way you . . . I got the impression . . .

He set the house on fire, Neil.

He set some curtains on fire.

Oh, I guess curtains aren't part of the house.

She'd had something with gravy. Her plate glistened, pearls of grease glowing like television pixels under the harsh hospital lights.

It was an accident.

I was here. You weren't.

It was like they were teenagers again. Whenever he said something she didn't agree with, something she did not like, she retreated into asseveration. *I am right. You are wrong.* If he kept pushing she'd get shrill and defensive. But he couldn't help it.

You were there, he said with dull incredulity. The night of –

I was *here*. I saw him. He was incoherent. His thoughts were disjointed.

It sounded like a word she'd borrowed from her husband, the psychiatrist, the psychologist, whatever he was.

Obviously he hasn't been quite right since the funeral, but that's hardly –

He was raving. He's still raving. You just don't want to listen. You're like *him*.

Neil leaned back in his chair and put his hands in his pockets. I guess I don't see it.

Go to the house. Wait till you see the house, she said, and showed him her teeth.

III

. . . one of those shy girls who hold themselves perfectly vertical when they walk, like a snorkel skimming across a lake. I'd like to make her buckle and sway like seaweed, flop about on the floor like a fish out of water . . .

. . . never thought I'd <u>miss</u> the war. But it's so. Especially the parts when the good guys were losing. Then it seemed like everyone felt as lousy as I did, which of course made me feel quite good . . .

. . . older, now almost archaic meaning of make love must certainly be the more accurate. That early, chaste phase of flirtation and flattery, when the thought of putting your hand on her knee still makes you drunk with lust and terror. This is when love is being made, surely – and not later, when you're finally permitted to post your letter . . .

. . . pompous windbag who verbosely criticizes the inadequacy of language to preserve the every shade and hue of his genius. All I mean is that all our words are dyed. Every utterance is a brush that paints the utterer. You can't say anything about anything without saying something about yourself. <u>That's</u> what I hate about language. It betrays you . . .

. . . flushed with pleasure at recalling how last night I made her laugh. Then I thought: Shouldn't I prefer it the other way around? Wouldn't it be nice, for a change, to recall how she made me laugh? . . .

Neil stopped reading. As though to catch his breath, he shifted his attention from the meaning of the words to the words themselves.

The ink was blue, though not always the same blue. Some of the pens used had left the pages sprinkled with splotches. The handwriting leaned heavily to the right, as though marching into a strong wind; its loops and strokes looked like so many toeholds put down for traction. Dashes and ellipses were preferred to paragraph breaks, as though to conserve paper, which made it difficult to know where one entry ended and another began. Some were separated by dates, but the year was never indicated. The notebook itself was brown and brittle; the corners of its cardboard cover were frayed. Some of the books were in better shape, their pages less yellowed. But the oldest here, he thought, might have been forty years old. More.

He fished another notebook out of the drawer, split it open at random, and read:

Sep 21. A very foolish and irritating woman came into the shop today and tried to persuade me that the plural form of the English noun flower should have an apostrophe. I launched briskly into a free tutorial on the possessive and elliptical functions of the apostrophe. "But I want it to look like that" was all she would say, again and again, like a Victrola caught in a groove. Instead of hitting her in the face or ear or about the neck as any rational person would do, I told her that we were having a special sale on quotation marks used for emphasis, and offered to set off the word Best in this fashion for no extra charge. —— That one should have to work in order merely to <u>live</u>, of all things, strikes me as a very dubious arrangement indeed. Like paying a tax on tax or tipping your executioner. I can't quite believe that on top of all the odious tasks I daily perform – waking, washing, shaving ("A daily plague, which in the aggregate / May average on the whole with parturition"), dressing, eating food, suffering fools, i.e. (make that e.g.) smiling and nodding and not hitting their faces while appearing to pay attention to the foolishness that comes out of them. On top of all this extravagant altruism, does it not seem outrageous that the world also expects me to <u>work</u>? That is, to do things I do not like in exchange for <u>money</u>, which I do not even <u>like</u>, since all it's good for is <u>paying for things</u>, things I do not even <u>like</u>, things like <u>soap</u> and <u>clothes</u> and <u>food</u>, things that I <u>require</u> in order to <u>stay living</u>, which I do not even <u>like</u>, necessitating as it does other things I do not like, things like having to work for my father – who I <u>do not like</u> – making and selling signs to people I do not like who are wanting to advertise the things I do not like in a language that they <u>do not even understand</u>.

A dash and a date separated this from what followed.

—— Sep 23. The double meaning of the word like. We only like that which is like us, that which we are like? I like those who like like I do. More to the point, dislike those who dislike unlike me. —— And what about girls? They're not like us, are they? They like unlike us, don't they? And yet we like them, or act like we do. Act like we like what they like. —— True too of literature: we like what we're like. Why do we read? Not for truth and beauty, but the opposite: for lies and ugliness, for reflections of ourselves. For glimpses that would make us less forlorn. For reminders that others read literature too, for evidence that we're not the only ones who sometimes feel like we're the only ones who feel like this. The good poem says something we wish we'd said, or wish we'd said first, or wish we could say better. Emerson (that raging twit) put it passably well: In every work of genius we recognize our own rejected thoughts; they come back to us with a certain alienated majesty.

The following was given a line of its own.

One should not look in a girl for what can only be found in a poem – nor vice versa.

His neck was cramped. There was a pain in his shoulder. How long had he been reading? Sunlight had begun to seep from the sky. The room had grown frigid.

He closed the window, turned on a lamp. Downstairs the television clucked and gobbled.

Dad? he called. LLOYD?

There was no reply.

He picked a new notebook out of the filing cabinet – green, this one, and ratty. He peeled back the book's cover, pulled towards him his father's chair, and was already halfway down the first page before he sat down.

May 17. Last night G. visited me in my bedroom, which made me happy, and we listened to my new radio box, which did not. The programme being aired (aired out more like it) was a specimen of what is called a radio play. One might think the inherent limitations of this format would rather constrain the action. Oh ho no. The radio playwright has heroically surmounted this challenge. How has he done that? Quite simple really. If someone does something with their body, someone will comment on it with their voice. Thus if a character walks across the room: Excuse me while I walk across this room old chap. If a character picks up a glass of sherry: – What's this then? – Why, it looks like a glass of sherry, Sergeant Bowles. – What's it doing here, blast it? – It appears to be being picked up by you, Sergeant. – So it is, Collins. So it is. —— Say what you will about the radio playwright, he cannot be accused of leaving too much to the imagination. To paraphrase one of G̶r̶e̶t̶e̶'s grumpy old syphilitic countrymen: If Nature had intended Man to think, she would not have given him radios.

The name had been crossed out, as though to conceal her identity – from whom? The ink was darker, fresher, almost black. It looked like some conscientious editor had gone back through these entries at a much later date, striking out the errors. And yet the name was still legible: Grete.

It was his mother's name.

G. I need hardly add seemed not to have disliked it as much as I disliked it, which is to say not nearly enough. In her defence however I suppose her English is not so very good as mine is good. And since, in lieu of speaking succinctly,

the radio voices spoke quite quickly, I suppose all her intelligence and attention, which might otherwise have been
channelled into incisive aesthetic criticism, had to be dedi-
cated to simply parsing meaning, ~~or rather divided between
doing that~~ . . .

Here, nearly half a page had been blacked out. Neil pulled
himself up to his father's desk and laid the notebook flat
beneath the lamp.

or rather divided between doing that on the one hand and
fending off my gently persistent attempts to remove her
brassiere on the other. —— She does this differently than
other girls, by the way. Instead of accusing me of not really
loving her, of being only interested in THAT (by which they
presumably mean that repertoire of things I could do to
them with their brassieres off), G. simply locks my offending
hand in her claws, smiles firmly but mysteriously, and stares
off over my shoulder or out the window, half dreamily, as
though intent on enjoying the sounds coming out of the
Broadspeak, and almost half wistfully, as though counting
the days until that time when she will no longer have to
resist. Or so I'd like to think. In fact . . .

There, mid-sentence, the censorship ended. The text went
on unconcealed.

~~In fact~~ I rarely know what goes on in her head. This is not
just the difficulty inherent in making sense of the motives or
rationales underlying the capricious behaviour of that
elusive creature, the female. That mystery, I often think, is

due to an absence of something (call it sense); this mystery, on the other hand, is due to an abundance. More goes on behind G.'s eyes – those TruVue stereoscope eyes with their illusory shifting depths, those many-faceted eyes of agate and topaz and jasper (<u>SORRY</u>) – more goes on behind them than she will or can say. Not that I think her mystery is due entirely to the language barrier, the perplexity introduced into our conversations by her constant stream of adorable neologisms and malapropisms. Some of these are quite delightful, actually. Her shadow she calls a me-hole, a me-shaped hole. Her tear glands are crying ducks. To respond in kind is to do something tic for tac. She pronounces mango – they had some in at Landmann's last week – like it's a Dear John letter: Man, go. When I do not want to go out away from the warmth and comfort of my bedroom, she accuses me of having Michelangelo legs, presumably meaning they are painted on. Her English, I might add, though not as good as my English, is inestimably superior to my German. I have to date learned three words. Schnee, which sounds to me more snow-like, whiter and softer and more frozen, than our wet, colourless snow. Gloves are Handschuhe, or hand-shoes. An airplane is if I'm not mistaken a Flugzeug, or flying stuff. Yes, German is unquestionably G.'s language. —— And let it also be said for the record, let it be written in posterity's register, that her accent, which she feels acutely embarrassed by, ~~gives me an erection~~. She says German is harsh. I'd prefer earthy. Consider our W versus their V: White is what I would wear were I to wed. Vhite is vhat I vould vear vere I to ved. W is wishy-washy, V is vivacious. W is the burbling of water, V is the buzz of electricity. German is broader, sturdier, has a lower centre of gravity, is

more like a pyramid than the redbrick block of flats that
is English. Take Yeah versus Ja. Our short A is closer to a short
E, theirs to a short O. Ours is higher, theirs lower, theirs
deeper, ours shallower. Yeah sounds like maybe. Ja sounds
like indisputably. German is the language of the syllogism.
Everything G. says in her mother tongue sounds like an a
priori dictum from Kant. Everything she says in mine sounds
like a Nobel Prize–winning physicist innocently repeating
back a filthy limerick to a rabble of mischievous schoolboys.
I tell her she must never lose her accent. She thinks I am –

I see you're getting a lot done.

Neil's heart skipped a beat. He hadn't heard the car,
hadn't heard the door, hadn't heard her come up the
stairs. To conceal his surprise he waited a moment before
turning around.

Just going through some of this junk, he said in what he
hoped was a casual, half-bored drawl.

Deanna gave him a look that he'd often seen on her face:
the one that announced that she could say a lot more, but
because others might not much care for what she had to say,
she would, out of consideration for them, resist the temptation to say it – for now.

The nurse is here, she said at last.

Oh? He stood and stretched. Where is she?

Without quite rolling her eyes, she lifted her gaze heav-
enward, pityingly. *He*, she said, giving the *H* a ferocious
emphasis, is downstairs watching cartoons with our father.

My father had expected scrubs or a white lab coat, but the
man wore a V-neck sweater and khakis. He looked more like

an amateur golfer than a nurse. He sat on the couch, as far as possible from my grandfather, staring at the television with skittish anxiety, like a suitor who'd run out of innocent things to say. He leapt to his feet when my father cleared his throat.

Hi, Neil Merchison.

My father thought he'd been misinformed. Actually, it's –

His name's Neil too, my aunt explained, possibly addressing herself to both men.

Right, said my father. Of course. Pembroke. Neil Pembroke.

They shook hands. The nurse's plump hand felt clammy, like something that had been growing in a cellar.

The other man giggled nervously. Great Neils think alike.

Slowly their gazes settled on Lloyd, who was looking at the television screen like it was something he was going to have to eat.

Perhaps we could move ourselves into another room for a bit, suggested the nurse, and talk in another room.

I'm not a baby, grumbled my grandfather. I know how to spell.

The nurse simpered. Well, perhaps then we could turn that TV off for a bit, if nobody minds too terribly much?

Lloyd said nothing.

Deanna strode purposefully forward and, with an air of righteous self-restraint, like a parent swatting a misbehaving child, switched it off.

That's better, said the nurse, then said nothing for a long time.

We'll clean the place up, Deanna reassured the nurse. Neil and I. So that's something you don't . . .

I was actually just in the middle of that, said my father.

What I usually do is start things out by coming four times a day, said the nurse. Once in the morning – for *breakfast* – once around midday – for *lunch* – once in the evening – for *supper* – and once at night, just before bedtime. For my grand-father's benefit, presumably, he pronounced the meals like they were items on a menu; "bedtime" he half-whispered. And from there, depending on your father's needs, we can do some fine-tuning. Though perhaps for the first week or two, due to the state of that knee –

My sister and I are in some disagreement about that.

Oh.

About our father's needs.

Oh?

Neil.

I don't think he needs a nurse.

I don't need a goddamn *nurse*, said my grandfather. What I *need* . . . He frowned, looked away.

Neil, we've been over this.

You've been over this. I've hardly begun to take it all in.

Whose fault is that? If you're never around. Never here to see what I see, what Eric sees, what anybody –

That man Eric is a damn fool, said my grandfather com-placently.

That – my father began to say, *is proof that he's in his right mind*, but stopped himself. Instead he turned to the nurse. We still have some discussing to do, as you can see.

We've discussed it to *death*. Who's going to stay with him? He can't walk. He can't get up or down the stairs. He can't fix himself anything to eat. You have to fly back, *I* can't afford to take any more days off work. Who's going to help him? Who's going to stay with him?

The nurse Neil was looking anxious and skittish again. Well, should I perhaps maybe leave you my number, and then we, if you, depending . . .

My aunt gave him a black look. You already *gave* me your number.

I can walk, muttered Lloyd. My legs aren't painted on.

My father looked at him. I'll stay, he said at last.

At which point Lloyd said – perhaps to my father, perhaps to no one at all, but with undeniable feeling – You're a goddamn ignorant fool.

My father nodded wearily, and, from force of habit, replied under his breath, Fuck you too, Lloyd.

But at that, with the rote articulation of those words, all the old anger and resentment and defiance arose within him, and suddenly all the questions that he'd been wanting to ask him – What did you do in the war? How did you and mother meet? Why did she never speak German? Why did you, why did we, never learn it? When did you stop finding solace in poetry? What happened to Pembroke *and Son*? If you loathed going to work so much, why were you never home? What did *your* father do to make you hate him? Why didn't you ever tell us about yourself? Why did you pour it all into notebooks? Who were you? Where did he go? – all those questions vanished from my father's mind.

What came flooding in to replace them was the crushing anxiety at being so far from home, so far from his office, while his business, his livelihood, was being methodically disman-tled by lawyers. They had an entire law firm at their disposal; my father had Troy Mackey, who looked like he cut his own hair. They advertised in *The Economist*, *The Atlantic Monthly*, and *Popular Mechanics*; my father, who could not afford a sixteenth of a page in the yellow pages, or even *The Winnipeg Free Press*, had to rely on bulk e-mail. They had offices in New York, Geneva, Taipei; most days he answered the phone himself. They boasted a product line of thousands, but did not, in fact, make the one item he manufactured and sold. They – they – were suing him – him – because the name of his company was, in the opinion of their lawyers, too much like theirs.

It happens all the time, Troy Mackey had told him, as though this would cheer him up. Big fish eats the little fish. Or in this case, big fish sues the little fish for trademark infringement.

His life was a speck of plankton passing through some whale's baleen and here he was, standing in his senile father's living room, preparing to lug him all around the house, cook his meals, clean out his basement, wipe his ass? Fuck you too, Lloyd.

You'll stay? My aunt was incredulous. You're going to cancel your flight? You're going to –

No, he said. Of course not. You're right. He nodded at his sister. You're right. You should know. You've been here. To the nurse he said, We'll work something out.

Then my father excused himself and went upstairs to use the phone.

Or maybe he used the one in the kitchen. I don't know. A lot of this is, perforce, speculation.

Yeah?
Andrew.
Dad.

We're not saying hello these days?

No. I don't know.

Look, I'm not trying to be a hardass here, but the thing is, as you know, sometimes I have to give clients my home number. "Yeah" doesn't sound very professional, does it?

Good afternoon, you've reached the home and private residence of Neil Pembroke, president of Springtek Electronics, how may I direct your call. Better?

Is your mother there?

I don't know.

Do you think you could find out?

Okay.

My father waited a minute. Andrew?

Yeah?

You're still there.

Yeah?

Are you going to go get your mother?

Right. Sorry. Is it *urgent*?

I'm calling long distance.

From the hotel?

I'm not staying in a hotel.

What, you don't stay in hotels anymore? Where are you, anyway?

It's not a business trip. I'm at Grandpa's. I'm staying at Eric and – No, I don't know, I'm not staying anywhere, I'm coming home. Look, could I *please* speak to your mother?

So, what, Grandpa or Deanna or wherever you're calling from doesn't have a phone plan? What are you doing *there* anyway?

That's not the point. Your grandfather's sick. *Andrew* –

Okay, shit, *sorry*. You guys never tell me *anything*.

My father took a breath. I'm sorry. Your grandfather, if you must know . . . Andrew?

But I was gone.

He waited. A minute, two. As his annoyance began to well up, a memory flashed through his mind. Walking home to our old house from the grocery store. He and my mother burdened with paper bags, leaving me, four or five years old, free to dash a few daring steps ahead – how far could I get without being reprimanded, without being called back? – before turning to wait impatiently for them to catch up. My mother gasping, dropping one of her bags, and then, in trying to catch it, dropping the other. Milk everywhere. A jar of pickles rolling away down the sidewalk. *Goddamn it, Peggy*. But then he saw what she – and I – had seen. Smoke. Thick, snowy, white clumps of cotton-candy spilling out of our kitchen window and into the sky. As soft, as innocent, as irresistible as falling snow.

Already the boy – what on earth was he thinking? – was running towards the front door. And the father was scream-ing, screaming the boy's name at the top of his lungs – screaming as though with hatred, as though he would cer-tainly kill the kid if ever he got his hands on him.

But that was wrong. Something was wrong.

We'd never had a fire. There was no old house.

Then a detail corrected itself in my father's mind. The man, the boy's father, had not said *Goddamn it, Peggy*. He'd said *Goddamn it, Grete*.

My mother picked up the phone. Neil? Will you talk to your son? I can't deal with him.

My father discovered he had nothing to say.

IV

It is sometimes said of good men that they died too soon.

The priest, a short sleek man who gave the impression of having been groomed entirely by cat's tongue, paused and frowned. For nearly a minute he stood considering the accuracy of this statement. Deciding at last that it would have to do, he went on, but no less haltingly, moving over the words of his sermon like they were nails or hot coals.

And it is sometimes said of evil men that they died too late. Now, this may be true for the world. But for the man himself the opposite is closer to the truth. The good man, destined for heavenly bliss, might justifiably resent having been so long waylaid. The evil man, on the other hand, from his very different vantage point, must certainly lament his not having been given a little more time to repent.

We are all, in our hearts, that evil man. What is it that St. Augustine says? "Give me chastity and continence – but not yet." We will make amends – tomorrow. And if not tomorrow, the day after. If not soon, eventually. Before we die, certainly. We are all, in our hearts, secretly planning our deathbed redemption. Even those of us who do not believe. What harm, after all, in a little last-minute apology – just in case?

To some of us this may not seem quite right. Should it be possible, should it be *allowed*, that a single act of contrition wipes out an entire life of sin – provided only that it comes last? No, something about this seems not quite "on the level." We may even secretly hope that God has the good sense not to forgive such scoundrels.

The congregation shuffled in their seats.

And what of the opposite? What of the righteous man who, on his deathbed, renounces his righteousness? What if your first sin is also the last thing you ever do? Should a bad end blot out a good life?

My father wondered what the priest knew, what he had heard. The death certificate was noncommittal. The obituary was brief, gave nothing away.

Had he, somehow, heard about the fire? Had Deanna, perhaps, told him something about disjointed thoughts? Had someone whispered that my grandfather had been found by his nurse at the bottom of the stairs? But the knee, the bad knee, that was surely the knee's fault, everyone agreed . . .

Or could he be referring obliquely to the will, which had caused my aunt and her husband such consternation? *We'll fight it* – those had been Eric's first words. *I can't believe he'd do this to us* were Deanna's. *He can't*, Eric had assured her. My father, who hadn't needed Troy Mackey to tell him the will wasn't worth the paper it was scribbled on, had said nothing.

One thing was certain. The priest was not talking about the notebooks. My father had told no one about them. And he never would.

The call, this time, had come in the middle of the afternoon.

The flight was the same outrageous price.

The study was immaculate. Books on the shelves. New curtains drawn tight. The trash can tucked under the desk. The filing cabinet locked. The key nowhere to be found.

My father had gone across the street and borrowed a crowbar from Delbert Mossbank.

The drawers were empty. The notebooks gone. Everything
– gone.

Here on earth, the priest went on, we live in time. Because
we live in time, because we forget, because today has never
been seen to follow tomorrow, nor yesterday to follow today,
we attribute special significance to the next thing, the newest
thing. "Modern" is a compliment; "antique" a slur. The word
"evolution" – which means only change, after all – has
become synonymous with "improvement." What comes later
is better, and what comes last is best of all.

In this world, last things are hallowed. Last things are
holy. That which can be followed by nothing can be
replaced by nothing, can be improved upon by nothing, can
be rendered obsolete by nothing. Last words, last acts, they
go on echoing long after they are uttered, like the twelfth
peal of the midday bell lingering in the silence that follows.
What comes last, lasts.

This is, in our hearts, what all of us believe. Trapped as we
are in time, we can't imagine it being otherwise.

But God is not trapped in time. To God, yesterday and
tomorrow are as today. God takes the entire span of our lives
in at a glance, as it were. Nothing is missed. Nothing is lost.
Nothing is forgotten. The record of our lives is written, as it
were, in permanent ink. The evil we do, have done, or will
do, is not erased by the good. But nor is the good blackened
by the evil.

Every second counts. A moment weighs the same no
matter where it falls. Our last days mean as much as all our
others – but no more. I hope – and here the priest struggled

mightily to find the right words – that this thought . . . may prove to be of some comfort, to some of you, here today. Amen.

Jesus Christ, Dad, I hissed, pull yourself together.

And, just like that, my father stopped. He wiped his eyes and was instantly calm – sombre, but calm. No trace of tears. No sign that he'd just been weeping. No sign that he'd ever wept at all.

PAST LIVES

I

After the doctors had come the "visitors." The gypsy woman was only the latest in a long line of such guests. There had been an acupuncturist, a dietician, a herbalist. There had been an animal magnetist who did nothing but pass his hands up the length of Grete's body, a gemologist who did nothing but place heated stones on her spine, a university student who did nothing but rearrange the furniture. There had been an astrologist who believed that sickness was only the result of neglecting to petition one's guardian planets and stars for good health, a reiki master who believed that it was due only to blockages of one's life force energy, and now this gypsy, who believed that it was caused only by unhappy memories from before one was born.

It was the nothing buts and the onlys that aggravated Lloyd most. More than their glib confidence, their unctuous assurances, their arrogant faith in the universal effectiveness of their own pet nostrum, more than their magical thinking, their dismissive ignorance of hundreds of years of medical science, their self-serving professional allegiance to miracles, that is, to those things which by definition could not happen – more than all this, what irritated him about these people was their shared conviction that there was at bottom *only one thing wrong* with Grete. The doctors they had gone through had shared many of these weaknesses and others besides – their tendency to treat their patients like walking case studies, their scattershot liberality with pharmaceuticals, their faith in the totemic power of diagnostic classification – but at least none of them could be accused of oversimplifying the problem. They had been trained in the complexities of the body. With biology there was no need for theology.

There had once been a time, thought Lloyd, before the microscope, perhaps, when the body had been nothing more than what it appeared to be: a scaffold of bone, a knot of muscle, ten pints of blood, a swath of skin to hold everything in. Back then, you could be forgiven for believing that there must have been something to make it all go. But as we came to know our bodies and to recognize that an arm was more than an arm, a leg more than a flank of meat, the idea of some divine breath bringing that meat to life became less necessary. We went from seeing ourselves as a phantom in a lump of clay to a ghost in a machine to nothing but an echo in the engine room.

The soul was an insult to the body. It took credit for all the body's accomplishments – denying that biography had any basis in biology, that philosophy had any link to physiology, or that metaphysics owed anything to metabolism – and blamed the body for every pain, fatigue, grey hair, and sneeze. But Lloyd had watched his wife's body grow frail and thin, had seen fevers break over her in waves, seen the violent spasms of retching, the heaving shudders, the turbulence in her guts churning right below the surface of her grey skin, and he knew that she was more than a little spark, a little flame. The belief that all Grete's ailments could be cured by treating some single, underlying vital principle was, as far as he was concerned, a throwback to the primitive animism of the soul. It was the most childish sort of wishful, and wilful, stupidity. In belittling biology it belittled the body, and in diminishing her body it diminished Grete.

Mind you?

Lloyd said nothing, gazed down at the bath mat for a few moments without blinking, then shifted his eyes again randomly, as though he'd been too deep in thought to realize he'd been looking at her.

Privacy, she muttered.

His knees began to wobble; he gripped the towel bar for support. Frowning, he took a slow deep breath through his mouth without visibly parting his lips. She was embarrassed by the smell, didn't like it any more than he did. But it seemed worse lately, even with the gluten-free flour, and that bothered him. It was as if even the blandest food was being converted to poison inside her.

Her posture changed, or her breathing.

Done?

She grunted. Without looking at her, he tore off a strip of paper, bunched it into a thick wad – she'd complained once that she could feel his "every little finger" on her – and swiped it between her legs.

Enough already. Genug.

He dropped the wad down between her legs, draped one of her arms around his neck, and lifted her to her feet. Was it his imagination, or was she a little heavier? Or maybe she was weaker, and clinging to him more tightly. More likely she was only being uncooperative, letting him do all the work as punishment for having looked at her.

With her free hand she grasped impatiently at the walker. He held her by the waist and twisted himself out of the way.

Okay?

Ja ja, okay.

Once she was secure, he reached down for her trousers. He tied them loosely; the sharp granite cliffs of her hips would keep them in place.

Eng, she complained. Too tight.

He loosened the knot, retied it in exactly the same spot. He waited, almost eagerly, for another word of complaint. But not today. She was already trundling through the door. After a quick look down inside, he flushed the toilet and followed her.

Hands, she trilled.

He went back to the sink.

She muttered imprecations, but waited.

And the light behind you, she reminded him.

Today was the visit from the gypsy.

Mrs. Jolliet was not, in fact, a gypsy. That was only his word for her. Something about the whispering looseness of her clothes, the black cataract of her hair, the wind-chime jangle of jewellery that accompanied her every movement made him think of vagabonds and campfire smoke. To the best of his knowledge she was a bank clerk in Encaster who had once been married to a tax accountant there. He should never have let her in the front door.

But he'd been discouraged, worn down to complicity, by the change that had come over his wife. Her search for a cure had become an undignified grasping at straws. Her desperation seemed less to him like overripe hope than curdled fear. He had never known her to show fear before, least of all of something as banal as death. He'd believed her to be too strong, too smart, too proud to succumb to that childish, superstitious dread. It was as though she had told him, at the end of a long day spent defusing landmines, that she was afraid of the dark.

He remembered the look on her face when the war had first reached them in her rented room above the theatre, the night they heard the first bomb drop, the ripping sound of the explosion both obscenely close and laughably distant, like a pornographic playing card held out at arm's length. He sat up, as though a spring in his spine had snapped taut, and stared stupidly at the window, which was of course covered over with mismatched squares of black cloth and black cardboard, and made somewhat less austere by colourful matchbooks and scraps of lace and the yellow cellophane in which he'd wrapped his immortal beloved "Blues in Thirds." Then he turned and looked down at Grete. She hadn't moved, but her eyes were now open. Her expression was not one of fear or even concern but almost, he thought, puzzled satisfaction. She looked like someone, on having woken, trying to recall the details of some beautiful dream. As it turned out, it hadn't been a bomb at all, but the scheduled demolition of the old train bridge. But in her apartment above the theatre, neither of them had known that it wasn't the end of the world.

It was happening to him too. These sudden bursts of isolated memory, moments without significance dredged up for no reason, random frames of his life that should never have been stored, let alone restored. Grete was not the only one who was sick.

Once, years ago, he had been stricken by the thought that nothing of his life – not a jot or a tremor of the rich uniqueness of his existence – would be preserved unless he wrote it down. Now, it was the idea that perhaps nothing, not even the most mundane event, could ever be completely forgotten that filled him with dismay.

They were late. The gypsy woman was not the sort to slavishly adhere to hours of the clock: he supposed it would detract from her self-image of intuitive mystic if she were to make appointments by the same mechanical means as everyone else. But most Sundays she – and the daughter and the dog – appeared before two. Today they were late, and as a result Grete was in an especially sour mood. She made him change her clothes twice, first because the material was itchy, then because she was too cold: the furnace was always on, the house was always the same sweltering temperature, but she had caught a glimpse of the thermometer through the kitchen window during lunch, and so knew it was cold out *there*. So for the third time that day he laid her out on top of her bare mattress – last night's sheets were already in the washing machine – and she played dead while he stripped the clothes from her tiny body.

Ach, gentle, she said, and, Ach, privacy.

I don't enjoy this any more than you do, was all he could bring himself to say. He would have liked to tell her that he had no desire whatsoever to look on what remained of her body. He would have liked to say that he considered the sight of her less a privilege than a penance. What irritated him most was the way she presented her shame as coyness. Don't look, she whined, as though there were nothing he would rather do, as though he were a dirty old man desperate for a peek. He might have forgiven this pretense if it had only been a habit. But she had never been coy. She had never had that mincing *pudeur* of other girls he'd known, with its implication that men were all a little nasty, a little dirty, for wanting to look – and so, by extension, was the body they wanted to look at. She might have thought him somewhat silly, somewhat tedious, but she had never expressed any surprise that he should take pleasure in looking at her. The most she had ever shown was a sort of bored bemusement that his gaze never grew sated, despite all the hours it spent feasting. She would never have accused him of lecherousness, as she seemed to be doing now. Now that no man, not even her husband, could have found her attractive, now that she had withered and shrunk, *now* she behaved like a shrinking violet. It was yet another of the deceptions she'd perpetrated on herself, and as these added up, the less of herself there remained for him to recognize.

He rolled her onto her right side, folded her left arm up like a chicken wing, poked the hand through the sleeve of her blouse, and eventually persuaded the rest of the arm to follow. She offered neither resistance nor assistance. He wondered, almost cheerfully, how undertakers managed. But corpses didn't groan if you handled them too roughly or not roughly enough, didn't sigh impatiently through their teeth, like someone hissing at an incompetent performance of her favourite play. He rolled her onto her back and buttoned up the blouse.

The ordeal of getting dressed for company was over, but it had taken its toll. She called for her wheelchair. But she was not content to lie flat on the bed like a dead thing while he fetched it. He had to sit her up and help her latch on to the walker first.

How much egg nog is left? she demanded when he returned.

I don't know. Half a litre.

We bought four litres last week only.

Maybe more, maybe a litre. Why?

But he knew why. It was a familiar, indeed formulaic argument. He would buy something that she did not like or could not eat and she would indict him for gluttony, for not leaving her any.

You drank three litres in less than even one week?

The incredulity in her voice was strained, but he did not consider this a mitigating factor. On the contrary, he was annoyed that even her cantankerousness was put on, even the fights she picked she picked out of habit.

It's been over a week, he said, as per the script of the argument. At least ten days, he added, though of course he had no more idea how long it had been since he'd last made the trip to the grocery store than she did.

Not the point. You take always more than your share.

He lifted her up and transferred her to the wheelchair. She

remained folded in the same seated posture, her dangling legs bent at ninety degrees, as he swung her through the air.

You know as well as I do you can't drink that stuff.

Not the point, she screeched, finding her indignation through repetition. What about company? What of visitors? If Madame Jolliet or her child today wants a glass of egg nog? And there is none?

Half a dozen rejoinders flooded his circuits at once, blocking one another at the bottleneck. Neither the gypsy woman nor her daughter had ever accepted any offer of food or drink in all the weeks they had been coming; if despite precedent either the woman or her girl were to request of all things a glass of egg nog, there was still at least a litre left that he could serve them; if he didn't drink the stuff, no one would; if he was seriously expected to leave untouched her half of everything they brought home, it would all go to waste; the very idea that there was "his share" and "her share" was simply idiotic, because no matter how much or how little either of them consumed they could always get more; and why did she insist on calling the woman, like some kind of Gallic oracle, *Madame* Jolliet, when she had quite clearly introduced herself as Mrs. Jolliet, had said that the name belonged to her dead husband, who had furthermore been Polish, and that she herself had come from a long line of Irish tailors? And as for the "child," she was obviously at least twenty and more likely halfway to her thirties, and why did a twenty-five-year-old woman follow her mother around like a shadow or a halfwit?

Grete was still enumerating the parallel universes in which one and a half litres of egg nog might be insufficient when

the doorbell rang. She stopped talking, then announced:
This shirt is too scratchy.

The girl was alone on the doorstep. From deep within the scarves and hoods that seemed designed to protect her small head less from the cold than from a heavy blow from some blunt object, she peered out at him almost beseechingly. Lloyd stood there, hand on the door, and said nothing. For some reason, his heart was thumping.

My mother, the girl said at last, and there was in her voice an apologetic tone that almost endeared her to him. She had to run back to the car, she said.

He nodded.

After some thoughts and second thoughts, she elaborated: She forgot something. In the . . . car.

She turned her entire body and looked back in the direction of the street – not like someone illustrating the location of the car to which she'd referred, but like someone waiting for a bus craning her neck out into the street in hope of seeing it approach. Perhaps she was only a child, he thought.

Come in.

She spent a few moments parsing this suggestion, scanning it for subtext, then nodded, and finally followed through on this unspoken agreement by stepping through the door. He regretted offering to take her coat when he saw how firmly ensconced within it she was; not for three or four minutes did she succeed in liberating herself. He waved her in the direction of the reading room, where, as she knew as well as he did, Grete received her visitors. He watched her make her way down the hall, charmed by the thought of the two of them struggling to make small talk. With her winter things off she looked twenty again, twenty-five.

The mother, Mrs. Jolliet, entered the house without ringing the bell, evidently taking her daughter's entrance as an extended welcome to herself.

Oh, she said when she saw him, as though surprised and even a little disappointed to find him of all people here of all places. Then, with a visible effort, she modified her expression till it seemed to say that she should have known better than to expect anything else.

He did not offer to take her jacket.

She avenged this rudeness by asking him to take her "Popsy" for a moment.

He took the clump of teeth and fur between his hands and held it there while the gypsy, with a roll of her shoulders and a toss of her head, shed her coat – which, from the look of it, had been made out of thirty or so Pomeranians just like Popsy.

Mrs. Jolliet scooped the dog up into her arms again and, after cooing and running her hands over him to ensure that he had not been physically damaged by the ordeal, lifted her head and aimed her grey eyes at Lloyd. He counted this look of hers – a look of pride and readiness and courage and almost preemptive defiance – among the several hundred things he disliked most about her. She was always challenging him with this look, letting him know that she expected nothing better than the worst from him and that she was prepared to withstand it.

Perhaps, Mrs. Jolliet began, with a show of struggling mightily, as whenever she spoke to him, to find the words that would penetrate his peculiar brand of wilful obtuseness, perhaps you will be joining us today?

No thank you, he replied cheerfully enough, taking special care not to pause after the "no."

But surely you won't be going for a walk in *this* . . . this . . .

He waited while she grasped about for a synonym for "weather."

. . . In this *weather*? she at last spluttered triumphantly.

I have a warm coat. The fresh air does me good.

Mr. Pembroke, she murmured, dropping her voice by an octave, as well as lowering her head by about six inches, I understand . . . I *may* call you Mr. Pembroke?

Instead of asking on what possible grounds she believed he might object to being addressed by what was after all his name, he merely muttered, Yes, Mrs. Jolliet.

She nodded solemnly and took a moment to file this verbal contract away for safekeeping before continuing. I realize that you do not necessarily . . . *subscribe* to the possibility of prior existences. Ah ah ah – please. Allow me to finish. As I said, I realize that you do not necessarily subscribe to the possibility of prior existences. There is no need to deny it. You are not the first skeptic I have crossed paths with.

She allowed herself a throaty chuckle at the thought of all the skeptics she had crossed paths with.

But I feel as though I should make clear to you, as I have to your . . .

She seemed to scan through some secret list of alternative and no doubt more exalted designations – "life partner," "soulmate," "co-pilot," "better half," "lady friend" – before settling finally, with manifest dissatisfaction, on the more prosaic "wife."

I feel, as I said, that I should make clear to you, as I have to your wife, that it is not always necessary to go back as far as previous incarnations. Do you follow me?

He did not but felt no need to tell her this.

I mention this for three reasons. First, to allay . . . suspicions. Some find it less than entirely . . . convincing if the recovery work remains firmly grounded in the present incarnation. Do –

Yes, he said, comprehending now. She was making excuses for why the therapy hadn't progressed any further, why Grete was still dredging up memories from her present life, and not past ones.

In my experience many blocks, as I call them, go much deeper. But the cart must not go before the horse. I'm sure this expression is familiar to you?

I think I get the gist of it.

Let me put it another way. One must take things in the proper order. One should not get ahead of oneself. One cannot –

I understand.

It is necessary if the recovery work is to proceed to clear the most recent blocks first. That brings me to my second point. It can sometimes be beneficial, in these early stages, when corroboration and . . . supplementation are still possible, to allow others to . . . how shall I put it?

Corroborate and supplement.

Precisely. As I was saying, it can sometimes be beneficial to allow others to corroborate and supplement, insofar as possible, the recovered material.

You think I should sit in on these sessions and help fill in the gaps.

She made a face that said she preferred her wording.

I wish of course, he said, that I could be of some assistance in Grete's recovery work.

Mrs. Pembroke, she said, lifting her head and fixing him with the look of preemptive defiance, might not be the only one to benefit.

But you see, I have a terrible memory.

But that, she said with some bewilderment, is precisely where I come in. I am, she said, a *guide*.

Let me put it another way. I like my memory the way it is – terrible. Do *you* follow *me*?

She dismissed this with a sweep of her chin. That only brings me to my third point. During this work many unpleasant things can emerge, unpleasant in this initial stage not only for the one recovering but yes, their loved ones too, their family and friends, and yes, of course this material can arouse bitterness and resentment and what I have called a head-in-the-sand attitude. I of course often bear the brunt of this resentment and am willing to do so. But it is important to recognize that the memory worker herself – your wife, in this case – is not doing what you might think of as dredging up the unhappy memories out of any malice or mean-spiritedness. Spite has no place in the work, except as a sort of dowsing rod to show where currents of pain lie buried.

Mrs. Jolliet paused and, for the first time in his memory, looked unsure of herself.

You understand what I mean by a dowsing rod?

I think, Lloyd said, the memory worker is ready for you.

Feeling altogether too much like a manservant, he showed her into the living room, where Grete – predictably, he now saw – was doing what she probably thought of as regaling her young visitor with the weather report from January 1967.

The more her body forgot, the more she remembered. This bothered him, the idea that there might be two kinds of memory, one somatic, one mental: habit, the memory of muscle, and recollection, the memory of mind. The detail and clarity of her memories seemed almost to suggest that they came from some place outside the body, that they relied on something less frail than grooves worn in nervous tissue.

But he would not think like that. He told himself that deterioration sometimes showed effects that looked like improvement, that illness sometimes mimicked health. He thought of idiot savants, swan songs, and supernovas, those dying stars that burned brightest before their collapse. All that Grete's recollections proved was that experience was etched deeply and that the mechanism that kept the past submerged until it was needed had, in her, begun to mal-function. Didn't the same sort of thing occur during fever, poisoning, insanity? It was only a sign of further decline.

Attention was precious; a person was at any given moment bombarded with so much information that any commentary from their past had to be exquisitely to the point; anything extraneous could only be a distraction. That was why memories were so difficult to revive: not because traces of experience faded or deteriorated with the body on which they were imprinted, but because it was to the body's advantage to keep its memories to itself. A crack had appeared in Grete's filter. It was a further symptom of an underlying physical ailment, and he could not blame it on the gypsy woman or her "therapy." He could not blame Mrs. Jolliet for his wife's transformation into the sort of dusty old chatterbox that he had always found repellent: the tedious bore whose every breath was spent reminiscing, the pathetic relic for whom current events were only shabby revivals of once brilliant and original productions, for whom every anecdote was a bashful request for one of her own.

Just outside town, Grete was saying, a horse froze clear through to the bone in under four and one half minutes.

Who, he wanted to ask, and not for the first time, who had had the scientific zeal and presence of mind to cut the beast open clear to the bone to verify this fact? And how had they arrived at so precise a figure as four and a half minutes?

Instead, as per custom, he waited for the visitors' polite astonishment to dissipate, then asked if he could bring either of them anything to drink or eat. The girl shook her head and smiled shyly at his knees, but the woman took her usual amount of time considering the question. By smoothing the dog's fur with her hands like it was some fuzzy crystal ball and staring into the middle distance as though consulting some unseen oracle, she was eventually able to arrive at a decision that was unlikely to imperil her or anyone else's spiritual well-being: gazing at him like he was a firing squad, she said that she believed that she would, in fact, if it was not too much trouble, like a glass of water. He said that he believed it would, in fact, probably not be.

Bring also those biscuits from Deanna, Grete called after him. And the cheese plate too.

I can help, the girl said, and sprang out of her chair – whether moved to sympathy by the arduousness of the task before him or simply tired of Grete's tiresome reminiscing he was not sure. Perhaps she was not such a halfwit after all.

In the kitchen she tried to make herself useful, but it was

done before he could say what needed doing. He handed her her mother's glass of water and looked around for something else that she could do.

Want some egg nog?

She hesitated. Is it light?

He didn't understand the question. Fairly, he said, thinking she meant the colour.

I love egg nog, she said at last, as though confessing to an obscene but not especially violent predilection.

He poured them each an egg nog. She took one without putting down the glass of water.

He watched her throat as she swallowed.

The body had an intelligence all its own. Even the halfwit had a certain grace and wisdom and health, could run and jump and sleep and swallow and fight off disease without a passing thought.

Perhaps she was twenty-five, after all.

II

What Lloyd remembered was that every Sunday afternoon he would walk to Molly's, the cafeteria where they would meet. They would sit at the counter or in a booth by the window and order malts. Then they would walk together to the theatre where she rented a room. They would enter through the alley door and sneak up the stairs, one at a time. Then they would take each other's clothes off, the muddy sound of the matinee feature reaching them through the walls.

Every Sunday at two o'clock he would walk to Molly's.

Is there anything sweeter than walking to meet a girl for whom nothing is sweeter than waiting to be met by you? The very streets seem to usher you along with a hand at your elbow. A shop chime tinkles flirtatiously at the door that nudges it, a cloud skims over the sky on its way to see its lover, the wind nudges the lindens knowingly, and a leaf, mustering all its courage, detaches from its branch and diffidently approaches the sidewalk waiting coquettishly below. Even the other girls you pass in the street seem lovelier, as perhaps mountains appear more beautiful when your home does not lie on their farther side.

It has become a custom, a force of habit. Every Sunday at two o'clock I walk the thirty or forty minutes to Molly's. The thought of what awaits me there renders the walk an exquisite torture and delight, one that I would fain cut short and fain prolong. The week leading up to each Sunday is like that walk – is that walk. The ambivalent gift of anticipation: waiting to see her, I am both not-yet-seeing-her and soon-to-be-seeing-her. And I am never, it seems, not waiting to see her – even when I am seeing her.

They would sit at the counter or in a booth by the window and order malts.

If I arrive first I sit at the window and watch the faces as they pass. I am filled not with tenderness exactly, but a sort of gentle tolerance of all these poor slags and slatterns who aren't her, verging almost on an affectionate sympathy for them in their abject failure, their hopeless inability, to be her.

If she arrives first she sits at the counter with her back to the entrance and orders a malt. She does not look up when I come in, so I must assume she does not look up when anyone comes in, and certainly does not look up, as I would, <u>each and every time</u> the door swings open to nudge the chime.

Not only does she not look up when I enter, she does not even look up to meet my glance in the cloudy mirror behind the counter when I sit down beside her. Instead she leans forward, arms folded like laundry on the countertop, and searches with slightly parted lips for her straw – unseeing, absentminded, pensive, aloof. But her posture betrays her: when I sit down, the muscles in her neck and back go taut. Her body knows I'm there. Only when she finds the straw does she look up and smile (or rather, smile and look up). My heart, meanwhile, has been crashing about inside my head and trying to climb out my ears, as if the fate of the world – the fate of something much greater than the world, the fate of our love – depended on the outcome of that careless, unseeing, absentminded search for that straw. I smile back at her in the fogged mirror, lift one hand in a limp wave, and feel for a second almost angry that anyone should be permitted to be so lovely.

They would walk together to the theatre where she rented a room. They would enter through the alley door and sneak up the stairs, one at a time.

In no hurry but our own, with arms and fingers linked, we walk the six blocks to the theatre. We enter through the back fire door to avoid Mrs. Petrov at the concession. (The hand-printed contract G. signed specifies, in block capitals that give the lie to the euphemism, "NO VISITORS.") In the dark of the interior we separate – the phrase that invariably enters my head at this moment is "reculer pour mieux sauter." I go up first, so that if ever I am to run across Mr. Petrov I can maintain, with a degree of plausibility that might be weakened if G. were in her room, that I was only looking for a restroom, a balcony, a better seat. But that has yet to happen: Sunday afternoons the proprietors of The Empress Grande screen matinees back to back, not even pausing long enough to turn the house lights up, and Mr. Petrov is rarely, if ever, seen to emerge from the projection room.

Her key clutched tightly in my left hand, the walls under my right reverberating with gunfire or saloon music or galloping hoof-beats, I grope my way up the steep narrow staircase blindly.

They would take each other's clothes off.

Sometimes we take turns playing dead, trying not to move or giggle, while the other undresses us. In the dim light of her garret we spend hours investigating each other's bodies, comparing skin, comparing scars. Here on the shin is where she was bit by a neighbour's dog when she was a child. Here just behind her right ear is where she was struck by something – a rock, a stick – while passing through a demonstrating crowd outside the factory where her mother worked. Here on her thumb is where she cut herself while chopping eggplant. And here below her knee is the coin-sized patch of glistening skin where for some reason no hair will grow. And here above her ankle is the slight concavity where I watch her pulse beat, and feel awe-stricken by the vastness of her heart's domain.

They would take turns playing dead. They would spend hours comparing scars.

These were the details he had written down so that he would not have to remember them.

Downstairs, Grete was calling. He no longer recognized his name in her call. The consonants, which of course did not travel through the walls or up the stairs half as well as the vowel, had been dropped, and the remaining diphthong had been stretched into two distinct syllables, the first a grumbling remonstration, the second an alarmlike screech of rising indignation: "Oh-*weeeeee*?" It sounded more like a yelp of pain or blame than "Lloyd." Maybe that was the point.

He tossed the notebook onto his desk, pushed himself out of the chair, and trudged downstairs, placing his feet with more care than necessary. His idiot son-in-law, a doctor only in name, had recently told him that more broken bones occur among the elderly following new bifocal prescriptions, due to slips while descending staircases. He'd put special emphasis on the greater risk of descent, as if this were some esoteric riddle and not simply common sense and common experience that going down a flight of steps was a more precarious undertaking than going up one. Lloyd did not wear bifocals but saw no reason to make himself a vindication of any part of one of Eric's statistics. Grete called out twice more on his way down. He felt a moment's flush of sour pleasure at the thought of her predicament if ever he *were* to fall and break his bloody neck.

She was right where he'd left her, sitting in the wheelchair in the back sunroom, swaddled up to her chin in a cocoon of cardigans and shawls and crocheted blankets. With only her head thus visible, the look of reproach that welled up in her wet black eyes when he appeared at the patio door struck him as especially cold and inhuman, almost insectoid.

I am cold, she said, her voice heavy with exasperation at having to articulate what should have been obvious. I want to go in.

The wheels on the wheelchair were, as far as she was concerned, decorative. Unless she was feeling her very worst, she refused to be rolled around the house like an invalid. He placed the walker before her and began unwrapping her arms so that she could hold on to it, but immediately she began complaining bitterly about the cold to which he was thoughtlessly subjecting her. He did not point out that the insulated sunroom was the same temperature as the rest of the house. The theme of his thoughtlessness sparked off a train of associations; as he half-carried her indoors, dragging the walker behind him with the heel of one foot, she began itemizing a few of the most salient or recent matters in which he had failed to think:

The back path still needs its shovelling off. It is an embarrassment looking like this.

As he guided her down the hall and into the bathroom:

You have not again called the pharmacist. You want I suppose me to become sicker with complications and contraindications?

As he moved the toothbrush around inside her mouth, avoiding as much as possible the flashing grey tongue:

You did not yet cancel the newspaper subscription. The two of us – ach, not so hard – we do not ever read one page or headline, you know.

And finally, as he helped her into bed:

Has this light been on all day?

He looked up. He supposed it had. They'd moved her bed, after she'd lost the ability to climb stairs unaided, into this room because of the amount of sunlight that it received. It was only at the end of the day, after the sun had gone down, that you would notice the far dimmer light.

He got up to turn it off, sat back down on the edge of the bed, and, as was his custom, waited in the darkness for her breathing to change. Only when he was sure she was asleep did he take off his own clothes and lie down beside her.

If it happened during the night, he wanted to be there.

He wondered how long it would take.

What would cease first: her heart, her lungs, her brain?

For how long after her heart had stopped would the pulse appear in the concavity above her ankle? For how long after they stopped receiving oxygen could the cells in the farthest reaches of her body go on struggling?

Would the organs shut down one at a time? Would each cell have to die its own solitary death? Was dying – even peacefully, even in your sleep – more like a prolonged, catastrophic shipwreck than the flickering out of a single light? Was death as intricate and manifold a thing as life?

Or would everything stop at once, in an instant – like magic?

III

It was a four-hour drive from Winnipeg to Encaster – five the way Morley drove – and she considered it a victory that they had spent the first three in silence. Isobel no longer cared to remember what they'd been arguing about – though whatever it was, it was not what he thought. She couldn't care less if he was hiding food from her, if that was in fact what he'd been doing – and it certainly looked that way, with the box at the back of the pantry behind the expired tomato juice and last year's inedible Easter candy. As far as she was concerned, if he wanted to go to the trouble of hiding her favourite cereal to ensure he'd get some before it was all gone, he was more than welcome. If it came to that, she could buy her own box and hide it in her closet, in the garage, in the trunk of the car. Nor was it ultimately his self-ishness or the possessiveness of his behaviour that irritated her, his belligerent attitude that there was a "hers" and a "his" – she would draw a line down the middle of the apart-ment if that's what he wanted.

The argument was not about this thing or that thing or *about* any one thing at all. It was about the fact that with him everything had to *be* an argument. She could not express dis-pleasure without him taking it as a criticism, an accusation, an indictment, and immediately launching into his defence or making his counter-indictment. Whether or not she had overreacted was not the point; the point was whether or not she should not occasionally be allowed to overreact. The point was that he was incapable of putting himself in her place, of imagining what she might be going through, of realizing that when she complained she was not necessarily asking for some explanation or expiation. She was expressing a mood, articulating a state of mind, advertising – though not in any vulgarly explicit way – the fact of her unhappi-ness. He was too thick to see that sometimes she was not after justice, but sympathy. At the very least a little patience, a little indulgence, a little liberty to be unhappy. Today especially, of all days, with her mother's funeral tomorrow.

Instead, he got his back up, and once Morley had his back up he could never back down. Even after two hours of arguing, ninety minutes after they'd originally planned to be on the road, he had still been, with the same mulish astonishment of the wrongfully accused, pointing out the disproportion between the lightness of the alleged crime and the severity of the prosecution, without ever once realizing what that disproportion proved: that it was not about a box of cereal at all. It made her want to scream. Instead, with the dignity of a martyr, she shut up. And he, the fool, did the same! As though that was what she really wanted all along, for the both of them to sit and stew in silence. Or perhaps he thought that this marked the end of the matter, that quiet was as good as peace. So, for her, each minute that passed like this was a victory, because it proved how little he understood her, how completely off the mark he could be. She nursed her anger like a seedling, taking care not to overwater.

The landscape was some help at first. The immense monotony of the prairies was like a persistent jab in the ribs, a constant reminder that nothing ever changed and that you were perfectly right to expect the worst, because that's all there was and all it did was come around again and again. The sky was as dumb and empty as a yawn, the bristling fields as flat and green as some giant's golf course. The sun did not move, did not seem to shine or give off heat or light, but simply hung in the air like a big white rock. The highway rolled under them like the reel of some interminable film; every song that came on the radio seemed to be playing for the tenth consecutive time; every service station they passed reminded her of a dozen just like it; every breath Morley took in through his whistling nose sounded like a sarcastic imitation of the one she'd just let out. At first it made her angry, but as the odometer turned over the miles her anger faded to depression and she found herself thinking about her mother.

"Turn here," she said, before she realized what she'd done, or what it meant.

"Where?" Morley's voice was thick with disuse, as though he'd been sleeping. She wouldn't have put it past him.

She shook her head; it didn't matter. "Up here. Next town."

It meant their argument was over.

She remembered how to get there before she realized where it was they were going. Morley followed her directions mutely, taking them away from the highway and into the centre of town. Something in her knew the place, knew the route. She knew but did not remember the crunch of gravel under the tires, the smell of compost and french fry grease and burning cardboard, the low sun at the end of each street scrubbing the contrast out of everything, turning the town the colour of salted butter. It was all familiar to her, and the sense of recognition was all the stronger for being incomplete. If she'd been the one driving she might have taken these turns automatically and ended up at the house without any conscious recollection of how she'd gotten there.

"Here," she said. "Stop here."

She rolled down her window and looked up at the house. Nothing had changed. Only, in her memory, the air was colder. It had been autumn then, or winter. She didn't remember the old woman's name but the husband had been called Lloyd. He'd looked about half the woman's age. She didn't remember what the woman had talked about but she remembered her voice: the deliberate syntax, the curious word choice, the accent that only flared up when hectoring the husband.

Morley parted his lips with an audible effort. "Know the place?"

She pretended to be lost in thought of a particularly deep and troubling kind. After a minute she leaned back in her seat and said quietly, "I used to come here with my mother."

Morley smacked his lips knowingly. "One of her . . . whatsits?"

"'Clients.'" She handled the word like a soiled handkerchief, pinched between quotation marks. "Yes."

"What did this one have?"

"I don't know. Something or other."

He chewed on this for a minute. "This one get better?"

She did not reply. None of them ever got better. And if any of them ever had, it wouldn't have meant anything. If they got better, it was because the sickness had run its course. If they improved, if they died, if they stayed the same, it had nothing to do with her mother. But for some reason her clients chose to look at it in the exact opposite way. If they improved it was because Mrs. Jolliet had helped them, they got no worse because Mrs. Jolliet had helped them, they died only because Mrs. Jolliet had not been given enough time to help them.

She wished her mother had been a charlatan, a callous con artist. But she'd been as deluded as any of her customers. To the very end, no doubt, she'd believed that the waking dreams – the wicked daymares – that she induced were actual memories, real traumas buried deeper than flesh or bone. Her mother had a gift for facilitating fabulation, that was all. She should have visited the homes of blocked novelists, thought Isobel, not the dying. Somehow, during one of her vacant trances, she'd muddled the notions of reincarnation and psychoanalysis and come up with the source of all evil: submerged unhappy memories; and conversely, of course, its panacea: remembrance.

Isobel distrusted recollection, and not just because of what she'd seen when accompanying her mother on her visits. Memories were unreliable, but more than that, they were painful. And not only memories of painful or unpleasant events, but memories in general. The content didn't seem to matter. Happy memories left her feeling as despondent as awful ones. There was something intrinsically depressing about the past. The sight of this house, for instance, which meant nothing to her, where nothing special had happened to her, this place that was without happy or unhappy associations of any kind – the sight of this house filled her with gloom.

It seemed an insult that the house hadn't changed. The effrontery of places, she thought, staying so much the same while we break down and fall to pieces. Memories did that too: they stood still. They were the fixed points along the shore that told the river how swiftly it was moving. Perhaps that was why they hurt: because they reminded her that she was travelling, always in the same direction, always away from something, always towards the same end.

The only difference was that no one lived here anymore. The grey paint was a little weatherbeaten. The grass of the

front lawn was nearly a foot long and overgrown with dan-
delions and purple prickleweed. The house was empty. There
were no lights on in any of the windows, which shone like
glassy eyes with the reflected light of sunset.

She could feel Morley watching her. Waiting, assessing,
knowing. His silence was as blatant a demonstration of
indulgent patience as if he'd said, "If you don't want to talk
about it, we don't have to talk about it; but if you *do* want
to talk about it, well . . ." Without having to turn around she
knew he was giving her the same kind of look her mother
had given her years ago, quite possibly in front of this same
house. A look that said she knew what was best for Isobel
but was graciously willing to let her come around to that
knowledge herself. "If you really don't want to go inside,
you don't have to go inside; if you really want to sit out here
in the car in the cold, you can sit out here in the car in the
cold; if you really don't want to come inside and say hello
to poor Mrs. Pembroke, who gets such delight in seeing you
every week, well . . ."

She got out of the car. That was something else that
memory did: made you feel like you were sixteen again. Like
the interim had been erased. Like everything you'd done
and worked for, all the distance you'd striven to put between
yourself and a place like Encaster, had been reduced to
nothing. Like everything since had been a dream. Like all
movement was an illusion. Like you were back where you
started. And where you started was the only place you'd ever
be, till the day you died.

The sun had mostly gone down, taking its yellows and
oranges and reds with it. The cool air seemed somehow
frantic, as though swarming with tiny particles or insects

too small to be seen. Her head was swimming. She needed a cigarette.

This alarmed her. It had been some time since she'd felt a craving. She'd been assiduously avoiding all the places where she used to light up – bars, cafeterias, the loading dock at work, Morley's balcony – because her body remembered those places and so prepared itself for the nicotine. It was this readiness that she felt as a craving – that emptiness somewhere between illness and hunger. To avoid this feeling, she'd taken to smoking only in novel and unfamiliar places, places she'd never return to anyway and so would not have to avoid. A place like this. The middle of nowhere.

But smoking in places like this had become a habit. So much so that her body could anticipate her – and prepare itself. The craving she felt here was indistinguishable from those she'd felt at any of her old haunts. There was now, it seemed, no longer anyplace she could go, new or old, novel or familiar, to escape or forestall the craving. Her body was one step ahead of her.

Morley killed the engine and got out of the car. After a minute or two he came around to her side as though by accident and stood there, hands in his pockets, looking up at the house, beside her.

For the first time that day, perhaps that week, she felt an absence of animosity towards him, a feeling that might have been affection if it had not been so heavily tainted with sadness. It was as if part of her was grieving for the departed anger.

Grief. Perhaps that was all that memory evoked: the simple sense of loss.

She remembered – why? – standing in the kitchen with him, drinking egg nog.

She remembered his eyes on her.

She remembered being drawn to him, without being able to say why – drawn to his withdrawal, drawn to his skepticism.

You don't buy into this, do you, she'd said.

Do you?

She'd shrugged, not wanting to appear too eager, too hungry. I don't believe in the transmigration of the *soul* or anything, if *that's* what you mean.

He'd looked at her for a long time, till the smile on his face expired. Then he'd said something. She couldn't remember the exact words, but the idea had struck her with force. He'd said something like: I think the soul would be too big to transmigrate.

She'd never thought of the soul as being big or little, or of having any particular size at all.

She'd been too dazed, too flustered, too flattered not to blurt out her own metaphysical aphorism, one she'd yet to share with anyone but her diary:

All I know is if there *are* other lives, past ones and future ones and what not, what's the point of worrying about *this* one?

Isobel felt an urge to tell all this to Morley, to explain to him exactly what was going on inside her. For a moment she felt as a visceral certainty the ultimate expressibility of every hue of emotion and shade of thought. This knotty sensation in her chest, for example, which was neither pleasure nor pain but something infinitely more complex: it seemed to represent both what Morley meant to her and the means by which she could illustrate that meaning to him. There was nothing that could not be said. She could tell him about the restlessness of the air, the craving for a cigarette, the accent of the Pembroke woman, the affliction of memory, which both proved and prohibited progress.

It occurred to her that if ever there was a lack of understanding between them it was due to nothing more complicated or nefarious than a lack of words. This time it would all come out in an effortless stream of luminous expression. She had only to open her mouth and begin.

She opened her mouth, but all that came out was a long, hiccuping wail.

"Oh Jesus," muttered Morley.

It was not too late. She could still explain. This too needed explaining, after all; this too was part of the explanation. Just as soon as she stopped sobbing, as soon as she got herself under control, she would tell him everything. Beginning, because she had to begin somewhere, with what was wrong. Beginning with that "Oh Jesus" – as though she was not entitled, not even today, to a few tears. She would begin by explaining what was wrong with that, wrong with him, wrong with her, wrong with them, and go on to what was not.

She had opened her mouth to begin again when he touched her. He pressed his hand down heavily on her shoulder, less, it seemed, to comfort than to constrain, and something inside her reacted. Her stomach went cold; the muscles of her neck and back went taut. Her body knew what was coming if she did not. Before she'd even spoken a word she felt it preparing itself for the inevitable argument, the battle whose rules of engagement had been set down so long ago that they were beyond the grasp of memory.

"Come on," he said. "Let's get out of here. They're probably calling the cops."

The house was not empty after all. A light had come on in one of the upper windows – or had been on all along, concealed by the glare of the falling sun.

Amy Young

CRAIG BOYKO's stories have been published in many of Canada's best literary magazines, including *Grain Magazine*, *The Malahat Review*, *PRISM international*, *Descant*, and *The New Quarterly*. A record-setting four-time nominee for the prestigious Journey Prize (which ties him with David Bergen for the title of the author with the most number of stories included in The Journey Prize anthology's twenty-year history), Boyko won the 2007 Journey Prize for "OZY," one of the stories included in *Blackouts*.

Born and raised in Saskatchewan, Boyko received degrees in English and Psychology from the University of Calgary. He now lives in Victoria, British Columbia.